SPITFIRES RISING

John Noble Thrillers
Book One

David Mackenzie

SAPERE
BOOKS

SPITFIRES
RISING

Published by Sapere Books.

24 Trafalgar Road, Ilkley, LS29 8HH

saperebooks.com

ISBN: 978-0-85495-670-8

CHAPTER ONE

Clydevale, New Zealand, 1938

The early morning autumn air was cold and still. Branches on trees drooped with the weight of a hoar frost, and frozen grass crunched underfoot. Out since first light, John Noble could feel the deep chill on his face, and around his neck. The thick woollen scarf he was wearing gave him little protection. The icy air managed to seep in everywhere. Given a choice, he would rather have been back in the comfort of the farm homestead, but that was not possible. First thing each morning, it was his job to check the livestock.

While John enjoyed working on the family property, something he had done since leaving school three years ago, he did from time to time wonder if a lifetime of sheep farming was for him. Trouble was, he had no idea what else he could do.

As he entered the last paddock to be checked, next to the river, he started thinking about what had happened the previous evening. He had been having dinner with his parents, seated at the large white-oak dining table in the homestead's kitchen. It was a room that was always warm, and consequently the focus of day-to-day family life on the farm. The heat came from the coal-fired range that seemed to burn there constantly. John's father, Cusack, had made an announcement during dinner.

'I'm going to buy Bill Cross's property. He's in trouble and needs to sell. The Depression has nearly sent him broke.'

Bill Cross was a neighbour who had a sheep and beef operation close to Cusack's farm. John understood the problem. The Great Depression, as it was being called, had hurt many since it had begun in 1929, nearly nine years ago. It was obviously still taking an economic toll.

'I want you to manage the additional land, John. It's a good opportunity for you,' Cusack had said.

John had immediately seen the value in what his father was offering. The farm was in the Clutha River valley, an area of high-quality agricultural land in New Zealand's Otago province. It was much sought-after, but John knew that if he committed and the Cross property was purchased, he would be working as a farmer for years, if not his whole life.

'Dad, I'm not sure at this stage if I want to work long-term as a farmer.'

'Christ, don't be such a clot, boy,' was the immediate response from Cusack. 'What else could you do?'

John was annoyed by that comment, but, deep down, he knew his father was right. He had no skills or experience other than farming.

John's mother, Lillian, sitting at the end of the table, shifted uncomfortably.

Recognising the conversation could become difficult, John diplomatically suggested he think about if for a few days.

'Let me mull it over, Dad, and then we can sit down and work something out together.'

'All right,' said Cusack. 'Let's have that talk soon and resolve the detail. The option over the property expires in twenty-one days. If we agree that you will take it on, we have things to sort out.'

John just nodded, knowing that he had merely postponed an argument.

The sound of an engine interrupted his thoughts. Faint at first, the noise slowly grew. It was not a very large engine, he decided, just a low-revving four cylinder. The sound seemed to be coming from the vicinity of the river, which formed the property's western boundary. The river was slow as it meandered past the farm and down the wide valley, but as it passed through a narrow gorge further upstream, it became fast-flowing, and large rocks lying just beneath the surface caused white water to erupt.

The surging waters of the gorge had presented an irresistible challenge to some of the teenagers who lived in the area, including John when he was home from boarding school. He had often spent time with others rafting on that part of the river, until a friend almost drowned. John had bravely jumped in and made a rescue, but that had counted for nothing when his parents found out what had happened.

'How many times have I told you, young Johnnie? Swimming in that part of the river isn't just risky, it's idiotic. I thought you would listen to me. You need to take notice of what you are told,' his father had said sternly, glaring at him.

John looked downstream, thinking the engine noise he could hear may have been Bob Smaill, motoring up in his small boat from nearby Clydevale. Bob sometimes came past the farm on his way to his favourite fishing spot, just a short distance further up the river. But there was no boat to be seen. The engine sound grew. Whatever it was, it was getting closer. Then John saw it.

A small, bright yellow biplane was flying towards him. John thought it was about two to three hundred feet above the ground. He knew it was a Tiger Moth. The aircraft was slowly weaving its way through the air. The pilot appeared to be following the course of the river.

Because the morning was cool and crisp, the engine sound carried clearly. So did the noise of the airflow, whistling through the various struts and wires on the aircraft's wings.

John was fascinated by the sight and sound of the little yellow aeroplane. As it went past him, he could see the leather helmet on the pilot's head. The pilot was sitting in an open cockpit, hunched forward as he flew. Then, as John watched, the noise of the engine suddenly increased, and the aircraft began to turn back.

Its left wing dropped to near vertical as it banked hard into its turn, under what John thought was probably full power. Once it had reversed its course, its wings were re-levelled and the Tiger Moth flew directly towards where he was standing. The pilot must have throttled back once the turn was complete, because the noise of the engine was much less now, right back to the original level he had first heard. John was enthralled.

As it reached him, the engine noise increased again as the aircraft entered another steeply banked turn, back towards the river. As he flew over, the pilot looked directly down at John and raised a gloved hand in a brief wave. Nearby sheep ran, frightened by the loud noise.

John waved back excitedly. The yellow Tiger Moth continued its turn. Once back over the river, the pilot resumed his curving and swaying flight path to follow its course downstream.

John felt a sudden sense of belonging, as if he had, in that moment, made a connection with the unknown pilot and his aircraft. He now knew what he wanted to do with his life. He would become a pilot.

He recalled seeing an advertisement the previous week in the local newspaper, the *Otago Daily Times*. The advertisement had invited interested young men to apply to join the Royal Air Force. Applications were to be made to the British High Commission in Wellington, and successful candidates would travel to the United Kingdom for training.

That evening, after completing his day's work on the farm and arriving back at the homestead, John went through the old newspapers his mother kept to ensure she had a ready supply of fire-lighting material. He soon found what he was looking for, and was relieved to see he had another week before the closing date for applications. He could get his to Wellington in time, if he caught the next morning's post.

That night he carefully wrote his application, making sure his handwriting was as neat as possible. He would give the letter to the postman tomorrow, and at dinner that night he would tell his father his plans.

'What do you mean, you're going to be a pilot?' roared Cusack when John revealed his intentions. 'What about the farm here, and the extra work that the Cross property will require? Who is going to help me? I thought we were going to discuss this.'

John tried to explain that he thought flying was what he had been looking for. 'In any event, Dad, Tom could work on the Cross farm in my place.'

Tom was John's younger brother. Away at boarding school, he was due to finish there in a few months. John thought Tom would be an adequate substitute, but Cusack did not agree.

'Tom? Too inexperienced. He couldn't run the Cross block on his own. No, I want you here working with me on the property, young Johnnie, and that's the end of it. You forget flying, you hear me?'

'Well, let's wait and see if I even get accepted for an interview,' John said, trying to defuse the tension. It did not work, and Cusack stormed out of the room, muttering about this nonsense needing to end.

Four weeks had passed since John had first raised with his father his wish to join the RAF, and there was still no resolution. Cusack would simply shut down John's attempts to talk about what he wanted to do, saying it was nothing but a young man's silly dream.

Then a letter arrived at the Noble homestead. It bore the Royal Insignia, beneath which was written: *British High Commission, Wellington, New Zealand.*

John's mother quietly passed it to him as she sorted through other mail. 'Good luck, John,' she said with a smile.

'Thanks, Mum,' John replied, patting her hand.

Taking the letter, he went to his bedroom to read it in private. He anxiously ripped open the heavy white envelope.

You have been accepted for an interview... the letter began. John was thrilled. He read on, giddy with excitement.

A Mr Pennicott, from the High Commission, would be in Dunedin on Thursday, the thirtieth of June, and he wanted to see John at two o'clock on that day. They were to meet at the Knox Church auditorium in George Street. *Please bring any driver's licence you may have, a reference from your current employer, and school reports for the last year of your schooling,* the letter concluded.

John doubted his father would agree to supply the reference, but he had to at least ask.

Later that evening, sitting at the dinner table, he summoned the courage to reveal his news. 'I have been invited to an interview for a career as a pilot with the RAF,' he announced.

Cusack said nothing and continued to eat, staring down at his plate.

'I'm going to Dunedin next week to meet someone from the British High Commission,' John persevered. 'I must take along some material, including a reference about my work, Dad. Could you provide that?'

His father still said nothing, but after a few moments he carefully put down his knife and fork, pushed back his chair, and stood up. Glowering down at John, he said, 'I thought this nonsense was over. Are you still pursuing it?'

John's heart sank. 'Ah, yes —' he began, but his father cut him off.

'All right, John, I recognise how keen you are to fly. I would rather you stayed and worked on the property with me, but if you are set on this path, I won't stand in your way.'

A week later, John was carefully parking the family car in George Street, Dunedin, near Knox Church. John had not spent much time in Dunedin, other than as a boarder at a local high school, but he had heard his father talking about the city and its citizens. According to Cusack, many in Dunedin were very narrow and strict in their view of life. John had seen how dismissive his father could be of such people, and he had picked up some of Cusack's attitudes. John had little time for anyone whom he thought had an overly conservative approach to life. In John's view, the status quo was there to be tested and should never be unquestioningly accepted, otherwise you risked a banal and mediocre life.

Too early for his meeting with Mr Pennicott, John strolled down to the town centre. In place of a traditional square, the centre of Dunedin was an open, eight-sided area known as the Octagon, with a large statue of Robert Burns in the middle. The pavements around the area were busy with well-dressed shoppers and office workers. John, wearing his best suit, fitted in well.

After wandering around looking into various shop windows for about thirty minutes, John made his way back to Knox Church for his interview. He had not been waiting long, when, at exactly two o'clock, a smiling, overweight man in a pinstripe three-piece suit came out of the office next to where John was sitting.

'Mr Noble?' he enquired, as he peered short-sightedly at John.

'Yes,' said John, standing up and reaching for the hand proffered for him to shake.

'Pennicott, British High Commission, Wellington. How do you do?'

'Pleased to meet you, sir,' John responded as his arm was pumped.

'Come in. Let's find out all about you and why you want to join the RAF.'

After Mr Pennicott had read Cusack's reference and noted the detail on John's driving licence, he looked through John's final school report.

'You seem to have done well at school, John. Your housemaster says you are intelligent and that you show leadership skills.'

'Thank you,' John acknowledged.

'And maths is a strong point for you — good. That's important for a pilot. You must be able to make weight and balance calculations, and plan flights that consider winds for navigation and fuel endurance. You up to that?'

'Yes, I think so, sir,' John replied.

'I note that your reference is from your father. Do you enjoy working with him on the family farm?'

'I do, sir,' John replied.

'So, why are you leaving?'

'While I enjoy farming, I want to do other things. Learning to fly and serving in the Royal Air Force would be very satisfying.'

'Given your father's reference, I presume your family is supportive of your plans, should you be accepted? You will be going to the United Kingdom, the other side of the world, and it will be a long time before you see them again. Is everybody, including you, going to be happy?'

'Yes, I am prepared for that, and my parents are supportive,' replied John, very pleased that his father had come around in his thinking.

Mr Pennicott continued in this vein for the next twenty minutes, probing and testing. Eventually, he said, 'Thank you for coming here today to see me, John. I have everything I need to make a recommendation. Is there anything you would like to ask me at this point?'

'No, sir,' John replied. 'Thank you for taking the time to come to Dunedin to interview me, sir. I am very keen to serve.'

'It was nice to meet you, John. We shall advise in due course whether you have been successful. You should hear within four weeks.'

John and Mr Pennicott shook hands again, and John left to drive back to the farm.

As he drove home, John spent some time wondering how he had done in his interview. He had been asked a lot of questions, not only about his life, but also about his ability to work in a structured service environment, with its rules and hierarchies. Mr Pennicott had even asked John about whether he would be happy living on the other side of the world, a long way away from family and friends. *Hopefully he was happy with all my answers*, John thought.

At the end of July, as the family sat around the dinner table, Cusack pulled a thick white envelope from his jacket pocket and handed it to John.

'You might have been waiting for this, I think,' he said to his son as he passed it over. 'It arrived this morning.'

John nervously tore open the envelope and scanned the letter. 'I'm in!' he shouted after a moment. 'I've been accepted.' His parents smiled warmly.

'Well done, John. Their gain is my loss, but I have decided I will be able to get by without you,' said Cusack.

'That's lovely for you, John,' Lillian added. 'When do you go?'

'A preliminary medical assessment is required, and if I pass that I must report at the High Commission in Wellington on the twenty-second of August. My ship sails from Wellington the next day.'

That was a lot earlier than Cusack and Lillian had expected. John would be gone very soon. They were also conscious of the news reports coming out of Britain about the rising power of Germany, and the belligerent attitude its leaders seemed to be taking with regards to matters in Europe. There was a lot of talk about the risk of war.

'You do realise you may get caught up in a conflict over there if this chap Hitler continues as he has done to date, John?' Cusack asked.

'Yes, I know that's a possibility,' John replied, 'but I would guess that everyone is working hard to ensure things don't get out of control.'

'Let's hope not, John. Congratulations on your success so far,' said Cusack, smiling.

CHAPTER TWO

On a bleak grey day in early October, John Noble arrived at RAF Desford, the site of No. 7 Elementary and Reserve Flying Training School. He had just spent the last five hours travelling from Southampton on a bus, and he was tired. It was the end of a long trip he had started some six weeks earlier.

John had travelled from New Zealand to the United Kingdom on a modern two-funnelled steamer, which had shown signs of wear and tear. Salt from constant sea spray had eaten into its paintwork. The cabins inside the ship were small, and some had no porthole as they were interior rooms. Luckily, John's cabin had been beside one of the open decks, so it had had a window.

It had been a long, tedious voyage. Since John was not a big drinker or keen card-player, there was not much to do every day, although he had demonstrated some prowess at deck quoits. There had been several other young men on board who were also travelling to the United Kingdom to join the services, but they were destined for the army or navy. John was the only one joining the air force.

After completing his arrival formalities at Southampton, John had been given a travel warrant by the officer in charge of service personnel arrivals. He was an older man, probably about sixty. John decided his grey moustache was much too big for his lean face.

'The bus outside is taking service inductees to their various destinations,' the officer had told him. 'You will see a sign in the front windscreen saying *Service Personnel*. Just show the driver this warrant. Make sure you say to him that you are for

RAF Desford as you get on. You will probably be one of the last to be dropped off, because you have the furthest to go, up near Leicester. I suggest you get yourself a sandwich or something for the journey. Got all that?'

John nodded. 'Yes, sir.'

'Good. Off you go then,' said the officer, and he moved on to deal with some of the other lost-looking souls who had just arrived from various Commonwealth countries.

John settled into the room he had been allocated at RAF Desford, which would be his home for the next twelve weeks. There was a narrow bed, a large wooden wardrobe with some wire coat-hangers that were bent out of shape, and, in the corner, a small desk and chair.

John saw a dark blue folder lying on the top of the desk. Picking it up, he found that it contained a brief outline of the school's facilities and the principal aspects of his course. He quickly scanned the course programme.

The first week did not look very interesting, with five days of lectures covering the history of the Royal Air Force and its traditions, structures, and hierarchy, as well as military law and discipline. Only after those initial classes were finished would the students go on to study core flying topics.

As he read on, he learned that there was accommodation for up to twenty-five students, although he knew there were only twenty on his course. The flying school appeared to be well equipped, and training aircraft were principally de Havilland Tiger Moths. John was delighted. It had been a yellow Tiger Moth over the family farm some months earlier that had ignited his interest in flying.

By the end of the students' first week at Desford, the initial part of their course, covering the general outline, expectations, and requirements of the Royal Air Force, had been completed. The Royal Air Force liaison officer attached to the course, Squadron Leader Phipps, now stood before them.

'That is your service introduction over, gentlemen,' he said. 'Now you can begin your aviation study proper, but you won't be flying for a while yet. Nothing is done in an aeroplane until you have successfully completed the required aviation subjects. After you have mastered the principles of flight, you will move on to studying weather and navigation. Don't want you caught in a storm or getting lost, or both, do we? Then it will be aircraft technical knowledge, comms, and air rules. When you have passed all the written examinations, we will let you get into an aircraft and start teaching you how to fly the bloody thing. Any questions so far?'

The students remained silent.

'All right,' Phipps continued, 'now your real training begins. Your first aviation subject is scheduled to take five days, with an examination on day six. To be clear, if you fail any exam, you will be given one day to review and revise, and then you will sit it again. If you fail the exam a second time, you will be transferred to some other branch of the service. Flying will not be for you. Alternatively, you may leave the service altogether, if you so choose.'

John's excitement was tempered by these comments. As he considered what the squadron leader had said, he made the decision to prioritise his personal success over any distractions. He had not come this far to end up undertaking administrative duties elsewhere, or, even worse, going home as a failed student.

'As you leave, you should pick up your copy of this text, and associated notes, covering your first subject. You need to read everything very carefully. It takes a lot of hard work to become an RAF pilot,' Squadron Leader Phipps warned, as he waved a small book bearing the title *Principles of Flight.* 'Gentlemen, be in this classroom tomorrow, please, at o-nine hundred, ready to start. Hopefully by the end of the week you will know all about why and how an aircraft flies, and some key tenets of aviation.'

Over the next week, John studied harder than he ever had before. He had been no slouch at school, but here he was even more driven. He wanted to fly, and relished every day of his study.

'Come down to the pub with us, John,' a classmate said to him after the third day of studying.

'No, thanks, I'm going to work this evening,' John replied. He felt he had not yet mastered everything they had covered, and he wanted to spend more time reviewing the material before the exam at the end of the week.

'Suit yourself, old chap,' was the response.

'You are being bit of a swat,' someone else said, but John did not care. There could be no failure, and he wanted good passes.

The second week of study involved aviation meteorology. Everybody on the course had passed the principles of flight exam, although a couple had barely scraped through.

'Take the warning if you nearly failed,' said Squadron Leader Phipps to the assembled student pilots, after those first examination results were made known. 'Two of you came within a mark or so of having to resit. A bit more evening study in place of visits to the Fox and Hounds for some of you, I think.'

They all took that on board, and there was less time spent in the local pubs during the next week of the course. The additional work and focus showed. Everyone passed the meteorology exam by a good margin. The squadron leader was pleased.

'That's a good result, gentlemen. Knowing your weather is key to planning safe operations. As I say to every class, it is much better to be on the ground, wishing you were in the air, than to be in the air, wishing you were on the ground. It can get dicey out there if you miscalculate regarding weather conditions, so read the forecasts carefully. We don't want to lose people, and we cannot afford to lose aircraft.'

John had known meteorology would be a very technical and demanding subject, and he was pleased to have already had a good understanding of weather prior to starting the course. He had acquired some knowledge from his experiences back home on the farm, as well as from some tramping in New Zealand's Southern Alps.

Whenever reviewing a weather map published in the newspaper at home, John had known how to anticipate poor conditions. Getting the timing of shearing wrong on the farm could cause high mortality rates among newly shorn sheep if a strong, cold southerly then came in off the sea, straight from the Antarctic. And an unexpected weather change when hiking in the Alps could prove fatal.

Finally, the ground school section of the course was complete. John had passed everything with good grades, and he felt sorry for those who had failed at some point on the course. Of the twenty who had started out, five of the students had not made it through all the examinations. The trigonometry of air navigation had caught some out, and aircraft technical knowledge had been too difficult for others. Because they had been dropped from pilot training, two had simply left the service. The remaining three had chosen to be reassigned to other roles, mostly associated with managing catering or supply. John was thankful he had decided at the outset to study hard.

To celebrate the successful end of their ground course, John and some of his classmates headed off into nearby Leicester to visit their favourite local pubs. They were in the third pub they had visited that night when the two men who had failed the ground course and left the service appeared. They were a couple of Geordies, which meant they came from Newcastle, one of John's classmates explained to him.

The Geordies were very drunk and loud. They saw their former classmates and started shouting across the room.

'You bloody swats!' one called.

They were belligerent and spoiling for a fight. One member of John's group went over to them, to suggest they calmed down. He suffered more verbal abuse for his trouble. The men came across the taproom, looking for an opportunity to confront someone.

John stepped forward. 'Come on, fellows, no need for this,' he started, before he was interrupted by the tallest of the two Geordies. Mick was his name.

'Bugger off, you bloody sheep farmer.'

John ignored that and again asked them to quieten down.

Mick's response was to swing the large beer mug he was holding at John's head. He missed. John had seen it coming and ducked down low. Then, still in a crouch, John stepped closer to Mick and, as he came up, delivered a short, sharp punch to the underside of Mick's chin.

Mick's head snapped back and he went down in a heap, his tongue bleeding where he had accidentally bitten it. The other Geordie backed away, cautiously watching John.

'Christ,' said one of John's friends. 'Let's go, now.'

The pub manager came out from behind the bar and strode angrily towards the group. He knelt next to Mick, who was starting to gather himself. The manager looked over at John, a grim look on his face.

'You'd better get out of here, young man. I heard and saw what happened, but these situations often have difficult ramifications, so I would go if I were you.'

John and his friends hurriedly left as Mick, now sitting up, glared at them.

CHAPTER THREE

Two days later, flying training for John and his classmates was about to begin. The weather was fine, and Squadron Leader Phipps was concluding his briefing before they took their first flight.

'Today's lesson is effect of controls,' he said. 'Go down to the stores and collect your flying kit, then move out to the airfield to meet me in front of the flight cab.'

The student pilots were starting to leave the room when the squadron leader called out to John to remain behind.

'I have had a report about a fight at the Brewers Arms the night before last, Noble, involving service personnel from this base,' said Phipps when they were alone. 'Do you know anything about that?'

John understood that Phipps already knew the answer to that question, since he had been asked to stay behind. 'Yes, sir. I was involved.'

'Listen to me, Noble, if you want to be an officer in the RAF, you do not get involved in bar-room brawls.'

'Of course, sir,' John replied, but made no further comment. There was no point in denying what had happened, he decided, and he was not going to claim self-defence.

'You risk your career with behaviour like that, Noble.'

'I understand, sir. It won't happen again, I can assure you.'

'It better not. You should know we contemplated your dismissal from the course over this, but when the adjutant found out exactly what happened we decided you could have a second chance. Consequently, it's just a warning this time, but if something like this happens again, you will be going home. Clear?'

'Yes, sir.'

'That's all. Go and get your kit and report to the flightline.'

'Sir,' John acknowledged as he spun around and walked out of the room. Once outside, he exhaled deeply. *That was too close for comfort*, he thought. *Always remember where you are and what you are doing, John.*

He made his way down to where the other student pilots were standing, near a line of fifteen Tiger Moth aircraft. Squadron Leader Phipps was already there.

'Gentlemen, this is what you have really been waiting for. Today you will fly. I will call your name and give you a number and name. The number is the registration of the aircraft you will be using. The name is that of your instructor. When you hear your information, go, find your aircraft, and introduce yourself to your instructor. He will be waiting for you beside your designated machine. Good luck with this part of your course. Fly well.'

Then he began calling out names in alphabetical order. After a short while, John heard what he had been waiting for.

'Noble, Airframe number H9467. Instructor C. Scott.'

John strode quickly down the flightline, looking for the aircraft bearing the number H9467 on its fuselage. He was excited. Now his flying career was about to start in earnest.

As John approached the Tiger Moth showing the registration number he was looking for, a man standing near the aircraft stepped towards him.

'Hello, John Noble?'

'Yes, sir,' John acknowledged.

'Good. I'm Chris Scott. I will be your flying instructor over the next eight weeks, so we are going to get to know each other quite well.'

'How do you do, sir?' John said as they shook hands.

'I am a pilot employed by a company contracted to the RAF to undertake elementary flying training. You do not call me "sir". I am a civilian, not a member of the service. Chris is fine.'

John, who was not enamoured with hierarchical structures, immediately felt comfortable with his flying instructor.

'Let's walk around the aircraft,' Chris said, nodding towards the silver Tiger Moth. 'I will take you through the pre-flight procedures.'

John was fascinated as Chris began by showing him all the important items on the aircraft that had to be checked as part of every pre-flight inspection.

'You need to check the control surfaces, ensuring they are secure and operating fully and freely,' he said, showing John how to manipulate the rudder, elevator, and ailerons from outside the cockpit. 'If these don't operate properly in flight, you will have your hands full, so always carefully check them before take-off.'

John nodded in acknowledgement, interested to see the various control surfaces he had learnt about in ground school. He moved them himself as he followed his instructor around the Tiger Moth.

'This is important, John,' Chris said, as he showed John how to draw some fuel from the aircraft's fuel tank through a check valve. 'You drain about an inch of fuel into this,' he went on, holding up a small glass tube, 'to allow you to make sure there is no water in the fuel. Any water content will separate and you will be able to see it in the bottom of the tube. Water in your fuel could cause loss of engine power, so you check this before the first flight of the day, and after any refuelling.'

'Yes, understand that,' John said. A small tractor back home on the farm had a fuel cap that water sometimes got through if left out in the rain. There had been occasions when he had found it necessary to drain the tank and refuel the tractor to be able to run its engine effectively.

After briefing John on some more items related to the operation of the aircraft — including how Chris would communicate when airborne, through a tube system — Chris announced they would go flying, and John's heart leapt.

When they were in the air, Chris asked John to take over flying the Tiger Moth. 'You have control,' he said, as he relinquished control of the aircraft to John.

To John, that simple statement meant the world. For the first time in his life, he was flying an aeroplane. There was a huge grin of satisfaction on his face.

John felt completely at home in the cockpit, manipulating the controls as instructed. After just a few minutes, he decided this was what he had always been destined to do.

Chris showed him how to make the aircraft climb and descend using the control stick's fore and aft movement, and by adjusting engine power. More power and stick back to climb. Less power and stick forward to descend. He also showed John how to turn the aircraft, by moving the control stick in the direction of the turn required. That made the aileron control surface on the wing on the outside of the turn drop down, while on the other wing a similar control moved up, into the airflow above the wing. Those control surface movements caused the aircraft to bank into a turn. John also discovered that it was necessary to press the appropriate rudder pedal when the aircraft banked, so the turn was balanced.

After an hour of what John considered pure pleasure, his first flying lesson was over. It seemed only a short time since they had taken off when Chris announced from the rear cockpit that they would return to land.

'That's effect of controls done. You now know what your cockpit inputs will cause the control surfaces to do, and how the aeroplane will react to the movements of those surfaces. We'll cover stalling next time,' said Chris, after they had taxied back into the area where the aircraft were parked.

John had carefully studied the aerodynamic explanation of stalling during ground school. As a result, he knew that stalling had nothing to do with the engine, but that it was actually caused by airflow over the wing, normally smooth and laminar as it passed over its upper surface, becoming turbulent and disrupted. That affected the wing's ability to produce lift, causing an aircraft to fall from the sky until actions by the pilot restored the smooth laminar airflow. The pilot did so by checking the control stick forward and applying full power.

Well, that's the theory, John thought. *Let's see how it works when we try it tomorrow.*

The next day, John was thrilled to be back in the air.

'Hold the nose up, hold it, hold it,' Chris instructed from the rear cockpit.

He wanted John to hold the aircraft in a nose-high attitude while engine power was reduced to an idle. The resulting angle of the aeroplane would disrupt the airflow over the wing surfaces, and an aerodynamic stall would follow.

John was apprehensive, but he did as he was asked. He felt the aircraft shudder slightly.

'Here it comes. Hold that, John, hold it. Look ahead at the horizon, hold your nose above it. Keep the stick back, keep it back.'

Then it happened.

Suddenly, the nose of the aircraft dropped down below the line of the distant horizon as the aircraft stalled. John found himself looking straight ahead at the ground far below, and he saw the Tiger Moth's altimeter begin to unwind. The aircraft was losing height as it fell, nose-first.

'Check the stick forward gently, apply full power, and recover to a climb,' Chris instructed.

John moved the control stick forward and pushed the throttle right in. As he felt the aircraft responding, he pulled it up into a gentle climb.

'Well done, John,' Chris said. 'That's a stall we induced and you recovered as required. Tomorrow we will stall with some power on, instead of reducing our revs right back to idle. Stalling with power on will cause one of the aircraft's wings to drop steeply, as if banking. Then you will need to use a different recovery technique, otherwise we will end up in a spin, which we don't want.'

When they had landed, and as Chris debriefed him, John realised he was sweating profusely.

Over the next two weeks, John learned and practised take-offs and landings, standard rate turns, steep turns, climbing and descending, power-on and power-off stalling, and engine failure procedures.

John and Chris flew a lot of circuits while practising take-offs and landings. A circuit involved the aircraft taking off, flying a race-track-shaped pattern around the aerodrome, touching down, and then, during the landing roll, putting on power and taking off again to repeat the exercise.

After one extended session of circuits, instead of reapplying power and taking off again, Chris asked John to stop and taxi back to the beginning of the grass strip. Once there, Chris told John to shut down the engine. In the quietness that ensued, Chris clambered out of his cockpit, stood on the bottom wing next to John's cockpit, and smiled at him.

'Go and do one by yourself, John,' he said.

John's pulse quickened. His first solo flight. He found that he was elated rather than apprehensive.

He got out of his cockpit at the front to move to the cockpit just vacated by Chris. If there was only one person on board, the Tiger Moth had to be flown from the rear cockpit because of balance limitations. After checking his straps were tight, he signalled to Chris that he was ready to start the engine. With a thumbs-up in reply, Chris swung the propellor. The engine coughed into life.

John was determined that this would go well. He glanced towards Chris, who was now standing on the edge of the strip, watching. He waved to John and then turned and walked away, back towards the area where the aircraft were parked when not in use.

John pushed in the throttle and the Tiger Moth began to bump its way along the grass strip. It started to feel light, skipping occasionally as its tail came up and flying speed approached. Then, when John saw and felt that the aircraft was ready to fly, he eased back on the control stick. The Tiger Moth lifted off and climbed away. John looked at the empty cockpit in front of him and shouted with delight. He was flying by himself.

John was grinning as he flew around the aerodrome's circuit and set up his approach to land. He reduced engine power. All was going well. He passed over the threshold of the landing strip at about fifty feet, and began to close the throttle and ease the control stick back towards him. That caused the aircraft to round out its descent. As the landing surface came up towards him, he looked along its length to maintain a perspective of his height above it, something he had practised so many times during his circuit sessions in the aeroplane with Chris. He wanted to hold off touchdown for as long as possible. Then it came. A gentle arrival followed by the rumble of wheels on grass and the airframe vibrating as the Tiger Moth rolled to a stop.

John didn't think he had ever felt so happy. He knew this marked a significant milestone in his journey as a pilot.

After completing their flying course, John and the other student pilots were summoned to one of the classrooms that had been used for their flying theory lectures. Squadron Leader Phipps was there, beaming as usual.

'Gentlemen, you are the successful ones. You have now completed your basic flying training.'

As well as those who had failed the ground school examinations, including the Geordie who had put John's career at risk, four of the students had failed the flying course and had already left. Despite being given extra time and flying instruction, they had not been able to get their performance up to a satisfactory standard. However, they had all accepted ground-based positions with the Royal Air Force.

'As successful pilot candidates, you will all now go through the officers' course at RAF Uxbridge,' said Phipps. 'It takes two weeks, and I'm sure you will all manage it without any difficulty. Once you've completed that course, you will be off to RAF Hullavington for your advanced flying training. Congratulations on getting to this stage, but make no mistake, there is plenty still in front of you. If you want to be awarded your RAF Wings, you have a lot to do yet. Good luck.'

CHAPTER FOUR

The base at RAF Uxbridge was busy. It was not just those undergoing their officer training courses who were there. A special operations centre was being set up, and a lot of people seemed to be involved. Some of the more prescient in the senior ranks of the Royal Air Force could see what was happening in Germany and had a view about what was likely to soon occur.

Consequently, an underground room was under construction. John was told it was to be the place from where fighter aircraft operations would be controlled in the defence of the southeast of Britain, should that be required in future.

Once he had settled into his room at Uxbridge, John began looking through the material he had been given to read in preparation for officer training. He was surprised by some of the topics and associated detail. There seemed to be a suggestion that they would be shown the proper dining etiquette to be observed while in the officers' mess, including when it was permissible to smoke, and subjects that should be avoided. Politics and religion were noted. *Crikey*, thought John. *I just want to fly, not get tied up in all this stuff.*

But he should not have worried. The things he learned about were not as petty as he had first thought, and much of what they were told just reflected common sense.

On the successful completion of the course at Uxbridge, Acting Pilot Officer John Noble, as he was now, travelled to RAF Hullavington. He was there for his advanced flying training. If all went well, it would culminate in John being awarded his RAF Wings.

The RAF station was in an attractive part of Wiltshire, not far from the town of Chippenham, and it was busy. Student pilots who had qualified at various other Elementary Flying Training Schools around Britain had now joined together here for the next stage of their flight education.

The first training sortie John undertook was in a new type of aircraft, a low-wing monoplane called a Miles Magister.

'This is the Miles Magister,' John's Royal Air Force instructor, Flying Officer Mike Tucker, told him. 'It is a relatively new aircraft and it's authorised for aerobatics.'

John looked at the aircraft, noting its clean lines compared to the strut-covered Tiger Moth biplane he had trained in. He noted that the Miles Magister had two open cockpits, positioned one behind the other, a tandem set-up with which he was familiar. There was a small windscreen in front of each cockpit to give some protection to the occupant from the wind-flow.

'These ailerons have quite a large degree of movement, as you can see,' said Mike, as he lifted the control surface on the left wing. 'And there are split flaps there,' he added, pointing to the rear inboard section of the wing. After a general briefing on the aircraft, it was time for John to begin his work.

'All right, John, pre-flight the aircraft for me, please, telling me what you are doing, and why you are doing it at every step.'

John remembered his previous training in pre-flight processes at RAF Desford, as well as the detail he had recently studied relating to the Miles Magister. He had spent time carefully going through the Magister's manual when he had first arrived at Hullavington. He methodically worked his way around the aircraft's wings, its fuselage, and its tail, telling Mike what it was that he was checking and what he was looking for to ensure safety. When he reached the front of the aircraft, he undid the engine cowling fasteners to check inside the engine bay.

'All secure, no nests,' he said. Then, after a further check, he went on, 'Oil level within limits.'

It was not unknown for birds to begin building a nest in the engine bay when an aircraft had been parked unused for a period, so "no nests" was an important check. A heated engine setting fire to a nest while airborne was something to avoid.

'Propellor secure, no blade damage.'

'I didn't see you check the fuel,' said Mike.

'Sorry, sir, I inadvertently omitted that check,' John acknowledged. Annoyed by his failure, John drained some fuel and looked at it closely. 'No water detected in the fuel, sir.'

'Good. Let's go flying.'

John and Mike clambered up onto the wing and made their way to their respective cockpits. John was in the front cockpit. Mike, as the instructor, was in the rear.

'I will fly initially,' Mike announced, as he signalled the airman waiting near the front of the aircraft to swing the prop, to start the engine.

After completing pre-take-off checks, which Mike guided John through, they started to taxi. On reaching the strip and receiving a green light from the station's flight control cab, Mike pushed in the throttle, causing the 130hp de Havilland Gipsy Major engine to roar. The aircraft accelerated along the grass runway in response. The Miles Magister's tail wheel came up off the ground. It was soon ready to fly. John could feel the bumping of the main wheels lessening, a result of the wings starting to lift the aircraft. Then the Magister became airborne, and the dark green grass of the strip's surface fell away as the aircraft began climbing.

John was delighted with the look and feel of the aircraft as they flew. He always enjoyed being in the air. Despite being a relatively new pilot, flying felt very familiar, and always pleasurable. In a book he had read recently, the author had talked about the rapture of flight. John knew exactly what that meant.

As the course progressed, the teachers and instructors had no concerns about John. He fitted in well and his flying standard was considered above average. He soon reached the point where he was due to undertake his first solo cross-country flight. For the first time, he would be flying many miles away from the usual operational area he was familiar with, and he would be responsible for his own decision-making during the entire flight. There would be no instructor close by to ask for advice.

The cross-country flight assigned to John involved him taking off from RAF Hullavington, tracking northeast to Chipping Norton, then turning south to fly to Andover. From a position above Andover, he then had to turn northwest and fly back to base. John knew the flight would take just over an hour, depending on the winds. He prepared with great care. He had heard the stories about those who had got lost, and he didn't want that embarrassment.

When John had been flying his solo cross-country sortie for some time, and was, by his reckoning, approximately twenty miles north of Andover, cruising at three thousand feet, he noted a weather issue. Looking to his left, towards where his map told him the town of Newbury was situated, he could see a significant deterioration. A line of large clouds paralleled his track, and heavy rain was falling from them. The rain obscured his view of the ground beneath the clouds.

The clouds themselves were huge, dark at the bottom, but with puffy white tops that seemed to be growing higher as he watched them. He recognised the signs. He remembered what he had been taught in his aviation meteorology classes back at RAF Desford. They were cumulonimbus clouds moving quickly, both vertically and horizontally. If he continued his track towards Andover, the clouds would soon envelope him.

John was not an experienced pilot. His total flying time was less than seventy-five hours. About forty of those were solo hours, but they had all been flown close to the aerodrome from which he operated. Now he was by himself over unfamiliar territory, in deteriorating weather.

He recognised that trying to continue to Andover as planned would have significant risks, but diverting would be difficult too. He was bumping along in an open-cockpit aeroplane with a storm approaching. He did not have the luxury of sitting comfortably in a classroom, reviewing maps, and making navigational calculations with no pressure. He could feel his anxiety growing.

John was still at three thousand feet. He could see the conditions were deteriorating rapidly and the air was starting to become rough. The Magister was yawing and lurching as the effects of the approaching cumulonimbus clouds were felt. Then John saw that the rain had reached him. His in-flight visibility was suddenly much lower. He estimated he could now only see about fifteen hundred yards ahead. If the visibility dropped any more, and he lost his horizon reference point, he knew he could become disorientated and lose control of the aircraft. John made his decision.

Reducing power, he began a descent, at the same time turning towards the southwest, away from his course to

Andover, but more importantly, away from the fast-approaching squall line. He saw a flash and heard thunder. The air was becoming very turbulent and he had to wrestle with the controls to maintain any semblance of balanced flight. After a few minutes of lurching and pitching through the roughness, the sky ahead began to lighten. John could see he was outrunning the line of weather that had closed in on him so quickly. The air was still bumpy, so he maintained a low power setting to keep his speed down as he continued to descend. *No sense in over-stressing the airframe, or me for that matter*, he thought.

Soon, John was flying in the clear, some distance ahead of the adverse weather that continued to follow him. Visibility had improved, but John was unsure of his position. His altimeter told him he was down to one thousand four hundred feet above sea level, although he could see he was still comfortably above the terrain in the area. Perhaps a thousand feet above ground level, he thought. He knew he needed to quickly establish his position and calculate a course back to his base. He decided to fly northwest, thinking that direction would be likely to take him somewhere towards RAF Hullavington.

John turned the Magister towards the right, altering his south-westerly heading by ninety degrees on his compass, back towards where he hoped the aerodrome he sought may be. He calculated his remaining fuel would only give him another fifty minutes' endurance.

After he had been following his course to the northwest for about fifteen minutes, John saw a large town in the distance, to the left of his track. When he got closer, John tipped his wing down to get a better look. He recognised the town of Chippenham, and realised he was only eight miles from base.

Just as well I have found where I am, he thought. *I was down to thirty minutes of fuel.*

Mike was there to greet him when he landed and climbed out. John told him what had happened.

'John, you did well, thinking your way through that weather — diverting, changing altitude, and planning a route recovery. Good for you.'

In the officers' mess that night, John had an extra beer to celebrate his safe return. He understood that his day could have ended badly if he had not made the decisions he had.

Finally, after weeks of intensive training, John and the other student pilots completed the course. Now, as newly qualified service pilots, they were about to receive their coveted RAF Wings.

Squadron Leader Phipps beamed through the entire Wings award ceremony, which was being held in one of the large maintenance hangars.

'Congratulations, gentlemen,' he enthused. 'You have studied hard and applied yourselves to developing your flying capability. You are now commissioned pilots of the Royal Air Force, and you have some special flying skills. That is something to be proud of. On the mess noticeboard there is a list of your postings. Some of you have been selected for fighters, and some for heavy aircraft. Good luck to you all.'

John eased his way through the cluster of pilots around the noticeboard, keen to see what he would be flying in the next stage of his career, and where that would be. He soon found his name: *Pilot Officer John Noble — 415 Fighter Squadron, RAF Station Catterick. Report at fifteen hundred hours, Monday 8 May, 1939.*

Fighters for me, John thought, *and not just any fighter.* They had all heard about a new aircraft the Royal Air Force was bringing in. It was something called a Spitfire, and it had a completely new level of capability. He was aware that 415 Squadron was one of the first fighter squadrons to get this new aircraft.

John was thrilled that he would soon have the chance to fly the Spitfire. During a recent chat with one of the flying instructors at Hullavington, who seemed to know all about the new aircraft, he had heard about some of its features. 'It has a terrific rate of climb, two and a half thousand feet a minute, and can cruise at three hundred miles per hour,' the instructor had said.

John was impressed. In his Miles Magister training aircraft, he was lucky to get much more than seven hundred feet per minute climb rate, and the Magister was going as fast as it could at one hundred and forty miles per hour.

What a difference, he marvelled. He could not wait to get to Catterick.

CHAPTER FIVE

'Welcome to RAF Catterick, Pilot Officer Noble,' the station adjutant said, smiling broadly.

A friendly chap, John thought. He had just reported to the adjutant on his arrival from Hullavington.

'I am Flight Lieutenant Gardiner,' the adjutant continued. 'I act as the principal administrator here, working closely with our commanding officer, Wing Commander Bland. You are the only pilot off the latest Wings course to be posted to Catterick, so that will help us get your operational training done relatively quickly.'

'Thank you, sir. I am looking forward to it. I understand I will be flying the Spitfire.'

'Indeed, you will, Pilot Officer. Four-one-five squadron has been re-equipped with Spitfires in recent months.'

'I have heard they are a very fine aircraft.'

'Yes, the Spitfire will be a quantum leap for you compared to what you've flown to date. You have some interesting days ahead as you learn how to operate it, but you will enjoy the experience. It is a great aircraft. You won't be introduced to any flying in the aircraft until you have completed the ground course for your rating on type. There's quite a bit to learn about the Spitfire's systems and procedures before you take it up.'

John acknowledged what the adjutant was saying with a small nod.

'The ground course should take you no more than four days,' Gardiner continued, 'and you will start on that tomorrow. Squadron Leader Bayliss will be your tutor. He will also supervise your Spitfire conversion and consolidation, as our principal flight-training instructor. I will introduce you to him soon, but for now, the CO wants to see you.'

'Sir,' John acknowledged, trying not to appear too excited about the prospect of flying a Spitfire.

Gardiner led him to the CO's office and made the introductions.

'Wing Commander, this is the new pilot Command promised, Pilot Officer John Noble. He has just gained his Wings at Hullavington. Pilot Officer Noble, this is Wing Commander Bland, Commanding Officer of four-one-five squadron.'

'Pleased to meet you, Pilot Officer. Thank you, Adjutant.'

Gardiner took his cue and left.

'Please, sit down,' Bland said to John, gesturing towards the empty chair in front of his desk.

John took a seat and waited for the CO to begin. He knew the rules for junior officers meeting senior officers in these circumstances. Speak when spoken to; don't initiate and try to run a conversation yourself. But Christopher Bland said nothing and began reading some papers on his desk. Sitting there, looking at him in silence, John began to feel a little uncomfortable. After a few more tortuous minutes, the wing commander looked up.

'I understand you have come from New Zealand.'

'Yes, sir.'

'What persuaded you to apply to the Royal Air Force and come halfway around the world to join?'

'I wanted to fly, sir, and when I saw the RAF inviting applications from New Zealanders, I thought it was an opportunity to pursue something I wanted to do.'

'What were you doing at that time?'

'Working on my father's farm, sir.'

'Oh, I see. How big was the farm?'

'About six hundred acres, sir. We ran sheep.'

'Hmm,' the wing commander murmured. 'Successful farmers, were you?'

'We did all right, sir,' John responded, slightly surprised by the question.

'Whereabouts in New Zealand?'

'A place called Clydevale. That's in the Otago province, which is in New Zealand's South Island.'

'A remote place, is it?'

'Relatively, so far as the nearest cities are concerned. It's a typical small New Zealand country village, sir. There's a general store, a garage, a church, and a pub. Not much else, apart from a sports ground.'

'I see. So where does one go to school, if living in Clydevale?'

'There is a local primary school, but secondary school requires a twenty-mile bus trip every day to a nearby town. Otherwise, there's a boarding school in the city.'

'Daily bus trip for you, was it?'

'No, sir, I went to a boarding school in Dunedin.'

'Oh, so the farm wasn't doing too badly then.'

John did not reply, but he thought the conversation a bit strange.

The wing commander must have thought the same, because he suddenly became more businesslike. 'Squadron Leader Bayliss has been assigned responsibility for getting you rated in the Spitfire. Once your initial training on type is over, and after you have completed your consolidation flying, you will be ready to start on air warfare tactics. At that point you become operational with the squadron. I pride myself on running a safe and efficient operation here. I want to see all my people operating competently and professionally. For pilots, that's expected as standard. You have been well-trained, but I always ask that every pilot guards against complacency and never undertakes any airborne shenanigans. Clear?'

'All clear, sir.'

'Do you have any questions for me, Pilot Officer Noble?'

'No, thank you, sir.'

'Very well, see yourself out. The adjutant will take you to the mess and show you where you will be living.' With that, Wing Commander Bland returned to looking at the papers on his desk.

John stood, saluted, and left, making his way back to Flight Lieutenant Gardiner's office.

'All done?' asked Gardiner as John reappeared.

'Yes, sir,' said John, deciding not to say anything about the strangeness of the conversation.

'I will take you over to the mess and show you around so you can get your bearings. Follow me.'

As they walked, John looked around. He saw a group of Spitfires parked in a dispersal area. Some airmen were digging and excavating the ground nearby, and he wondered what they were doing.

'Slit trenches and gun pits,' Gardiner said, answering John's unspoken question. 'The general view is that we need to prepare in case the Germans get more belligerent and something develops.'

John just nodded. He had read the newspaper articles about the political instability in Europe. Hitler and his cohorts were ramping up their National Socialist agenda. He had also seen the reports about the British Prime Minister's attempts to appease the Germans, something that was not going well, it seemed.

Gardiner spent about twenty minutes showing John around the officers' mess and pointing out the location of important airfield facilities — the maintenance hangar, met office, briefing room, and aerodrome control cab. It was early afternoon, so there were not many people to be seen in the mess. Some would be engaged in operational activity, others busy with administrative duties, Gardiner explained.

'You will meet them tonight. Normally they will start to gather in the mess bar for a pre-dinner drink at about eighteen hundred,' he told John. 'Dinner is at eighteen thirty. Sit wherever you like, apart from the top table. That is Wing Commander Bland's table, and he chooses who joins him there.'

'Thank you, sir,' said John as Gardiner left him.

John went to the room he had been allocated. It was quite spacious and comfortably furnished with a well-cushioned armchair. A shared bathroom was just a short distance along the corridor. His accommodation was on the first floor of the mess, with a view over the airfield. As he leaned out of the room's window to look around, John noted the nearby windsock bordering the operational area. In the absence of any wind, it was hanging limply, so white and pristine he thought it must have been brand-new.

After settling into his room, John looked at his wristwatch. It was just after six o'clock, time to head downstairs and meet his fellow officers.

John pushed open the main door to the bar. He was struck by the noise of multiple conversations and the grey, smoke-filled air. Many of those present were puffing away on their favourite brand of cigarette.

'Ah, Noble, come and let me introduce you to some of your fellow pilots,' said Gardiner, when he spotted John. He introduced him to a group of five men, all enjoying a dark-looking ale. 'Gentlemen, let me introduce Pilot Officer John Noble, a new pilot who arrived today, joining us off Wings.' Then he went around the group. 'This is Greg Somerville. He was on the Mark II Fury for six months, and managed not to bend one, so we let him move to Spits.'

Everyone laughed. They all knew how difficult the Fury was to land in a crosswind.

'Nice to meet you,' Greg said, grinning at John.

'And this is Richard Cowles. He has also been on the Fury, and did manage to bend one,' Gardiner continued.

'Tell the whole story please, Adjutant,' Richard pleaded. 'I had an engine failure, and had to land out, with only rough terrain to select for my arrival back on terra firma.'

More chuckling from the group.

'Sure, Richard,' said Greg, 'and in your case, the firmer, the less terror.'

That set them off, with loud guffaws directed at the hapless Richard.

'And this is Roger Barton,' said Gardiner, 'our Spitfire aerobatic ace.'

'Good to meet you, John,' Roger smiled. 'I hear you are a Kiwi, joining us from down under?'

'Yes, that's right. I arrived in the UK in early October, and I am thoroughly enjoying my time here.'

'This is Charlie Ross,' Gardiner continued, introducing a short, stout young man.

'Pleased to meet you, Charlie,' John said, shaking his hand.

'Charlie is our mountaineer. Always out climbing in any high terrain he can find, when we give him some leave,' Gardiner added. 'And last but not least, meet Craig Thomson.'

'Hello, Craig.'

Craig smiled in response, and was starting to say something when Greg interrupted.

'Here, have one of these,' said Greg as he thrust a dark ale into John's hand. 'Welcome to RAF Catterick.'

'What did you do before coming to the UK, John?' Roger asked.

'I was a farmer. I worked on the family farm in the south of New Zealand with my father.'

'So, how did you end up as a pilot in the RAF?' Roger continued.

'I responded to an invitation that appeared in New Zealand newspapers, asking interested parties to apply.'

'Ah, part of the Commonwealth Scheme,' Roger responded. 'Well done. Good to have you here.'

'That's quite a transition, from New Zealand farmer to Royal Air Force pilot,' Richard commented as he finished off his ale. 'Was it difficult for you?'

'Christ, ignore him, John,' Greg interjected. 'What you need to understand about Richard is that he is, despite appearances, exceptionally well-bred. He has an "Honourable" at the beginning of his name, and he went to the best school and university, of course. But we all ignore that, just like we ignore his view that you must be special to fly.'

'No offence intended, John,' Richard chuckled. 'It's all in jest.'

John smiled and nodded, uncertain whether Richard was being sincere.

'I'm from a farm too,' Craig volunteered. 'Folks had a property on the coast north of Berwick, which is not far from here.' He then spent the next few minutes describing to John everything he could about his farming experiences. John guessed he had a reputation for talking, something confirmed when Charlie, who was behind Craig, winked and smiled at him. Then the group was joined by another pilot, a squadron leader, according to his insignia.

'Evening all,' he said in a relaxed tone.

Looking at John, he held out his hand. 'You must be John Noble. I am Alastair Bayliss, your instructor on the Spitfire.'

'How do you do, sir?' John responded, quite formally.

'Flying training is a serious business, but that doesn't mean we are not going to have some fun,' said Bayliss.

'I am looking forward to it.'

'The Spitfire is turning out to be a significant step up for us, and it is an absolute delight to fly, as you will find out.'

A gong sounded suddenly. It was loud and insistent. John heard an official-sounding call from the doorway.

'Gentlemen, dinner is about to be served.'

'Speak later,' said Bayliss as he turned to make his way to the dining room.

The mess bar quickly emptied as the assembled officers put down their glasses, whether finished or not. No-one took their glass with them to the dining room — that was one of the rules. Fresh glasses would be provided as the officers dined.

John was invited to sit with the pilots he had just met, although he noticed Richard Cowles was no longer with them, nor was Alastair Bayliss. No-one sat down immediately. They stood behind their chairs, waiting. The reason for that soon became clear to John. After just a few moments, Wing

Commander Bland entered the room, strode to the top table, and positioned himself behind the chair at its head.

Flight Lieutenant Gardiner, who was also at that table, then called to the room, 'Gentlemen, you may sit.'

John saw that both Alastair Bayliss and Richard Cowles were seated at the top table with the CO.

Greg saw John looking. 'Only senior officers or important people are asked to sit with the boss, John,' he whispered. 'Richard gets an invite because of his title, not because of his rank. He's just a Flying Officer — that wouldn't be enough on its own.' Greg grinned.

John understood what Greg meant. He had discerned the sort of person Bland was when he had been introduced to him on his arrival at the station.

'We aren't senior enough, nor important enough, to be asked to the top table,' Greg went on.

Just then, Gardiner appeared at John's shoulder. 'Pilot Officer Noble, Wing Commander Bland would be pleased if you would join him at his table this evening,' he said.

Greg laughed quietly and winked at John.

'Follow me,' said Gardiner as he moved off, with John falling in behind him.

'Pilot Officer Noble, thank you for joining us. Please sit here,' said Bland, indicating the chair next to him. 'You of course know my adjutant, Flight Lieutenant Gardiner, and I think you have also met Squadron Leader Bayliss and Flying Officer Cowles.'

'Yes,' said John, nodding a greeting to them.

'May I also introduce Squadron Leaders David Sidey, Tony Smallbone, and Michael Howarth?'

'How do you do?' John said to each, as he shook their hands.

During dinner, Bland resumed quizzing John about his background. He wanted to know about New Zealand farming methods, and whether a farmer with a reasonably sized property could earn a satisfactory income from grazing stock.

John skirted the income questions, but happily talked about farming techniques and what he and his father had found improved productivity on the farm.

'Much different from the way you do things on your estate?' Bland asked Richard.

Richard was happy to talk about crop and animal management, but he too avoided any comment on finances. It soon became clear to John that Richard, or at least his family, farmed a substantial property in Norfolk.

'Good to see you again, Pilot Officer Noble. Best of luck with your conversion training. Goodnight,' Bland said as he left the table at the end of dinner. Everyone in the room stopped talking and stood as he left, resuming their seats and chatter once he had departed.

John smiled at Richard, raising his eyebrows slightly.

Leaning over to John, Richard said quietly, 'So now you know what drives our CO, John. You were being examined to see if you were of the right stuff socially, as he sees it. We all know what he's like. If you found him difficult, don't worry about it. We all do, and we just ignore him when he's being a prat. You might have noticed the other senior officers at the table didn't join in with the conversation either. They could see what was going on and kept out of it.'

John nodded, grateful for the insight, but he did find himself wondering if Bland's personality might adversely affect the squadron. *How will his outlook affect his capacity to bring a balanced view to his role as commanding officer*, John asked himself?

Anyone who knew Wing Commander Christopher Bland understood that he was a complex character, someone always quick to talk about his own flying and leadership skills, but often dismissive of others. Few of those who flew with him considered he was particularly capable, as either a pilot or a leader. His elitist approach to life, seen in his social behaviour, meant that he was considered an unpleasant person by many.

If you were wealthy, or socially important, Christopher Bland would be your friend, but not so if you were from what he considered to be an ordinary background. Then, you would be tolerated, but he would remain distant and make little effort to engage in any pleasantries. In fact, quite the opposite on some occasions, when he could be rude or dismissive. The fact that he held rank as a Wing Commander, but had been given only a single squadron to command, indicated that some at RAF Fighter Command had probably recognised his failings as well.

CHAPTER SIX

Within the first few days of joining the squadron, John had recognised that all the pilots had a special camaraderie. As the newcomer to the squadron, he had been readily welcomed and made to feel comfortable, and he enjoyed the company of the other pilots. Often, as they relaxed in the bar of the officers' mess before dinner, stories would be told. Sometimes they were about a young woman someone had met at a local dance or in the pub, and sometimes they were about difficult flights. John particularly enjoyed hearing the flying tales. He liked to take in everything he heard about the Spitfire. Some of the pilots' experiences provided valuable insight for someone new and inexperienced.

Just a few days after John had arrived at RAF Catterick, he had been fascinated by a story he heard Greg Somerville telling in the bar one evening. It seemed that about a month earlier, on a particularly cold day, Greg had struggled to get back to the airfield. There had been a severe build-up of ice on his aircraft. Despite the Spitfire's capabilities, the conditions could have brought it down.

'I don't mind admitting that I was bloody frightened,' Greg said to the assembled group of pilots, who stood listening to him in silence. 'The ice on my Spit not only added weight, but it also disrupted the airflow over my wings. I felt the bloody controls snatch a couple of times too, a result of icing on the control surfaces causing imbalance, I decided. Thought I was going to lose the aircraft. The ice just kept building. It was getting thick on the front cockpit window. Looking out the side, I could see it was also forming rapidly on the leading edge of both wings. Damn scary, I tell you.'

'Crikey, what does a fellow do in those circumstances?' Richard asked.

'Well, doing nothing is not an option. Take my word for that,' replied Greg. 'The aircraft was clearly overweight and losing lift. I could see its performance reducing. Full power and the aircraft would only just hold altitude — it wouldn't climb, despite the aircraft's nose-up attitude, and my airspeed was reducing steadily. The controls felt soggy, except for the occasional sudden jerk.

'I lowered the nose, planning to descend to warmer air to get rid of the ice. That also meant I was able to reduce the exposure of the underside of my wing and tailplane to the ice. I did it all slowly and carefully. I didn't want to make any sudden control input, changing the aircraft's attitude too quickly. I was thinking about the risk of an aerodynamic upset. Being unsure of my precise position and forced to descend while in cloud, I also worried about a bloody hill looming up in front of me.'

'Christ, Greg, what a pickle,' Richard interjected.

'As I descended, I turned the aircraft on to an easterly heading, thinking the risk of high terrain in that direction was less than if I headed west.'

'Good thinking, Greg,' Richard said. Others nodded. They were all thinking of the Pennines to the west of Catterick.

'Because I was worried about high terrain in the area, I stopped my descent as soon as I saw the ice beginning to melt and fall away. I didn't want to go any lower than necessary while still blind-flying and unsure of my position. Suddenly, I popped out of the cloud. Most of the ice had dropped off by then, and I was able to see I was near Sunderland. I turned south and flew towards the airfield, but when I got closer, I could see I was going to have to deal with more poor conditions. I thought about a diversion, but decided there was nowhere else within range. I was down to twenty minutes of fuel, at most. The cloud ceiling looked to be no more than two hundred feet, with patches lower. The control cab reported it as a two-hundred-foot base. Drizzle was reducing my visibility to around four hundred yards. I knew I was right on the margin for visual flight.

'I was being bloody careful. I dropped my flaps to slow the aircraft down, and then used my established ground markers to work out where I was in relation to the runway. I got in, but let me tell you the bad weather approach and landing were a walk in the park compared to the icing encounter.'

'Well done. Good stuff. Lessons there for us all, I think,' said Richard.

Over dinner that evening, John found he was sitting next to Greg.

'What an experience you had with the icing and poor aerodrome visibility,' John commented, keen to hear anything that would help him develop his flying skills and judgment.

Greg was happy to give John some guidance. 'You have to watch it around here when a north-easterly flow is forecast, especially if they are going for low stratus, reduced temperatures, and higher humidity than normal. It's a dangerous cocktail leading to marginal ceilings and reduced visibility, and of course the likelihood of icing conditions at higher levels.'

'You've flown in and out of Catterick for a while, Greg,' John said, 'but I'm not sure how I would find my way into the airfield in conditions like that, not being as familiar with the area.'

'Sure, John, I understand. You will soon get to know your way around. In good weather, I went out and established some ground markers that would help me position myself when visibility was poor. For example, when the easterly vector is in use, I use the double road that runs past the western side of the aerodrome and follow it, north or south, depending on the direction from which I'm approaching. I do that until I reach a point from where I know I can turn safely towards the field, even though I might not be able to see it at that stage. The turn-in point is where the pedestrian and cycle bridge crosses the river. It's right next to the double road. When I see that bridge, I turn east, and I know I'm on a short final approach into the aerodrome. The field is very close by then, and will come into view through the murk in seconds. You won't run into anything on a short approach in poor visibility if you stay at or above four hundred until you can see to land. Maintaining that height has you about two hundred feet above ground level as you come in and there is nothing over one hundred feet high immediately west of the aerodrome. So, marginal, but safe.

'Thanks. I see the value in known ground position markers in low visibility conditions.' John realised that doing what was being suggested would require care and precision. Flying in poor meteorological conditions at two hundred feet above ground level demanded extreme caution.

'Yes, and provided you have a cloud-base of no less than two hundred feet, it's safe enough because you know where you are. I wouldn't do it if I didn't have a least four hundred yards' visibility, though, and you need to have the aircraft slowed right up. Reduced power, with flap and gear down. The aerodrome is close to your turn-in point and the landing threshold will appear at the last moment, so you have to be ready, in landing configuration.'

John nodded, making a mental note to avoid flying in weather conditions of that sort, at least until he had more experience in the Spitfire and had become more familiar with the environs around the airfield at Catterick.

The day John was due to take his initial flight in the Spitfire was fine, and there was no wind. He was relieved. He knew he would have enough to focus on, taking a Spitfire up for the first time, without having to worry about a crosswind or a gusty landing approach.

Squadron Leader Bayliss was waiting for him in the briefing room.

'Good morning, Pilot Officer Noble. Ready for your first flight in a Spitfire?'

'Yes, thank you, sir,' John replied, trying to sound calm. He had more than one hundred hours' flying time, but he knew the Spitfire represented a significant advance on the aircraft he had flown to date.

Having completed the Spitfire ground course, John was familiar with everything in the aircraft manual. He had all the required power settings, procedures, and speeds clear in his head. Following discussions in the mess with experienced pilots, he also understood the various nuances of the Spitfire at different stages of flight. Nevertheless, he still felt apprehensive. There was no dual cockpit in a Spitfire, so a pilot's first time flying one was a solo venture from the outset. No instructor could accompany him on his initial flight to guide him and advise him in the air. Lectures and briefings on the ground were all that were available, and, of course, a lot of preparation by the pilot.

'Natural to be a bit nervous,' Bayliss said. 'Take comfort from the fact that you have been well trained, both in the air and on the ground.'

'Sir,' John acknowledged, surprised that the squadron leader had noticed that he was nervous.

'We will start with a walk around the aircraft,' Bayliss continued, leading John out of the briefing room and walking across the newly mown grass towards a lone Spitfire parked a short distance away.

John was surprised that the squadron leader had not given him a detailed briefing. The reason for that soon became apparent.

'You won't be flying the aircraft this morning, Pilot Officer,' said Bayliss as they reached the Spitfire. 'What I want you to do is pre-flight it, then get into the cockpit, strap yourself in, and sit there confirming the position of every switch, button, wheel, handle, and lever. Talk yourself through, aloud, what they are for and when you would use them. I want you, by the end of the morning, to be able to describe the cockpit and all its controls and their various purposes just from memory.'

'Very good, sir.'

'Any questions?'

'No, sir.'

'Right-oh. I will stay with you during the pre-flight walk-around. After that, you can climb aboard and I will leave you for about an hour while you spend time on your cockpit familiarisation. When I get back, I will ask you to come into the briefing room and describe the cockpit in detail, telling me what everything in there does, when, and at what speed where there are limitations applying. Let's make a start.'

John began his pre-flight inspection. As he moved around the Spitfire, he felt a sense of personal attachment. He liked the way the aircraft sat on its main undercarriage, nose inclined upwards, as if ready to climb into the sky. The banks of exhausts along each side of the nose signalled the raw power of its Merlin engine. John had been told that engine made one of the sweetest sounds known to pilots.

He was also aware that the long nose in which the Merlin was housed would limit forward visibility on the ground. That was overcome, according to the instruction manual John had studied, by weaving the aircraft as it taxied, while looking along each side of the nose in turn to check the way was clear. Similarly, when landing, a curved approach was to be flown, the manual had noted. Without that approach profile, the runway would not easily be seen over the nose.

After John had completed his pre-flight walk-around and inspection, Bayliss left as planned and John climbed up onto the port wing and lowered himself into the cockpit. He immediately felt a strange sense of familiarity, even though it was his first time in the aircraft.

Strapping himself in, John began checking the position and function of the various controls. The throttle, complete with a rubber grip, protruded from the left-hand wall of the cockpit. Immediately in front of the pilot's seat, the primary instrument cluster provided critical information about airspeed, height, rate of climb, and orientation. A compass indicated direction. John also took in the large trim-wheel, a control that allowed the aircraft to be kept in balance longitudinally while in flight, the short lever used to lower and raise the wing-flaps, and the selector for undercarriage extension and retraction. The engine instruments John saw on the lower left and right-hand sides of the panel would tell a pilot all he needed to know about his engine's performance and health.

The aircraft's control stick was positioned directly in front of the pilot. At the top was a padded, round, grip. On the upper left-hand side of that grip there was a button. That was it, John thought. *The* button. Pressing it would unleash a barrage of fire at whatever was in the Spitfire pilot's sights.

He continued his cockpit familiarisation, working left to right through all the switches, levers, handles and controls, over and over. After doing that for nearly an hour, John felt totally familiar with the Spitfire's cockpit controls and layout, and was confident he would perform well when Bayliss tested him.

The squadron leader soon returned. 'So, Pilot Office Noble, did you get the cockpit sorted and fixed in your mind, and have all the limiting speeds nailed?' he asked.

'Yes, I think I have it all clear, sir,' John replied.

To his surprise, Bayliss did not then begin testing him. 'Very good,' was all he said, followed by an instruction to get some lunch and to be back at the aircraft, ready to go, at 1400 hours.

As John ate lunch, a large omelette that completely covered his plate, Richard Cowles sat down beside him.

'Hear you are about to fly the Spit,' he said cheerily. 'Scared?'

'Moderately apprehensive,' John replied with a smile.

'Ha, good answer. That sums it up. We've all been through it, so I know what you mean. A suggestion for you: take charge of the aeroplane. Don't be timid and wait to respond to what it does. Take charge and drive it with purpose, and it will do what you ask of it.'

'I will. Thanks.'

'Enjoy your first flight, John. See you tonight.' Richard got up and left.

John finished his lunch and walked back out to the field to meet the squadron leader.

'Fed and watered and ready to go?' Bayliss asked as John arrived back at the aircraft.

'Yes, sir. Ready to fly.'

'You may not fly today. It will depend on how things work out.'

John was surprised but said nothing.

'About two months ago, Wing Commander Bland implemented a new procedure for squadron pilots taking their initial Spitfire flight,' Bayliss explained. 'Fighter Command was concerned about the rate of training accidents occurring across its fighter squadrons. Here at four-one-five, we now put our pilots through some additional exercises prior to their first flight on type. The CO is determined that his squadron will have the lowest training attrition rate in Fighter Command.'

John nodded.

'Consequently, before you actually fly it,' Bayliss continued, 'you will undertake some practice runs in the aircraft, while it remains on the ground.

'The procedure we have adopted is that you accelerate the aircraft along the runway, as if taking off, but then abort at about fifty miles per hour. When you close the throttle to abort, bring the aircraft to a stop slowly. No need for heavy braking — there is plenty of room. The exercise is intended to give you some familiarity with the Spitfire's behaviour under full power while on the ground. Also, you can get a feel for controlling the aircraft as it would be in the landing roll, when you are bringing it to a stop after your run.

'When you put on power to begin the take-off roll, you will find the aircraft wants to swing left much more strongly than anything you have flown to date, so be ready with your right rudder input to keep it straight. During the roll-out, after cutting power you will also need to ensure you hold the aircraft straight. That might mean a bit of dancing on the rudder pedals. Don't want any ground-loops.'

John grinned. That would be embarrassing, but he understood the risk. The Spitfire had a narrow undercarriage track, so a pilot could lose directional control if he was not careful, especially if there was a crosswind. *Glad there is no wind today*, he thought.

'There is some initial stuff to do after starting, before undertaking the speed runs,' Bayliss continued. 'First, of course, you conduct your standard engine ground-checks and run-up. You need to be quick with that; a Spit can overheat quite quickly, so keep an eye on your pressures and temperatures. The aircraft is fitted with the two-pitch propellor blades, so you should also exercise the pitch change mechanism to ensure it is operating properly. We expect to have full constant speed propellors soon, but for now it's just the two positions. After that, you carry out some simple taxiing exercises, swerving the aircraft from side to side slightly as you taxi at low speed. That is to enable you to practise maintaining an adequate lookout for any obstructions in your path. There might be fixed objects in your way, or even another aircraft taxiing. You wouldn't necessarily see them if you weren't weaving to enable your forward view. The nose of the Spitfire restricts what you can see ahead when the aircraft's tail is on the ground.'

John was familiar with all of this. He had studied the Spitfire's Pilot Notes carefully.

'Then, after doing that relatively straightforward stuff, you go on to the practice runs I talked about. As I said, this is something the CO has recently implemented. What you are to do is accelerate the aircraft as if making a take-off run, but then you abort the run before getting anywhere near airborne.

'The control cab will give you a green, clearing you to start each run. They have been briefed about what you are doing. Any questions so far?'

'That's all clear, thank you, sir. How many high-speed runs do you want me to do?'

'Depends on how you are handling the aircraft. If you are keeping it straight and are tidy with the tail coming up and setting down, and you can bring the aircraft to a stop without over-braking and risking tipping it onto its nose, I would think maybe three or four runs. That should leave you, and me, comfortable that you are ready take it up.'

John smiled. He was confident he would complete the exercises with no problems.

Strapped in tightly, with his parachute pack pressed against his lower back, he started the Spitfire's engine. It coughed and spluttered initially, its propellor moving only slightly, but then it burst into life with a roar and the propellor whirled so fast its blades became invisible. Smoke, and some momentary flame, came out of the bank of exhausts along each side of the nose cowl. It was something John had expected. He had seen Spitfires belching like that before as they were started. John let the engine warm up before easing the throttle handle forward to increase power, all the time watching the temperatures and pressures. He soon completed his ground checks. Then he began taxiing, keeping his speed low as he pushed each rudder pedal in turn, setting up a weaving path over the ground. As the Spitfire turned one way then the other, John would lean towards the opposite side of the cockpit to peer along the edge of the long nose, checking the way forward was clear. He soon mastered the taxiing technique.

'That all looked fine,' Bayliss said after John had returned and shut down the engine. 'Now the practice take-off runs, but as I said, don't allow the aircraft to become airborne, and keep an eye on engine temperature. And remember, before every run, turn towards the control cab and await your green.'

'Yes, sir,' said John, climbing back up onto the wing and into the cockpit.

By the third run, John was feeling comfortable. He had been a bit slow adding power on the first run, and did not get the aircraft's tail up properly before deciding it was time to cut the power and stop. He had been over-cautious with the required slight check-forward on the control stick, to help the tail come up. He had read the warning in the Pilot Notes about the risk of a prop strike if too rough with that movement, and he had let that affect him. On the second run he fed in more power earlier, and more quickly. John found he had to put a lot of pressure on the right rudder pedal to keep the aircraft straight. After a short acceleration, the tail had come up as he wanted, and then gently lowered itself when he cut the engine and brought the aircraft to a stop. On the third run, he felt much more confident. Everything went exactly as he planned, but he was a little slow in reducing the power. Just as he started to close the throttle, he felt the aircraft skip and lift, before settling back down onto the ground. He had only risen a few inches, and just for a second or so, but he realised he might have just completed his first flight in a Spitfire.

Taxiing back in, he was feeling very happy with his progress. Squadron Leader Bayliss was also pleased.

'That looked all right, Pilot Officer Noble,' he said.

John could hardly keep the grin off his face as he answered. 'Thank you, sir. I'm looking forward to taking it up.'

'Very good. Unfortunately, I can't let you fly this afternoon. First Spit flights must be signed off by Wing Commander Bland, on my recommendation as your instructor. I am ready to give that recommendation, but realistically the CO won't be able to review it with me and authorise your flight today, so tomorrow will be your day.'

John was disappointed, but said nothing. He could wait another day, he decided, but he knew what would be on his mind as he tried to sleep that night — his first flight in a Spitfire the following morning.

CHAPTER SEVEN

Early the next day, Bayliss met John in the briefing room and confirmed that the wing commander had signed off late the previous afternoon on John taking the Spitfire up. After a quick review of flight procedures and the airborne exercises to be undertaken, Bayliss sent John off to the flightline.

As he approached the area where aircraft were parked, John could see the Spitfire he was to fly. It was sitting alone, separate from the other machines being readied for the day's operations. As John walked towards it, he was not nervous. No, this was like meeting an old friend.

He felt nothing but pleasurable anticipation as he sat in the cockpit, the engine quietly grumbling at high idle. When he had completed all his checks, and the engine was warmed, John lined up for take-off. His clearance flashed green from the control cab. He pushed the throttle of the Spitfire forward and set take-off power. His aircraft began to accelerate rapidly. As the airspeed indicator approached eighty-five miles per hour, he gently eased the aircraft's control stick back, just a fraction, as specified in the Pilot Notes he had reviewed. The Spitfire responded, lifting off and climbing easily towards the east. Everything John had heard about the aircraft seemed accurate so far. Plenty of power, smooth and crisp in its control response, and wonderful visibility.

Bayliss's brief to John after he had told him he would be flying the Spitfire today was simple.

'Just fly it around for a while and get the feel of it. Try some stalling, but not below four thousand feet above ground level,' he had warned John.

In a fully developed stall, a Spitfire could flick into a spin if a mistake was made. Because a pilot would quickly lose altitude if that happened, it was important to ensure stalling was undertaken at a height sufficient to allow recovery.

John cruised along at seven thousand feet. Even though he had not set the power high, he saw his indicated airspeed was two hundred and seventy miles per hour. He had never travelled so fast in his life. The air was smooth, with no bumps at all. John moved the control stick left. Dutifully, the Spitfire's port wing went down, its starboard wing came up, and the aircraft banked into a turn to the left. He gently pressed the left rudder pedal when he saw, from the Spitfire's turn and slip indicator, that his turn was not balanced. The aircraft's tail had been slipping into the turn.

John decided to steepen the Spitfire's angle of bank in the turn. *Fifty degrees to the horizontal will be good*, he thought. The aircraft's nose began to drop. A result of the steepness of his turn, John realised. He stopped the nose from continuing to fall by bringing the control stick back towards him some more to hold the nose up, and by slightly reducing his angle of bank at the same time. The Spitfire continued around in a tight circle. *It's like this machine is on rails*, John thought, impressed with its smoothness and the ease with which he could accurately hold it in the steep turn and maintain his chosen height.

After rolling out on a north-easterly heading, he could see Middlesbrough in the distance, and beyond it the North Sea, bright and blue in the sunshine. John banked the aircraft into a right-hand turn to fly south past the North York Moors. Looking down, John could see wooded river valleys winding their way through the moorlands. He decided he would take a closer look, and fly through the wide valley he could see below. He rolled the Spitfire into a steep descending turn.

A whistling sound, as the airflow around his cockpit canopy increased, was the first warning John got that he was too fast. He glanced at his airspeed indicator: 355 mph, and increasing. He needed to react to prevent an overspeed. *Christ, what a slippery machine,* he thought as he reduced power, levelled the wings, and slowly eased the control stick back. He had not noticed the speed building after he had put the Spitfire into a power-on diving turn.

'Stupid bugger,' he said out loud, chastising himself as he sat alone in his cockpit nearly a mile above the ground. He knew the overspeed would not have happened in that way with a similar manoeuvre in the Magister. Now he appreciated, even more, that the Spitfire was in a different category. He needed to get to know this aircraft a lot better before he tried any "special" flying. His plan to descend and wind through one of the moorland valleys at low altitude, and fast, would have to wait for another day, when he was more experienced with the Spit.

John decided it was time for some stalling. The Spitfire was relatively benign in basic stalls, as he had expected. When its nose dropped at the stall onset, a standard recovery process, checking the control stick forward and adding power, soon got the aircraft flying again. Satisfied with that exercise, John decided to move on to fully developed stalls. The increased power and steeper nose attitude involved would cause more than just a pitch-down of the nose, he knew. In a fully developed stall, the benign characteristics of a basic stall would be replaced by one wing suddenly dropping steeply, almost putting the aircraft on its side. John was aware of the consequences if a pilot reacted incorrectly when trying to recover from that position.

Conscious of the fact that he was new to the Spitfire, John was being extra careful as he entered his first fully developed stall. He found himself reciting out loud the procedure he had to follow as he went through the required recovery process.

He need not have worried. It went well, and John felt very pleased with his performance.

As he touched down at Catterick, John reflected on his morning's flying. He thought the aircraft flew beautifully. He had not identified anything he did not like about the Spitfire. As everyone had been saying, it would lift RAF capability by a large margin.

John did recognise, however, that it would be foolish for an inexperienced pilot to take the Spitfire for granted. Nice as it was, it could get you into trouble if you were careless or clumsy.

'That go okay, Pilot Officer?' Bayliss enquired as John jumped down from the Spitfire's wing after parking in the dispersal area.

'Yes, thank you, sir. It's a very pleasant aircraft to fly.'

'Very good. Apart from the stalling, I left the content of your familiarisation flight this morning largely to you.'

'I did the stalling sir,' John responded, 'both basic and fully developed stalls. They went as expected.'

He had decided he would say nothing about the steep spiralling descent that had led to a near overspeed incident.

'All right,' continued Bayliss, 'that has got you started. From now on, your training in the Spit will be more structured. I will task you each day with the activity I want you to undertake. When we get through that over the next few weeks, your basic consolidation training will be complete, and we will move you into service training. That training will begin with the various types of formation we use, which are normally dependent on the phase of flight or the circumstances. Then it will be on to specific operational techniques. As well as some low-flying sorties and air warfare exercises, you will undertake some oxygen climbs to high altitude.'

'Yes, sir,' was all John said, feeling very pleased that he would soon be engaged in serious service training.

'Come to the briefing room at fourteen hundred, please, and I will go through the detail of what is proposed.'

Roger Barton was in the mess dining room when John came in for lunch.

'Hello, John. Congrats on taking the Spit up. Now it's consolidation training for you, I expect, so lots of study and practice over the next few weeks.'

'Thanks, and yes, Squadron Leader Bayliss has confirmed I'm on to that now. I will be joining the rest of you once I've completed it.'

'Did you enjoy the Spitfire?' Roger asked.

'Oh, yes. It's everything I thought it would be. Looks good, handles well, and the performance...' John trailed off. He had realised he was sounding a bit like an over-enthusiastic trainspotter.

'Yes,' said Roger, 'although anything would be a performer after the Tiger Moths and Magisters you flew before you came here.'

'I hadn't expected the high-speed ground-runs required before taking the Spit up for my first time' John said. 'Alastair Bayliss told me it was a new procedure laid down by the CO.'

'Oh, that,' Roger responded. 'Yes, we think the boss has misjudged it, putting that procedure in place to help reduce training risk and keep the squadron's record clean. Most of us who've been flying the Spit for a while doubt that it is a sound aviation practice. We think a new pilot charging up and down the runway like that probably adds to the risk of an incident, rather than reducing it. Don't think the exercise has any real training value, but that is what the CO wants, so that's what we get.'

'I did wonder,' John responded, a nod of his head acknowledging what had been said.

'John,' said Roger, moving on, 'because the Spit is in an entirely different category from what you have previously flown, a couple of tips for you.'

John looked at him expectantly over the bowl of steaming hot leek and potato soup a mess steward had just put in front of him. He was keen to hear anything the squadron's aerobatic expert had to say.

'When I get into the aircraft,' Roger continued, 'I like to think of myself as part of it, not simply as a person sitting in it. I know that may sound a bit strange, but next time you fly, adopt the mind-set that you have strapped the aircraft onto your back.'

John nodded. 'Thanks, Roger. I understand how that might feel. I will do that next time.'

'And, the other thing, John. When you get to aerobatics, use clouds as your markers. Find some clouds with reasonably level tops sitting at a safe height above the ground. Fly just above those tops and make a note of your altitude. Then climb up far enough to give yourself room to complete your aerobatic sequences without coming back down into the cloud. Treat the level of the cloud tops you have identified as the surface of the ground. Practise away, and if you bungle one of your exercises, and inadvertently enter the cloud, you will be all right.' Roger smiled. 'But you will know that you would have been dead if it really had been the ground.'

'That's a good idea,' said John, as he pictured the exercises.

'A few of us are going into the village for a few beers at the pub this evening. Want to come?'

'Yes, thanks, I would like that.' John smiled. He was pleased he had been invited to join them. As the new pilot in the squadron, he was busy with his type rating and consolidation on the Spitfire, flying separately from the other pilots who were undertaking operational training. It was good to be asked to socialise with them.

They had been in the pub for about an hour when John first saw her. A tanned young woman, with blonde hair that finished in ringlets trailing down to her shoulders. Her features were finely chiselled, but that did not make her appear stern. She wore a constant smile as she engaged in an animated conversation with the two women she was with. They were at a small table near the far end of the bar. John was fascinated. He thought she was the most attractive woman he had ever seen.

He tried not to look across at her too much. He did not want to be caught staring. Forcing himself to look away, he returned to his comrades' discussion about the risk of war, and what it would mean for 415 Squadron if the Germans started anything.

A few moments later he could not help glancing back in the direction of the woman who had caught his attention. To his dismay, she had gone. Her friends were still there, but there was no sign of her. *Bugger*, thought John.

'Look what Hitler has done in Czechoslovakia,' Richard was saying. 'I don't think he will stop there. First the Sudetenland, now the rest of the country. He's a madman. He will go to war to get what he wants, and that could eventually affect us here in Blighty.'

'Maybe, Richard, but I think Chamberlain will still be looking for a way to try to satisfy Hitler and maintain peace,' Greg replied.

'Wish I had your confidence in our PM,' was Richard's retort. 'He hasn't done well so far with his Munich Agreement, certainly not as far as the Czechs are concerned.' He turned to John. 'How does someone from the other side of the world view Germany's aspirations, John?'

'Well, we are a long way away, so we don't feel so threatened. Nevertheless, if it goes bad over here, as part of the Commonwealth we would probably be drawn in,' John replied. 'The old saying "give them an inch, they take a mile" comes to my mind when I think about what Germany's been doing. Getting Sudetenland just seems to have encouraged Hitler to take more, which he has now done, marching into Prague in recent weeks. The big risk for us all, I think, is that he wants more than Czechoslovakia.'

'Agreed,' said Charlie. 'He appears to be driven by a view that Germany was badly treated by the surrender requirements of the Great War, and he needs to right some wrongs. That could involve more than we have seen to date. I'm with you on this, Richard. Hitler is trouble, and I'm not confident Chamberlain can deal with him.'

'I do hope you are both wrong about that,' Greg responded. 'God, it's a worry. Let's have another drink.'

Richard laughed. 'Greg, when will you stop addressing every worry you have with another drink?' he asked.

Greg grinned. 'Probably never, and certainly never after having to fly close formation with you.'

As they continued to drink and talk, John looked around the bar. He wondered if many of the others there spent their time, when at the pub, worrying about the politics of Europe. Probably not, he decided. They look to be enjoying themselves, not bothering about what might be being planned hundreds of miles east of here, in Berlin. Then he saw the woman he had noticed before. She was at the bar, trying to carry three tall glasses back to her table. She was finding it difficult with just two hands.

John went across to her. 'Hello, can I help you with those?' he asked, nodding at the glasses.

The woman looked at him, smiling. 'Oh, thank you. They are all gin and tonics. Expensive waste if I drop one.'

John picked up one of the glasses and followed her to the table at which he had seen her earlier.

'Here you are, ladies,' she said to her two friends, 'G and Ts safely delivered, thanks to this charming man who offered to help me carry them.'

'Happy to have been of assistance,' John said with a smile. 'My name is John.'

'Mary,' said the woman, holding out her hand, which John shook.

'Pleased to meet you, Mary.'

'And this is Phoebe and Liz,' Mary went on, introducing her friends. 'John, that accent — where are you from? Australia?'

'New Zealand. You weren't far off.'

'Come and join us,' Phoebe said.

John returned to his group's table, picked up his glass, and told them he was having a drink with some young women he had just met. Amused looks from his fellow pilots were followed by not entirely unexpected comments.

'Three of them? Bit greedy, John.'

'Don't you be late home now, darling.'

'Make sure your gear is down before landing, John.'

There was lots of laughter from the group as John walked away, ignoring the ribald commentary.

He soon discovered that Mary, Liz and Phoebe were nurses. They all worked at a hospital near Thirsk.

'And you, John, what do you do?' Mary asked.

'I'm in the RAF,' John replied.

'Oh, what do you do there?'

'Bet you're a driver,' said Liz. 'You look like a driver to me.'

'No,' Phoebe chimed in, 'I reckon you are a cook.'

'I am a driver, of sorts,' John answered. 'I drive a Spitfire.'

'A Spitfire pilot. I might have guessed,' said Mary.

'How so?' asked John.

'You just have that look about you. Spitfire pilots tend to exude confidence. Maybe overconfidence,' she added with a mischievous grin.

'John, take no notice,' Phoebe cut in. 'Mary had a bad experience with a Spitfire pilot based at Hornchurch. He suddenly decided he didn't want to go out with her anymore and dropped her with no warning. She dislikes pilots as a result, particularly Spitfire pilots. Come on, Mary, don't be rude to our new friend.'

'Sorry, John,' Mary replied. 'Silly of me. I need to move on. It's not you.'

Over the next hour they continued chatting. They covered a wide range of things, including the possibly imminent war, and how it was affecting their lives.

'We are getting a lot of training on how to manage trauma injury from blast effects. The authorities must be expecting that we will become involved in war, otherwise they wouldn't be requiring that particular focus from the health services,' Phoebe said.

'I think it shows they are worried about bombing. Do you think so, John?' Mary asked.

'I suppose all sorts of preparations will be underway in many parts of Britain, given what's happening in Europe at present,' John replied, thinking about a comment he had heard in the mess earlier that week. Someone had been talking about the need to intensify the RAF's air defence training "for when Jerry arrives with his bombers." John didn't want to say too much now, here at the pub. All members of the squadron had been told that discretion should always be maintained about things such as their squadron's activities, size, and training. You never knew who may be listening.

Just then, Liz reminded Mary and Phoebe that they were due at Liz's parents' home for supper.

'We are off, John. Nice to meet you,' said Mary, getting up from the table.

John was disappointed that their evening was over. He felt he had just been getting to know them, and Mary in particular. She saw his disappointment and took the initiative.

'I live with my parents just outside Thirsk. Well, just with Mother really, unless Father is home on leave. We are on an estate about two miles north of the town. It's a big, white, two-storey house right next to a small lake. You can probably see where I am quite clearly from the air, so waggle your wings if you ever go over in your Spitfire.'

'Ha, shall do,' said John with a smile.

Mary hesitated, then scribbled down a telephone number and handed it to John. As she and her friends left, John re-joined his fellow pilots at their table.

'All set now are you, John? Got a date to meet her again?' asked Craig.

'Settle down, lads. It was just a chat with some pleasant young women, not an attempt to establish a relationship,' John said. But he knew that was not true. He would like to see Mary again, and he now had her telephone number and knew where she lived. She had made sure of that, and John hoped they would meet soon.

CHAPTER EIGHT

The weather in north Yorkshire was kind to aviators during most of May 1939, with few days having conditions that adversely affected flying operations. Consequently, John progressed rapidly through his Spitfire consolidation phase. When he got to the more advanced part of that training, he particularly enjoyed low-level flying. It was something Bayliss was keen for him to practise, and he set John several low-level cross-country flight tasks.

'It will hone your planning, dead-reckoning skills, and your aircraft handling competency,' he said. 'Once you have completed that part of your training, I am going to have you do the high-altitude climbs I mentioned. I'll get you to go up to twenty-nine thousand feet. If it's not too warm, the Mark One is good to a service ceiling of around thirty-one thousand, so twenty-nine is perfectly achievable on most days.'

John had completed the oxygen course, so he was confident about a climb of that magnitude.

'When you do it, at the top of the climb try some manoeuvres to get the feel of the aircraft up there. But a word of caution: the air is thin at the height you will be flying, so don't throw the aeroplane around as you might at lower levels. Don't want you falling out of the sky because you lose control in the rarefied atmosphere.'

Soon, John's consolidation training was almost complete. He was becoming proficient at aerobatics, and his high-altitude climb had not presented any problems. John had been tentative with his control inputs when at extreme altitude, not wanting an upset, but in the end, he had decided the Spitfire remained perfectly flyable at that height. Today he was on a low-level navigational exercise.

John quickly glanced down at the small map on his knee. A brief look was all a pilot could afford when flying low and fast. This sortie would be John's last exercise in the Spitfire before joining other members of the squadron in their regular operational training. He noted that he was going to pass relatively close to Thirsk. A small diversion off track, no more than ten miles, and he would be close to where Mary lived, he calculated.

He banked his Spitfire right, passing close over the top of a row of tall poplar trees. Rolling his wings level, he aimed straight at the point where he believed the small lake showing on his map might be situated. Somewhere nearby would be a large, two-storey house. A few minutes later, at approximately one hundred feet above the ground and indicating two hundred and eighty miles per hour, John picked out the house he was looking for. It was relatively easy to see. The large white building stood out in the green and yellow fields, and, yes, there was the adjacent lake. John increased power to the maximum continuous setting allowed. He screamed across the colourful countryside, directly towards Mary's home.

As he rapidly closed in on the house, John pulled up sharply. He might have hit the double chimney protruding from the house's roof otherwise, he was so low. As he passed through four hundred feet, he dropped his starboard wing, hauling the aircraft into a tight right-hand turn. Completing his orbit, John rolled out on a heading that would take him back to Catterick. He could not stop grinning as he flew back to base. He had enjoyed that piece of flying. *I hope she was home*, he thought. It was not the wing-waggle she had requested, he had been too fast for that, but a high-speed tight turn around the house in a low and noisy Spitfire would impress, surely?

When John arrived back at RAF Catterick and parked his Spitfire, Bayliss was waiting for him, looking cross.

'What the hell were you doing, Pilot Officer?' he shouted. 'I send you on a low-level sortie along a planned route and you divert to beat up someone's house!'

'I apologise, sir. It was the house of a friend who had asked me to make a fly-past if I was ever in the area.'

'Three things, Noble.' Bayliss was so angry he had dropped the use of rank when addressing John. 'One: we do not respond to personal flyover requests. We have a training and ops schedule to run — no exhibition flying. Two: we do not divert from planned routes unless it is due to weather or other circumstances. And three: an extremely low, high-speed approach followed by a pull-up into a tight turn, which is apparently what you did as you flew just above the roof of the house you were beating up, is an unnecessary risk. We cannot afford to lose any aircraft or personnel for the sake of a stunt.'

John was surprised the Squadron Leader was able to describe his flying so accurately. He found out how he knew when Bayliss continued his tirade.

'And, Pilot Officer, if you do plan to do something stupid like that, you certainly don't do it over the home of a senior officer in Thirteen Group, particularly when he is home for a few days' leave. Wing Commander Bland has had a very irate Air Vice-Marshal on the telephone, complaining about dangerous flying by a four-one-five squadron Spitfire.'

Oh, Christ, thought John. *Pity Mary didn't tell me who her father was.*

'That is all for now. Wing Commander Bland is deciding what steps he will take. In the meantime, dismissed.'

John saluted and left. He knew he had pushed the boundaries with his flyover, but normally there would not have been any problem. From some of the stories he had heard, quite a few of the lads had done something similar. *Just my luck to startle a Thirteen Group senior officer*, he thought. *Bugger. Just have to see where this goes.*

'Today, gentlemen, we are going to discuss some of Fighter Command's proposed air warfare tactics,' Squadron Leader Michael Howarth announced at a training meeting later that week. All the pilots of 415 Squadron were there, including John; he was now one of the regular squadron pilots, following completion of his Spitfire conversion and consolidation flying. They were in the main briefing room, where an area of desks and chairs had been set up for use in training lectures. It looked like a school classroom, right down to the blackboard, chalk, and dusters that Howarth would use to sketch examples of various types of formations and positioning techniques. John knew that Howarth was an experienced pilot, who no longer flew, a result of losing his medical following an accident with a drilling auger. Now he used his experience to act as a ground instructor, schooling the squadron pilots on aerial warfare tactics.

'You will all be aware of the general air warfare philosophies developed and set out in the Air Fighting Manual, but you won't be familiar with all the detail. I am going to cover some of that this morning,' Squadron Leader Howarth continued. 'The air attack plans in the Manual are based on what Fighter Command considers to be the best options for the various scenarios we expect you will encounter. They have been designed after much thought and consideration by a panel of experienced pilots. Obviously, none of the plans has been tested in battle, because we have no current aerial warfare experience. Nevertheless, they are our best view as to what we might encounter and how we should react.

'Depending on the number and type of enemy aircraft to be intercepted, and their relative position, you are to use the air attack plan best suited to the circumstances. While some plans involve line astern ops, we do make a lot of use of three-aircraft "Vic" formations. We will have you operate in Vics when you go out for this afternoon's air exercise practice.'

There was a murmur of acknowledgement from some of the squadron pilots. They were all familiar with the requirements of Vic formations, where two aircraft flew behind the leader, one to the left and the other to the right. The Vic leader had it relatively easy in these practice sessions, the pilots thought. He flew along straight and level, while the two aircraft following him had to concentrate on maintaining formation with him. They would do the real work this afternoon.

'As you all know, gentlemen, a Vic leader's task is to look out for enemy aircraft. When he spots something, he calls it, and the squadron is to position itself for the appropriate form of attack. That will be based on whichever of the various attack plans your leader considers appropriate. In the air, he will choose the plan that is best suited to the number, type, height, and position relative to you, of the enemy aircraft encountered. Remember also that the priority will be to stop the bombers. They can do the real damage, so we must limit their ability to get through.'

For the rest of the morning, Howarth took the assembled pilots through different scenarios they may encounter. They had to identify the best response for various situations using one of the available air attack plans formulated by Fighter Command.

John found himself wondering about the value of having pre-ordained attack plans. A fixed response to a dynamic situation did not seem sensible. He appreciated there were some six specified plans to consider using in different situations, but, even so, the inherent inflexibility of those pre-determined arrangements remained. *No plan can anticipate exactly what might unfold*, he thought. *It's flawed thinking. In the air, facing the enemy, we need to be ready with a response based on what we see, not simply choosing one fixed scenario from a damn book.*

The thirteen Spitfires of 415 Squadron had been airborne for fifteen minutes. They were out over the sea, about five miles off the coast from Hartlepool. Conditions were relatively clear, with only some low cloud back to the west, building against the Pennines. Squadron Leader Bayliss was in command of this training exercise. He was flying a thousand feet above and slightly behind the squadron's twelve aircraft, so he could observe them. The squadron aircraft were flying at five thousand feet, proceeding in four Vic formations of three aircraft each.

As they flew north, paralleling the coast, Bayliss followed them. The Vic formation on the left, which was closest to the coast, was designated red section. The other formations, further out, were, in turn, yellow, blue, and green sections. Red and yellow sections were "A" flight, while blue and green sections were "B" flight. John was flying as red two, paying close attention to his leader, Charlie Ross, who was flying as red one. Craig Thomson was red three.

Bayliss called the leaders of A flight, detailing an imaginary situation to which they had to respond.

'Red leader, yellow leader, enemy aircraft, twenty plus bombers, three thousand feet at your ten o'clock, go.'

'Yellow one, this is red one,' Charlie, flying as red leader, called in response. 'Follow me, turning left, ten o'clock, bandits at angels three. Attack plan two.'

'Wilco, red one,' the yellow leader responded, as he led his section down behind red section, but slightly out to the right of that section's flight path. That positioned his section to attack the imaginary bombers further back in the group of hostiles reported for the purposes of the exercise, while red section attacked the leading aircraft. It was air attack plan two, in action.

The two sections conducting the mock attack sequenced themselves well as they flew towards where the enemy aircraft would have been if this had been real, rather than an exercise.

'Very good. Red and yellow sections reform, please,' Bayliss called. He then did something similar with blue and green sections. They responded as required, and once again the squadron leader was satisfied with the way the Spitfires planned and executed their attack sequence. Next, they practised their scatter reaction. This was what they had to do if caught unawares while flying in formation.

During the morning's lecture, Squadron Leader Howarth had warned the pilots of the dangers of enemy fighters using the sun to mount a surprise attack. It was difficult, if not impossible, for enemy aircraft to be seen when they were diving down out of the sun, he had said. If the squadron was caught like that when flying together in formation, they would be easy pickings until they had time to respond.

'The first you may know of an attack,' he had said, 'is when bullets start shredding your aircraft. You won't have seen them coming against the sun. If you are ever the subject of a surprise attack when in formation, you must scatter, but in an organised way. We certainly don't want anyone reacting randomly and unpredictably. Apart from affecting your ability to evade and then quickly re-gather into an attacking position where possible, it risks a mid-air collision.'

The instruction to quickly cease formation flying in the case of a surprise attack was "break, break, break."

'Break, break, break!' Bayliss suddenly called. One thousand feet below him, twelve Spitfires responded with their pre-planned scatter manoeuvre.

Red section rolled left and dived to the west. Yellow section also rolled left, but maintained a tight turn to effectively reverse course, and head south at their current height. Blue and green sections took similar avoiding actions, although green section climbed after initially turning right. Within a minute, there were four separated Vic formations, all in different positions, on different headings, and at different heights. If this was real, after scattering when attacked they would now be looking to reposition to engage with enemy aircraft, hunting as four separate Vic formations of three aircraft each. Satisfied for today, Bayliss called an end to the training exercise.

'Back to base, please, tail-chasing your section leader.'

The squadron pilots enjoyed this sort of flying exercise. Each section leader would fly along, turning steeply, climbing, descending, whatever he wished. His two section members, now flying in line astern, had to stay on his tail, following his twists and turns. It was excellent dogfighting practice.

In response to the tail-chase instruction from Bayliss, Charlie Ross, red one, applied full power and dived towards the coast. John, as red two, followed close behind, with Craig Thomson, red three, following him in turn.

Their airspeed built quickly and they were soon crossing the coastline bound for Catterick, low and fast. People walking on the beach below stopped to look up as three Spitfires sped low overhead, one after the other, their Merlin engines howling.

As John watched, he saw Charlie pull up into a steep climb. He followed, determined to stay close on his tail. After just a few seconds climbing, the nose of Charlie's aircraft pitched down sharply. John pushed forward on his control stick to stay with him. As he did that, the smooth hum of his engine faltered momentarily. He had expected it. The steady flow of fuel to a Spitfire's carburettor could be interrupted by the sudden weightlessness of a push-over manoeuvre. One of the problems of not having fuel injection, John knew. He also knew that it would be a dogfighting disadvantage for pilots of Spitfires if they did end up duelling in the air with German fighters. The Me 109s had fuel injected engines, so would not suffer fuel flow interruption in that way.

John saw Charlie enter a steeply banked turn to the left. John did the same, to follow, but then lost visual contact with Charlie's aircraft. He added more power and tightened his turn, trying to catch up with red one, but still, he did not see him come into view as he continued in his turn.

Damn, where's Charlie got to? John asked himself.

He held his aircraft in the steep turn, its nose carving rapidly along the line of the horizon. As he looked ahead, John expected to see red one come into his line of sight at any moment, but there was nothing. Even looking up, through the top of the cockpit canopy as he went around in his turn, he could not see Charlie.

It was a mystery. John knew that with what was effectively a maximum rate turn he should have seen him by now. He rolled level, looking left and right, trying to sight Charlie. Still, he could not see him. Then, he sensed a shadow, just before he saw the belly of a Spitfire, close above his cockpit.

"Jesus!" was all he had time to say before he felt and heard the mid-air collision that took his aircraft's tail off.

John's Spitfire was uncontrollable, and immediately pitched down into a steep dive. Speed was building rapidly as the aircraft arrowed towards the ground.

'Oh no. Please, no!' John screamed. 'Got to get out. Move man!'

He closed the throttle and reached for the lever that would open his cockpit canopy. As soon as the catch was released, the canopy was gone, ripped from the aircraft by the force of the air rushing past the doomed Spitfire, in its high-speed plummet.

John struggled to undo his straps. Looking out he could see the surface of the ground below, rushing towards him at a terrifying speed. Staying below the level of the cockpit's front windscreen to give some shelter from the torrent of air, he gathered himself, feet off the rudder pedals and on to a small ledge just below the front of the seat. Then, with a huge effort he pushed his legs down as hard as he could, effectively ejecting himself from the cockpit. If his Spitfire had still had a tail, he might have hit it and been killed as he baled out, but it was gone.

Tumbling through the air, clear of what remained of his aircraft, John pulled his parachute's ripcord. There was a satisfying *crack* and sharp jerk through his harness as it opened, and filled with the air that would arrest his fall. John realised he had been very low by the time he had managed to exit his aircraft.

Hope I'm not too low for this chute to work, he thought. Moments later John landed heavily. He tried to cushion the impact by ensuring his legs flexed as he hit the ground, hoping that would absorb some of the shock. He deliberately rolled to one side as he landed, trying to divert some of the downward energy resulting from his arrival. He recalled being told to do that during his brief and rudimentary bale-out class at Hullavington.

It was all very quick. The last things John was aware of, before he lost consciousness, were flexing his legs, rolling sideways, and a huge impact on his right shoulder and thigh.

CHAPTER NINE

The squadron pilots were assembled in the briefing room. They had been there since landing, following completion of the day's flying exercises.

Flight Lieutenant Gardiner came in to speak to them. 'Unfortunately, Pilot Officer Noble and Flying Officer Ross suffered a mid-air collision during the last exercise. Pilot Officer Noble's tail was ripped clean off and he had to bale out, but I'm pleased to report that he is all right. He has suffered a knock to his head, and some other minor injuries, mostly just cuts and bruises. He was unconscious when he was collected from a hay paddock near Sedgefield. His aircraft came down close by him, and as you would expect it was destroyed on impact. He is going to be okay, but will spend another twenty-four hours in hospital under observation to make sure there is no ongoing issue with his head knock.'

The pilots responded with a mix of whoops and applause, happy that their friend had survived and did not appear to be too badly hurt.

Gardiner continued, 'I also want to note that Flying Officer Ross did well to get his badly damaged Spitfire back safely, after the incident. I have spoken with the maintenance sergeant and he has reported that it's a miracle the aircraft could even be controlled, let alone landed safely. So, well done.'

There was more applause from the pilots.

Two days later, John was back, and appeared none the worse for his experience. He was sitting with the other squadron pilots in the briefing room, awaiting the arrival of the CO.

Bland was to brief them on the current situation in Europe, and what it might mean for them at this stage.

'Attention!'

All the pilots stood at that call, making a lot of noise as chairs scraped loudly on the floor. Wing Commander Christopher Bland entered and walked to the front of the room.

'At ease, gentlemen, thank you,' he said as he turned to face them. 'I have an update on what is currently being anticipated regarding Germany, and its intentions, but first I want to comment on what happened in the training exercise on Tuesday. The mid-air collision between two of our Spitfires should serve to remind you all that we constantly face risks in some of the things we do. Fighter pilots are highly skilled but operate in situations that can bite.' He paused. 'The safety officer is progressing the normal enquiry into what might have contributed to the incident, but the message I have for each one of you is this: whenever you fly, think carefully about what you are doing and try to anticipate risks and how you could mitigate them. Just to be clear, I am talking about our current training operations here. I appreciate our risk appetite will be different if we become involved in war.'

There were a few nods from some of the pilots, while others just sat in silence. John thought the comment unfair, at least to the extent that it suggested a lack of care and failure to assess risks by the pilots involved. He and Charlie had simply been undertaking an established training exercise, and they had not been reckless. In John's view, if the exercise was not safe, the leaders of the squadron should change things, not simply suggest that pilots may have failed to identify and mitigate risks.

'Now, enough said about that. Lessons will be learned by some, I'm sure,' Bland said, looking directly at John.

He's blaming me. John was well aware his CO seemed to have some antipathy towards him.

'I also want to confirm with you something all commanding officers have been asked to raise with their squadrons by the Air Chief Marshal,' Bland continued. 'He issued a note to us all this afternoon, from Bentley Priory. I will summarise its key points.'

There was a stir among the pilots in response to that comment. What did the man responsible for guiding Fighter Command want them all to hear?

'The Prime Minister had hoped that appeasing Germany may prevent the war we wish to avoid. As you are probably aware, and for obvious reasons this cannot be acknowledged publicly by us, the Munich Agreement has not been successful in stopping Germany taking the steps it has regarding Czechoslovakia.'

John wondered if the wing commander was going to tell them that war was about to begin. He seemed very serious and worried.

'As you will all be aware, Hitler, not content with the Sudetenland being ceded to him as part of the Munich Agreement, ordered his troops into the remainder of Czechoslovakia, mid-March. The view of the British Government is that a wider war is now very likely, as Germany is signalling further expansion. Consequently, the Royal Air Force is to accelerate its preparations and be ready for war within six months. Training Command is producing new pilots as quickly as it possibly can, and our aeronautical industry is building fighters and bombers around the clock. As a country, we need as much time as possible to prepare for any offensive

Germany may begin. In that regard, while not achieving what was hoped for, the Munich Agreement has at least given us the precious commodity of time.'

The room was quiet. John was not surprised by what had been said. Further German moves had been expected by most.

'Here at four-one-five squadron, we are going to bring forward some of your training so far as it relates to war-operation exercises,' Bland continued. 'I want the squadron battle-ready within three months, so you are going to be doing a lot of training, hopefully assisted by some good summer weather. We must use that time wisely. Gentlemen, our preparation, and your skills and commitment, are going to be key. I thank you in anticipation of your efforts to be ready. We will give you all the assistance you need. Good luck to you all. Thank you.'

To John's surprise, everyone started clapping, but he recognised the patriotic stirring they had all felt.

Over the following weeks, the squadron flew a lot of training exercises. A particular favourite among the pilots was practising attacks on imaginary enemy formations. Sometimes, they would jump actual aircraft, flown by pilots of other squadrons acting as the enemy for the purposes of the exercise. Honing dogfighting techniques with fellow squadron pilots was another activity they all looked forward to, often starting with the tail-chasing that had led to the mid-air collision of two of the squadron's Spitfires.

During this time, the Royal Air Force was training pilots as quickly as it could, and the squadron received some new recruits. Two Wings graduates arrived in the last few days of August, Pilot Officers Jack Peters, and Derek Laing. John immediately felt a connection with them. He had recently been through what they were now about to do — convert to Spitfires.

'Nice to meet you, Jack, and you, Derek.' It was the first night in the officers' mess for them, and John could see they were feeling their newness. He had approached them as soon as they had come in, and acted as their host throughout dinner.

'Where are you from, Jack?' John asked as they ate.

'An area you have probably never heard of. A village at the end of Loch Shin called Lairg. It's a couple of hours northwest of Inverness. My folks have a farm there, and I was their labour.'

John smiled. He was familiar with that proposition. 'And you, Derek?'

'I'm from the city,' said Derek. 'London. I worked as a clerk in a broker's office before deciding to join up.'

'You will enjoy four-one-five squadron,' John said. 'Good bunch of blokes, and we get to fly Spitfires for our day job. Hard to beat.'

'Absolutely,' replied Derek. 'Both Jack and I are looking forward to the Spit. We have heard they are terrific aircraft to fly.'

'We are both as keen as mustard,' Jack agreed.

John smiled, thinking of his own excitement when he had first arrived to be trained on the Spitfire. He knew what they were feeling.

'Well, good luck with your type rating and follow-up consolidation. Look forward to flying with you when you are fully on-squadron,' John said, as he savoured the gravy-covered roast beef and Yorkshire pudding that was tonight's dinner in the mess.

John made an extra effort with Jack and Derek over the following days, talking to them in the bar or over dinner most nights. He was keen to ensure all was well with the new arrivals and that they felt supported. They got to know each other well, and as the three most recently arrived pilots at 415 Squadron, they formed a special bond. John was always keen to hear how their flying was progressing, and he warmly congratulated them when they took their Spitfires up for the first time.

'Well done, Jack and Derek,' John toasted them in the bar.

'Thanks, John, much appreciated,' said Jack. 'Thought we might have a pint at the local tonight, after dinner, to mark us flying the Spit. Will you come too?'

'I'd be delighted to help you mark that occasion,' John replied.

That evening, the three young pilots had a wonderful time celebrating Jack and Derek's first flight in a Spitfire. John smiled a lot during the evening at the pub, as he listened to them talking excitedly about the aircraft. He understood their enthusiasm.

When John came into the dining room for breakfast the next morning, a Friday, he found the other squadron pilots already there were clustered around the radio, listening intently.

'What's this about?' he asked as he went over to the group. He was met by several "shushes" from those listening to the radio. John sat down and listened.

'The invasion occurred at four forty-five this morning, Polish time. German forces have crossed the border at several points, using armoured and air elements...'

John was not surprised Poland had been invaded. He knew this was probably the beginning of a larger conflict. The British Government had made it clear that if Germany escalated its military activities, then war between Britain and Germany would be likely. Everyone's worst fears appeared to be becoming reality.

Later that morning, Wing Commander Bland gathered the pilots in the briefing room. 'This is it, gentlemen,' he said. 'What we all hoped could be avoided has now occurred. Germany invaded Poland in the early hours of this morning.'

The pilots remained silent.

'Fighter Command has ordered all squadrons to war-operation standby status. The adjutant will brief you on the detail of what that requires. I am sorry, but he will also be confirming that all leave is cancelled, and pilots are asked not to leave the station's grounds, even temporarily, until we have more clarity on what may now happen. The British Government is communicating with Berlin, and we remain hopeful that something other than war may result. I understand we should know more about this by midday on Sunday. I don't want you to think me over-dramatic, but we are at a critical point so far as being able to maintain peace is concerned. We must prepare for the worst. Your accelerated and intensive training in war operations in recent months reflects that. You may now be required to put that training into practice. We will soon know, but I am confident this squadron is as well-prepared as it could be. Adjutant, carry on please.'

With a curt nod, a grim-faced Bland stepped down from the small dais at the front of the room, and walked out briskly. As he went, he looked neither left nor right. He was clearly upset by the developments in Europe and the prospect of war.

Flight Lieutenant Gardiner stepped forward and began speaking. 'War-operations standby means we act as if we are at war,' he said. 'That means no-one leaves the station, aircraft on the ground are to be dispersed around the airfield when parked, and they will be kept fully fuelled and armed. Consider yourselves on a twenty-minute response time. Observer stations will be manned, as will gun-pits.'

There was a buzz around the room as people took that in.

'This is what you have all been preparing for, and luckily in this squadron we have a group of pilots who are relatively experienced with the Spitfire, and in air warfare manoeuvres. Our two latest joiners, Pilot Officers Peters and Laing, still have some work ahead of them to get through their consolidation training, but that shouldn't take too long. Getting that done will be given priority,' he said, looking towards Jack and Derek.

They nodded in unison. John looked over at them and smiled encouragingly, but he realised that much of RAF Fighter Command was not yet ready to successfully engage with experienced Luftwaffe pilots. He knew 415 Squadron was better placed than many to go to war, if that was what was required, but there were some horror stories about other squadrons. In some, more than half of the pilots had less than twenty hours' flying experience in a Spit, and no air warfare training at all. *In that case, I suppose, set air attack plans may be better for the inexperienced*, John grudgingly acknowledged to himself.

'I'm going down to the lounge,' Richard called as he banged on the door of John's room on the first floor of the mess. It was Sunday morning, and just forty-eight hours since they had heard the news of Germany's invasion of Poland. 'The PM is broadcasting something later,' he said as he carried on down the hall towards the wide stairway that led to the lounge.

By the time John got there, most of the squadron pilots had arrived and pulled up a chair or squeezed onto a sofa. They were all intent, listening to the radio broadcast by Prime Minister Chamberlain. He was just starting as John walked in.

'*I am speaking to you from the Cabinet Room at Ten Downing Street,*' John heard as he sat down.

No-one in the room said anything as Neville Chamberlain continued, outlining how the Germans had failed to provide the requested assurance that they would withdraw from Poland. The Prime Minister went on, reciting the events and facts relevant to how things had got to this stage. Then, all the men who would have to fly their Spitfires into battle in the event of war heard him say what they had hoped he would not:

'*Consequently, this country is at war with Germany.*'

They were all stunned. It had been expected, given Hitler's statements and actions to date, but that made it no easier. War had been declared. The things they had been practising were now to be used in real life. They would have to fly their Spitfires against the Luftwaffe.

That afternoon, Bland again met with the squadron's pilots.

'This morning, the Prime Minister's announcement moved us from simply preparing for war, to being involved in war. Fighter Command will be promulgating directives as to individual squadron roles and required operations. These will be available by Tuesday, and we are to implement our directive on receipt. In the meantime, we are to patrol out over the North Sea, from abeam Newcastle upon Tyne in the north, to abeam Hull in the south. We will run patrols in response to any reported sightings of inbound aircraft, as well as scheduled patrols at times to be notified. We do not expect any enemy aircraft activity over or near the UK at present. The Germans appear to be fully committed to their attack on Poland, so if we do see anything, intelligence considers it will be limited to long-range surveillance aircraft. Back here, please, at o-seven hundred hours tomorrow. We will have for you at that time some patrol rosters and tasks. This is it, gentlemen. What you have trained for. Until the morning. Thank you.'

John looked around the room. Most of the pilots were now talking animatedly, seeming excited by the prospect of battle, rather than apprehensive. He could see that Jack Peters and Derek Laing were looking less comfortable than the others. He felt for them. They were relatively inexperienced and still had some training to complete. They would be aware, he knew, that they were not ready to come up against Luftwaffe fighter aircraft. He resolved to support and help them prepare as much as he was able.

CHAPTER TEN

John and some of the other squadron pilots were in the officers' mess at Catterick, talking about the progress of the war. It was now over three months since the German invasion of Poland, and no significant enemy activity had yet been seen over Britain. 'War was declared at the beginning of September, but now, months later, nothing's happening. Absolutely bloody nothing. No wonder everyone is referring to it as the phoney war,' Greg grumbled.

'I agree with you on this occasion,' Richard replied. 'Patrol after patrol over the North Sea, but not a sausage.'

The other pilots sitting in the group nodded their agreement.

'Well, there won't be anything today, I can guarantee that,' John said. He was confirming what they all knew — no-one in four-one-five squadron would be flying in the current conditions. They would all have to remain on the ground today. The weather they could see through the window: low cloud, strong, gusting winds, and passing hailstorms, was too extreme. It was so bad that the squadron's Spitfires had had to be securely tied down, in case a gust got under a wing and tipped one over.

'That's for sure,' Richard said. 'Wouldn't like to try and go up in this.'

'Even if we could, what to do,' Greg asked, 'in this phoney war?'

'Apparently the Germans see it the same way. I understand that if we were in Germany, we would be referring to this as *Sitzkrieg*, the sitting war,' Richard continued.

'What I don't understand,' said John, 'is why we have the rule that we must not cross the coast into Europe when on patrol, and enter the airspace there — French, Belgian, Dutch, whatever.'

'Ha, I can tell you why, John,' said Roger.

'Okay, let's hear your view, Roger. Your colleagues at Fighter Command have briefed you personally, have they?' Richard said, winking at John.

Roger ignored him and proceeded to tell them why he thought they were banned from crossing into Europe. 'The government doesn't want to risk any more aircraft than those already committed to the support of the British Expeditionary Force. While Britain has committed some fighters to be based in France, the rest are being held back here in England. That's to ensure we don't weaken our ability to provide air defence if the Luftwaffe arrives overhead here, at some point.'

'Sounds plausible,' said Richard. 'Anyway, whatever the reason, the fact remains we are banned from crossing the coast right along the other side of the Channel, so this discussion is largely academic.'

The listening pilots nodded their agreement.

'And how is it going with you and Jack?' Richard suddenly asked Derek, changing the subject. 'Are you enjoying doing the operational stuff with the squadron now that consolidation is behind you?'

'Yes, all going well, thanks. While consolidation is complete, Squadron Leader Bayliss has said there is one piece of that still outstanding: an extended low-level cross-country exercise, which we haven't had time for yet, being so busy practising tactical engagements.'

'Good to have done that, focusing on as much dogfight-type flying as you can,' Roger said. 'I know it's not real, but flying practice sequences of extreme aero manoeuvres as if to get someone off your tail or to get behind your adversary will be great for the day you face the enemy, Derek. Everything you are taught and practise will help you put your aircraft exactly where you want it in an encounter.'

'I'm sure that's right,' Derek answered. 'We don't have time to pre-plan and prepare for dogfight manoeuvring as we engage. I think it's going to be about instinctively knowing what is required and being able to execute that without much thought.'

'Correct, and for that reason, continuously working on aerobatic sequences is highly valuable. It means there's much less chance that in a real dogfight you will bungle a manoeuvre and lose control. Stalling in a max rate turn or dropping out of a loop when dogfighting with the enemy would probably mean you had just flown your last encounter. We should keep practising while this phoney war gives us more time to prepare,' Roger continued.

'That's correct, Flying Officer Barton,' said Alastair Bayliss, who had just come in and was standing behind him, 'and it's not just the new recruits who should practise. Every one of you should be doing as much as you can to keep honing your skills.'

They knew he was right. The fact the war had not yet come to Britain had provided the RAF with more time to get its pilots ready. If the Germans had kept advancing after taking Poland, things might have been a lot more fraught. That was something they all understood.

The following morning, a briefing for some of the squadron who were going out on patrol was being delivered by Squadron Leader Sidey. Squadron Leader Bayliss, Greg, Richard, Charlie and John were there.

'The six of us will be operating this morning's patrol in sector four,' Sidey said as he began the briefing. 'Take-off is at o-ten-thirty hours. Our aircraft will carry maximum fuel. The patrol is planned to take one hour forty. We will fly in two Vic formations, which I am nominating as red and yellow sections for this patrol. I will lead red section. Squadron Leader Bayliss will lead yellow section. Airborne, we will head towards Middlesbrough. Crossing the coast outbound, we will track southeast towards Rotterdam for forty-five minutes, then turn northwest and return to Catterick. Climb to fifteen thousand feet for this patrol. Our task is to look out for any other aircraft, and, if we spot anything, to close in and identify it. If it's hostile, we will engage, following the rules of engagement we have been set by Fighter Command. Any questions, gentlemen?'

After a moment's silence, John raised his hand.

'Yes, Pilot Officer Noble?'

'Would it be better if we flew the patrol in a different formation? Flying in two Vics means only two sets of eyes are available for scanning. It's only the leaders who can look out for other aircraft. The rest of us are busy maintaining our formation position. If we patrolled in a way that didn't involve close formation flying by two of the three aircraft in the Vic, we could have more eyes searching for enemy aircraft.'

Sidey was silent for a moment before replying. 'We have used the patrol formation specified by Fighter Command for a while now, and that has served us well, so, no, I don't think we will modify our approach. Thank you for the suggestion.'

But John would not be put off that easily. 'I understand we are familiar with Vics, but if we are tasked with patrols to look for enemy aircraft, wouldn't it be better to have more of us scanning than just the section leaders?'

'That's been perfectly adequate in the past, thank you, Pilot Officer.'

Sidey's tone indicated to everyone in the room that he was not interested in the point John was making. John should have left it at that, but it was not in his nature to avoid discussing something he considered important.

'I have heard the Luftwaffe used an alternative patrol formation in Spain, with some success. It's called a *Rotte*.' John paused, trying to gauge the squadron leader's reaction to what he was saying. Sidey's face was stony, but John continued, 'The *Rotte* is a two-aircraft formation, leader and wingman, that allows more flexible operational —'

'I am not interested in what the Germans did in Spain, thank you Pilot Officer,' Sidey cut him off. 'We will continue with our practised and specified methodology.'

'Very well, sir.' John realised he was going to get nowhere with his suggestion today, but then he had another thought. 'If we stay with Vics, what about flying a wide formation? That would free up eyes for lookout,' he said.

'Pilot Officer Noble, the issue is settled. We will be flying in our normal formations. If no-one else has anything to say, go and get your aircraft ready for take-off at o-ten-thirty.'

John put up his hand again. 'I wonder whether patrolling at more than fifteen thousand feet may assist us with interception of anything we spot?' he asked.

'Fifteen is adequate,' was the abrupt response.

'If we were higher, say twenty-five thousand, we could better intercept other aircraft,' John persisted. 'Any enemy aircraft on a reconnaissance mission is likely to be high, and if they are above us we would have to climb after him. That limits our speed and risks us not being able to catch up.'

'That hasn't been an issue for patrols to date, Pilot Officer. Today will be at fifteen thousand, as I have said.'

John thought about saying something more, but then just nodded. He recognised that he could not take any of this further today.

The pilots all left the room and began walking towards their aircraft, which were parked in the dispersal area about two hundred yards away. As they walked, Greg fell into step alongside John.

'John,' he said, 'I agree with your comments. Opening the Vics wider or adopting something like the German *Rotte* is well worth some thought by Fighter Command. And yes, being higher would increase a patrol's interception capability, but for Christ's sake, don't confront people like that at a briefing. The squadron leaders don't appreciate being told how things should be done, particularly by a relatively new pilot like you. If you must raise that sort of stuff, do it carefully. Be suggestive. That's the only way I can see you being able to develop your ideas.'

John said nothing, as Greg continued.

'You won't get a full discussion about the pros and cons of any idea you have by raising it out of the blue at a briefing, as you did today. Get them engaged over a period and you have a much better chance. If you can get them to the stage where they think something was always their idea, then something might happen.'

'Yes, you're right,' John acknowledged. 'While I think some of the Fighter Command war-ops planning is just untested bureaucratic nonsense, I agree it was naïve of me to push my views like that. I will keep my mouth shut at briefings in future.'

Fifty minutes after take-off, just before the patrol was due to turn back to Catterick, Sidey called a sighting.

'Single aircraft, multi-engine, eleven o'clock at about ten miles, estimate angels twenty-four. Everyone climb please, and follow me for interception.'

John, number three in red section, saw Sidey's Spitfire pitch up as power to its Merlin engine was increased and the aircraft's nose was raised to a climb. John followed suit, stealing a quick glance as he did so, to see if he could also identify what had been sighted. He did not have time to scan fully and didn't see anything. A few minutes later, he stole another quick look. There was nothing for a moment, but then he saw it. *Looks like a Dornier Do 17*, John decided, noting its distinctive pencil-like fuselage and twin tails.

As they continued to climb towards it, the German aircraft turned towards the Dutch coast. The pursuing Spitfires had closed the lateral distance to about three miles at this point, but they were still some three thousand feet below the Dornier. The estimated height of twenty-four thousand feet had been wrong. It was more like twenty-seven thousand feet, they now realised.

'Break off pursuit.'

The call from Sidey was unexpected. *Why has he done that?* John asked himself.

'I can complete the intercept, red leader,' John called.

'Negative, red three. Break off the pursuit.'

John had already started tracking further to the right, diverging from the flightpath of the remainder of red section.

'Red three, where are you going?'

'I can bring guns to bear on him in short order, red leader.'

'Red three, understand this: you are ordered to break off and reform.'

John continued after the Dornier.

'Red three, do you read? Break off now.'

'Affirmative, I read you, red leader, breaking off.' And with that, John turned back towards his section and was soon easing himself back into his number three position.

'Returning to base. Follow me,' was the call as they turned on to a heading that would take them back to Catterick.

After the patrol landed, the pilots gathered in the briefing room. It was a standard procedure to debrief those involved in every mission. After completing a general review of the patrol, Sidey turned towards John.

'Pilot Officer Noble, I wasn't happy that I had to order you back, more than once, from your attempt to intercept the Dornier we were pursuing. I had called a break-off. What on earth were you thinking?'

'Sir, I would have been in range to shoot in no more than another one or two minutes, so I thought I should go ahead and close in on him. We had been pursuing since your sighting, and we were almost on him when you called the break-off. I could have got him before my fuel got too marginal.'

'I didn't call it because I was concerned about fuel.'

'No, sir?'

'No. I called the break-off because if you hadn't been so intent on the aircraft you were chasing, you would have seen that he had crossed the Dutch coastline. Standing orders for Thirteen Group squadrons prevent us from going after him once he does that.'

John was mortified. He had not noticed exactly where they were. He had thought the break-off call was related to fuel. He knew their consumption rate would have gone up significantly during their climbing chase.

'I am sorry, sir. I hadn't appreciated that Dutch airspace was so close.'

'A lesson to be learned. Always maintain positional awareness, Pilot Officer.'

'If we had been patrolling at a higher altitude, as I suggested at the pre-flight briefing, we would have had much less climbing to do and more speed. Then we would have caught him before the coastline.'

The room went totally silent. The other pilots seemed stunned by John's challenge.

Sidey was clearly angry. 'Thank you, gentlemen. Dismissed. Pilot Officer Noble, remain behind, please.'

John's fellow pilots got up and left the room, mostly averting their eyes. Greg, however, stared at John and mouthed 'careful' as he left.

When all the pilots had left, Squadron Leader Sidey began. 'Let's get things straight here, Pilot Officer Noble. Like every other officer in this squadron, you are to comply with orders. You breached that requirement twice today. You didn't break off when I first gave that command, and you entered a banned area when you crossed the Dutch coastline. These matters are serious.

'Now you have compounded things by arguing and being disrespectful. I'm not about to discuss with you whether our patrol altitude should have been higher. I am simply going to remind you that after you raised it at the briefing, it was dismissed. That should be the end of it. It's not appropriate for you to bring it up again at the post-flight debrief. Your attitude is almost petulant, and it is certainly insubordinate.'

As Sidey spoke, John accepted that he had been out of order. 'I apologise, sir. I realise now that I was wrong to speak like that. It won't happen again.'

CHAPTER ELEVEN

Operations the next day were affected by poor weather, similar to the conditions the squadron had experienced earlier in the week. All flying operations were cancelled at thirteen hundred hours.

Later that afternoon, John was called into the CO's office. When he arrived, Squadron Leader Sidey was also present.

'Take a seat, Pilot Officer,' said Wing Commander Bland. When John was seated, he went on, 'I've called you here to let you know that you have been temporarily taken off war operations. Instead, you will be supervising the completion of some outstanding training exercises by Pilot Officers Peters and Laing.'

John was stunned. 'I'm sorry, sir, I don't understand,' he said.

'Explain it to him please, Squadron Leader,' Bland said curtly, looking to Sidey.

'Pilot Officer Noble,' Sidey began, 'we are happy with your flying standard, and your aerial warfare skills have developed well. There is no issue with you on the operational side. Our concern is that you seem to have forgotten we have a command structure, and that you are obliged to follow instructions given to you by your senior officers.'

John was silent. He did not understand why Sidey was saying this to him, nor why it had to be done at a special meeting with the squadron's senior officers.

I've had my disagreements when querying some operational matters, but nothing so serious it justifies this, surely? What's going on? Is this Bland having a crack at me again? John wondered.

'Take yesterday's patrol, as an example,' Sidey continued. 'I briefed you on an operation we were about to undertake. A patrol tasked with looking out for any enemy aircraft over the North Sea. You raised the question of effectiveness of Vic formations when patrolling. I didn't mind you asking the question, but I wasn't happy when you persevered, even after I had told you no change would be made. It was entirely inappropriate for you to keep arguing the point at that stage, particularly at a briefing being held immediately prior to a war operation.'

'I'm sorry, sir, I did not intend to cause an issue. I just wanted to voice my concern.'

'Maybe, Pilot Officer, but you went further. You argued about the effectiveness of the patrol height I had chosen, fifteen thousand feet. You suggested it would not assist the interception of any enemy reconnaissance aircraft flying higher than that level. I had selected that altitude having regard to forecast cloud, but when I confirmed that was to be our operating level you made it clear you did not think it appropriate.'

'I accepted at the briefing that fifteen thousand was the height at which we would operate the patrol, sir.'

'You did, eventually, Pilot Officer, but you may recall that when we landed, at the debrief, in front of everyone else you suggested that the interception of the enemy aircraft had failed because we were too low. You were being openly critical of the fact I had kept to my plan of patrolling at fifteen thousand. As I said to you at the time, that's unacceptable insubordination. It's also disruptive to the team spirit we try to foster in this squadron.'

'Looking back, I accept I was out of order with that comment, sir. I apologise.'

'Thank you, but unfortunately what I have just outlined is not the end of my concerns. You will recall that I had to call you multiple times to stop you continuing to chase the Dornier we had spotted. One call should have been all that was needed. I know you thought I was mistakenly thinking your fuel state was becoming marginal to carry on after the enemy aircraft, but as you now know, my concern was based on something else. Standing orders require we do not cross the European coastline, and you were about to do that. Quite apart from not responding initially to my radio call that you stop your pursuit, you demonstrated a complete lack of positional awareness. It came as a surprise to you that you were about to enter Dutch airspace, and that is not good enough.'

John said nothing, but as Sidey spoke, he could see that he had been out of order on the ground, and not performing to the standard expected of an operational Spitfire pilot in the air. As someone who always sought to avoid mediocrity and failure, in any form, John did not like it.

Sidey continued. 'The bottom line, Pilot Officer, is that when raising questions about any features of a mission you consider may not be appropriate for some reason, you do it in a measured and respectful way, and you accept the decision made after your comments have been considered. You do not get involved in an open disagreement with a senior officer at a pre-flight briefing. And, on completion of the operation concerned, you certainly do not continue your disagreement, or lay blame for some perceived failure, because you feel dissatisfied with the mission outcome.'

John remained silent. He realised, listening to Sidey as he had listed his complaints against him, that he had been wrong to do what he had. *Asking the question is fine, John,* he told himself, *but once answered, do not continue arguing the point, and never, ever, follow up concerns by effectively telling a senior officer "I told you so."*

John resolved to be more careful in future, and to do everything he could to avoid clashing with the squadron's senior officers.

'We want you to spend some time considering how best you might fit in with squadron disciplinary requirements,' Sidey continued. 'Your attitude is not acceptable and your behaviour is not conducive to maintaining the *esprit de corps* we have built among the pilots. It's disruptive, insubordinate, and has no place in our squadron.'

'Yes, sir,' John replied. The squadron leader was clearly very unhappy with him. John had always considered he was respectful, and a team player. Not in this case, he could see, with the benefit of hindsight. He had let his concern with the effectiveness of squadron operational arrangements, and his response to that, get him into a difficult situation.

In the mess that evening, John approached Jack Peters and Derek Laing.

'Jack, Derek, just to advise you that I have been assigned to complete your outstanding consolidation training exercises. The ones that got held up when it was decided you should go into some of the air warfare exercises early, before everything on your consolidation flying was finished.'

'Oh, all right, John. Did Squadron Leader Bayliss not want us again?' Jack asked, laughing.

'Probably not,' John said with a grin. 'If you can get me your logbooks later, I will review them overnight to see what you've been doing and where you are up to. We will have a chat in the morning about what we must do to finish your programme. I understand it's principally the low-level cross-country work.'

The next day, John went up to practise some aerobatics. It had been a while since he had looped, rolled, and stall-turned a Spitfire.

As he increased power on take-off, his Spitfire quickly gathered speed. The aircraft's tail came up and soon after that, with a slight rearward pressure on the control stick, he lifted off. Once airborne, John checked forward on the stick and held the aircraft down, letting his airspeed build as he continued low across the airfield. John remained at about thirty feet above the ground. As he saw his airspeed indicator passing through two hundred miles per hour, he pulled the column back, firmly. The nose came up in response, and he noted that he was being rewarded with a climb rate of nearly three thousand feet per minute. John rolled the Spitfire into a gentle turn, continuing to climb as he flew east, towards the coast.

As he passed through five thousand feet, John reduced power and began his pre-aerobatic checks. In his early days, he had used a written checklist to ensure he did not overlook anything, but now that list was no longer needed. Everything he needed to do was fixed and clear in his head. He started going through the various items.

Height? Sufficient for the exercise — *yes.*

Area? Not over an aerodrome or a town — *checked.*

Loose items? Checked. Nothing that might fly around the cockpit when I manoeuvre.

Harness? Secure, he confirmed, tugging at his straps to test them.

Engine instruments? Temperature and pressures? All in the green.

Then John made some gentle inputs on the control stick. His Spitfire responded as expected. 'Controls operating correctly,' he muttered to himself.

He went through the remainder of his checks, before finishing with a good scan of the area in which he was flying. He did not want any conflict with other aircraft operating in the area as he went through his aerobatic sequences. Too much of a collision risk. No other aircraft could be seen.

Finally, his checks were complete. *Ready to go*, he thought.

Whenever undertaking aerobatics, John always followed the advice Roger Barton had given him some months ago. He would imagine himself as part of the aircraft itself, rather than as a person sitting in the aircraft.

I will start with a loop, he decided.

Pushing the stick forward and adding some power, he put the Spitfire into a shallow dive. His airspeed built rapidly. As it reached his target speed, John hauled back on the stick and thrust the throttle right forward. Full power. The Merlin engine sang. The aircraft's nose lifted quickly and he was soon going up vertically, but only for a moment, as he continued to hold the stick back — then he was inverted at the top of the loop. Now he released some of the back pressure he was applying to the control stick and reduced power as the Spitfire continued its loop and began descending vertically. Then John added power and again increased his pull on the stick, causing the Spitfire to come out of its earthward plummet and ease its way back to level flight.

'That loop was all right, John,' he said to himself. He found talking out loud helped his focus.

For the next thirty minutes, John went through various aerobatic sequences. He thought they all went reasonably well. *I will finish with a stall-turn*, he thought, *then go back to Catterick.* John set the Spitfire up for this last manoeuvre.

From a dive, to build airspeed, John pitched the aircraft up into a vertical climb, applying full power as he did so. His airspeed started to drop quickly as he held the aircraft in its climb. As his speed continued to decrease, moving towards its stalling speed, John cut the power and stood heavily on his left rudder pedal. That caused his Spitfire to pivot to the left, effectively rotating around the tip of its left wing.

The stall turn manoeuvre was intended to allow the aircraft to transition from travelling straight up, as it climbed, to straight down, as it dived. Its essence was a one-hundred-and-eighty-degree pivot around its horizontal axis, from nose vertically up to nose vertically down. But John was a moment too slow with his control inputs during the pivot, and the aircraft stalled partway through the manoeuvre, flicking the Spitfire onto its back. It entered an inverted spin, taking John by surprise. He had never been in a spin where he was upside down.

Looking at the surface coming up to meet him through the top of the cockpit canopy, John knew he had a major problem. His rate of descent was increasing rapidly as he spun down, inverted. He was not sure he would be able to recover control before impact. He was desperate, frantically making various inputs, trying to regain control and prevent a crash. The surface was getting ever closer. It was now probably only a thousand feet below him.

He managed to get the aircraft the right way up, and to stop the spin, but he was still going down. His Spitfire was plummeting earthwards in a steep nose-down attitude. John was not confident that he had sufficient height left to recover. He pulled back on the control column and added power. That helped, but still, he was not recovering quickly enough to avoid a crash. Even though he risked a high-speed stall in doing so, John pulled the control stick back even more, and put on full power, trying to stop the aircraft's dive towards the ground. He could feel the heaviness in his body, a result of the extreme gravitational load he had created with his attempt to pull out.

The Spitfire's nose slowly came up as it responded, and John managed to get the aircraft into a level attitude. But it was still descending, a result of its inertia. He realised he may be unable to prevent his aircraft crashing into the surface. *Dammit*, he thought. *Come on!*

To say John was angry with himself would have been an understatement. But he was very pleased he had been using the top of a level piece of stratus cloud at two thousand feet as a proxy for the ground's surface. Pancaking into a cloud did not have the consequences that would have resulted if it had actually been the ground. *Live and learn, John, you idiot*, he thought, as he set a course back to the aerodrome.

Later that afternoon, John summoned Jack Peters and Derek Laing. They were to carry out some of the consolidation training they had postponed earlier to allow them to participate in aerial warfare practices.

'Gentlemen, your programme today is your outstanding low-level cross-country navigation exercise,' John told them.

He saw the two men glance at each other, grinning in anticipation. He understood their excitement: sitting in the aircraft as it flew fast and low was always a joy. The Spitfire's Merlin engine, set to high cruise power, would be making a beautiful noise.

'The route you are to plan and fly is Catterick to overhead Pickering,' John continued, 'then across the moors to overhead Whitby, and up the coast to a position abeam Hartlepool. Once there, to Carlisle via the Tyne Valley. Overhead Carlisle set heading for Penrith, and then through the Stainmore Gap, and back to Catterick. Fly the route at three hundred feet above ground level, but don't cross any built-up areas at that height. Either skirt those areas or pop up to one thousand feet above ground level if planning to fly over them. I don't want people calling the station complaining about low-flying aircraft frightening their dog,' John continued.

Both Jack and Derek chuckled, although they did find it surprising that from time to time people would complain about noisy, low Spitfires. After all, there was a war on.

'Your tasked height is also your minimum height above the terrain. If you can't maintain three hundred feet above ground level at any time due to weather, find a clearer route. Divert or simply turn around. Don't just keep going with a cloud-base that's not working. Similarly, with in-flight visibility — not less than three thousand yards, please, gentlemen. You can only see about twenty seconds ahead in that visibility. If it falls below three thousand yards get out of there, with a quick one-eighty.'

John's reference to a steep turn reversing direction was noted by Jack and Derek. They both knew poor visibility made for difficult flying conditions when low. Things could change quickly, visibility sometimes deteriorating so fast that a pilot could lose all outside reference in seconds. They both understood the reason for John's comment. Flying blind at three hundred feet would be no picnic.

'Get your weather briefings from the met officer and be ready for take-off in ninety minutes, please.'

The weather briefing indicated relatively benign weather along their route — little wind and no cloud other than some broken cumulus at three thousand feet, well above the level at which they would be flying. There was also the possibility of some low stratus forming in valleys, particularly those in the Pennines.

Derek and Jack told John that they had agreed Derek would lead the two Spitfires as far as Carlisle. As a result, he was responsible for the pre-flight preparation from Catterick to Carlisle. Jack would then take the lead from Carlisle back to Catterick, and he would complete the pre-flight work for that segment. The pilots also noted that they had decided to fly with a separation of a minimum of one hundred yards. Flying low and fast was demanding at the best of times — no point in adding the need to maintain a close formation position.

'You both ready to go?' John asked after their initial briefing.

'Yes, we are,' Jack replied. 'We have the en route weather and the forecast shows that conditions will be suitable for the exercise. We can depart as soon as aircraft checks are complete.'

'Yes, I've seen the forecast,' John said. 'Looks all right, so off you go, and report to me when you get back.'

Just over an hour later, John was in the ops room, waiting for the two pilots to return from their exercise. He looked up when Derek came through the door.

'Good exercise?' asked John.

'Yes. Very good. All went well, although there was a bit of low cloud affecting us as we came through the Stainmore Gap.'

'Where's Jack?'

'Should be here soon.'

'All right, let's make a start on the debrief. Jack will just have to join in when he arrives. From the beginning, please.'

Derek had just begun when the ops room telephone rang. The duty orderly who answered called out to John.

'Pilot Officer Noble, somebody wants the duty officer. That you, sir?'

'Yes, that's me,' John said as he went across to take the telephone from the orderly. 'Pilot Officer Noble speaking. Yes. What? I'm listening.'

After a few moments, John looked across at Derek.

'All right. We will come out. Be there in an hour.'

After hanging up he said nothing for a moment, before turning to Derek.

'Jack's aircraft has crashed in the Stainmore Gap. A farmer heard the impact and went looking. He found the wreckage strewn along a field near a high rock outcrop that Jack appears to have clipped. Police are on their way there. Jack didn't survive.'

'Jesus,' was all Derek could say.

John did not say anything, but he was wondering why Derek had simply said that Jack should be arriving soon, when he had come in after completing the exercise. Why did Derek not know that the aircraft he was with, flying as its number two, had crashed?

'I will advise the CO and adjutant,' John muttered, trying to gather his thoughts as he hurriedly left the ops room. *How could this have happened?* he asked himself. It was unbelievable.

As he made his way around the mist-enshrouded site, at the top of the Stainmore Gap, John was shocked by what he saw. Smoking pieces of aircraft wreckage that had previously been Jack Peters' Spitfire were scattered across the tussock. A deep gouge ran across the ground, starting with a slightly deeper ground indentation where the aircraft had first impacted. The gouge, three to four inches deep, was about one hundred yards long.

Jack's body, or what was left of it, could be seen, blackened and charred, in the remains of the cockpit. John felt a deep sense of loss. He was shocked by the accident, and was determined to find what had caused it.

After making a few notes, John left the crews to clean up the site and recover Jack's body. He returned to Catterick, planning to set up an interview with Derek as soon as possible. *I need to know why this happened,* he thought.

Back at Catterick, Derek was still in the ops room when John returned. Derek was clearly anxious, and wanted John to tell him what he had seen.

'Could you see from the wreckage at the site what might have occurred?'

'Too early for cause, Derek,' John said, but he did go on to briefly describe what he had found. Derek listened quietly.

After outlining what he had seen, John asked, 'Derek, how is it that you had no idea Jack had crashed? When you first came in, you told me he would be with us soon.'

'We got separated.'

John paused, before going on to say what he thought should now be done.

'All right, we need to go through this in detail. I'm sorry to ask you to talk about this so soon after the event, but we should do it while everything is still fresh in your mind.'

'That's fine. I understand,' Derek responded, with a weak smile.

'Thank you. Take me through it please, step by step, from the beginning. We will get to the separation of the two of you as we proceed. Outline the operational detail on each the sectors of the route, weather encountered, and decisions made as you proceeded. Also, think about whether there is anything, looking back, that may have unexpectedly affected any part of your exercise.'

With a nod of agreement, Derek began.

'We took off from here at ten-thirty hours, planned for the low-level cross-country approved; Catterick, Whitby, Hartlepool, Carlisle, Penrith and back to Catterick. That last sector was to be via the Stainmore Gap, through the Pennines. Planned time en route was one hour.

'We flew at three hundred above ground level, as briefed. Planned airspeed was two sixty, to be reduced as required. For example, we flew at two-twenty as we followed a valley through the moors to Whitby.'

'Why did you do that?'

'We were winding through the valley, flying low. I was lead at that stage, and I thought it appropriate to do the valley transit at a lower airspeed. It had some narrow areas and a number of twists and turns, although nothing too tight. There was no weather issue, but I decided to make the call to slow up as we went through. Just precautionary, probably not strictly necessary.'

'That's just sensible airmanship. Sounds reasonable to me. Carry on,' said John.

'As far as Penrith, the flight was standard. No weather of any concern. Straightforward navigation, and we kept clear of any high obstacles.'

'So, you had no concerns about anything at all, as far as Penrith? You were able to maintain three hundred feet above ground level with no difficulty?' John asked.

'No trouble maintaining our minimum height, correct.'

'Everything was normal, with no surprises?' John confirmed.

'Ah, er, yes.'

John wondered about the slight hesitation in Derek's response, but decided it was nothing.

'And then, from Penrith?'

'Jack had taken over lead by this point. Passing Penrith, I could see some stratus ahead, in the Pennines. As we got closer to the valley we were to use to pass through the Pennines at low level, it has the Stainmore Gap at its high point, I saw there was more stratus there. It was not sufficient to dictate any consideration of a variation of route or procedure, well, not at that early stage anyway.'

John detected there was something in that expression that might indicate an issue, so he pressed, 'Are you saying that you saw conditions change shortly after that?'

'Yes.'

'And that caused you to start re-evaluating low-level passage through the Gap?'

'Yes.'

'Describe that to me please.'

As he said that, John recalled that when Derek had first come in after completing the exercise he had made a comment about some low cloud in the Stainmore Gap. He had said nothing about it affecting their flight though. Why had he not mentioned any concern about low-level stratus then, John wondered? Given what had occurred, he would need to reconcile that with some follow-up questions, if Derek did not clarify it, he decided.

'As we approached, I could see that as we went further into the valley, the rising terrain was going to force us up closer to the base of the low-level stratus we could see ahead, around the top of the Gap.'

'Tell me what happened as you approached the Gap itself.'

'I was looking carefully, trying to see if we would have a sufficient margin at the top of the pass to allow us through safely. I was conscious that to preserve our three hundred feet above the ground we were already having to climb. The terrain rises towards the southeast, the direction in which we were flying, and that was pushing us up closer to the cloud base.'

'Did you and Jack discuss the conditions?'

'I called him, and suggested we abandon low level passage and go through in the clear air above the stratus. That was perfectly doable.'

'What was his response?'

'He thought the low cloud was at a sufficient height to allow us through, with sufficient room for safe passage. He said we should proceed, noting it was good wartime training.'

'What airspeed were you flying?'

'Still the standard two sixty, and I thought that faster than we should be in the conditions. I suggested we bring it back to two ten, but Jack didn't think that necessary.'

'But you did think it necessary?'

'Yes. I had suggested reducing speed because I was feeling uncomfortable with the conditions on this part of the route. We were getting tight, squeezed between the cloud and rising terrain, and going faster than was safe in my opinion. There were occasional encounters with lower patches of cloud that we couldn't avoid. When that happened, we were momentarily blind, but never for more than a second or two.'

'So, Jack wanted to continue low level, despite the conditions, and did not think a speed reduction was necessary?'

'Yes. I was becoming increasingly concerned, but Jack thought it was all completely manageable.'

'I see,' John said, wondering why Jack had adopted the attitude Derek was describing. He was not sure if it was inexperience or bravado. Maybe both, he decided.

'In the end I called to Jack that I was out. That was when we separated, as I climbed up above the stratus, and then made my way, in clear air, back to Catterick. He acknowledged what I was doing, but he chose not to take the same action.'

'What did he say when he acknowledged your advice that you were not continuing at low level?'

Derek hesitated. 'Oh, he just made it clear he did not think that was required.'

'All right. One last thing. Were you and Jack both quite clear about the minima I had set, and how to respond if it looked like it might be infringed?'

'Yes. You even reminded us at the briefing about making a one-eighty if necessary. The weather we saw en route was as forecast. No significant wind, good visibility, and some medium level cloud above our planned operating height. The risk of low stratus in some higher passes noted in the forecast did eventuate, and that was what we encountered in the Stainmore Gap.'

'Describe the conditions in the Gap for me in a bit more detail please. I want to know what you both saw as you approached.'

'There was some mist clinging to the tops of the hills around the highest parts of the Gap, and it was close to the ground at the summit, where there is a saddle that has to be crossed. That mist on the hills was quite a height above us as we entered the area, so not a problem. Some stratus had formed in the valley itself though, and, as I said, because the ground rises from the northwest towards the southeast, we were being pushed up towards it as we went further in to the pass.'

'Did you consider there was sufficient room to remain under the cloud, and clear of the ground by the required three-hundred-foot margin, as you approached the top of the Gap?'

'Initially, I did think that, but as we got closer it became apparent that we might have an issue maintaining that margin.'

'Jack was leading as "training one" at that stage?'

'Ah, yes, he was leading as number one on that leg.'

'Did he raise any concern about the clearance from cloud in the Gap, or was he confident that it was of no significance, despite the comments and queries you said you made?'

'No. He said nothing to indicate a concern. Quite the opposite. He said he thought it was okay. I didn't, and eventually abandoned low-level passage. Jack showed no interest in slowing down, and wanted to proceed across the saddle notwithstanding the cloud sitting on or very close to much of the ground there, so I took my own initiative. I climbed out, passing through some cloud as I did so, but there was no option for a one-eighty degree turn at that point — it had got too tight with the low cloud.'

'All right, thanks, Derek. Now I understand why you didn't know Jack had crashed when you first came back. What you have said gives me some useful insight into what occurred. The squadron safety officer will probably want to interview you for the accident report that he will complete. Just tell him what you have told me. From what you have said you acted appropriately throughout: questioning what you were doing, suggesting alternatives, and eventually, climbing away from the danger.'

CHAPTER TWELVE

Two days after the accident, John was summoned before Flight Lieutenant Gardiner.

'Pilot Officer Noble, we have scheduled a panel hearing on Thursday next week to investigate the accident involving Pilot Officer Peters,' Gardiner told him. 'The hearing will commence at eleven hundred hours, in the main briefing room. A panel of three, chaired by Wing Commander Bland, will consider the matter. The other panel members are Squadron Leader Bayliss and Flying Officer Cowles. I will be the hearing clerk.'

'I understand, sir,' said John. He was nervous. He knew Bland did not like him, and now this, a formal hearing scheduled regarding an exercise John had been responsible for overseeing that had gone badly wrong. It was not the norm, John knew. It did not seem to matter that Britain was now at war. The CO had decided he would hold a formal hearing into the accident that had killed one of the members of his squadron, Pilot Officer Jack Peters. The usual, and relatively brief, squadron safety officer investigation process was not going to be used in this case, despite RAF Command deciding some time ago that fully reviewing matters around a training accident at a panel hearing was a disproportionate response when on a war footing. It tied up too much critical resource. That had been the instruction from the top, but it seemed that Wing Commander Bland had decided he would ignore it, and John thought he knew why. Bland did not like him, for some reason.

There had been several examples of the CO's antipathy that John could recall. The most recent had been a particularly unpleasant incident in the officers' mess. On that occasion, Bland had been trying to impress his table by expounding on some opera he had attended. His audience had included the people in the squadron he liked to keep close, those he saw as socially important.

John had walked past the group, and Bland had called out to him.

'Pilot Officer Noble, you ever attend the opera when you were back on the farm in New Zealand?'

Taken aback by the question, John had replied hesitantly, 'Ah, no. Haven't ever been to the opera, sir.'

'Ha. No surprise there, Noble. Never mind, on you go. I will continue discussing the performing arts with these gentlemen. You clearly wouldn't have a contribution to make on the topic if you joined us.'

John had nodded, smiled awkwardly, and moved away. It had been obvious that the CO's rudeness had made everyone in the vicinity feel uncomfortable.

Now John could sense trouble again. Bland pushing for a full panel hearing into Jack's accident, something not normally done, was probably aimed at him. Finding John responsible in some way, as the officer in charge of the exercise, would no doubt give Bland some satisfaction, he decided.

'You will be assisted by Squadron Leader Smallbone,' Gardiner continued. 'He is appointed to be your Hearing Friend. Effectively he acts as your counsel, helping you to prepare and give evidence. Squadron Leader Sidey will be Presenter, putting the agreed facts before the panel and examining witnesses.' Gardiner paused. 'So that you understand what is required, this is how it will run: Pilot

Officer Laing will be asked to speak, as one of the pilots on the training flight that day. Then you will be asked to tell the panel about all relevant arrangements and matters regarding the sortie from your perspective, the briefings you provided et cetera. You should be prepared to answer any questions Squadron Leader Sidey, or any of the panel members, may have about what you say. Clear?'

'Yes, sir.'

On the day of the hearing, there was low cloud, limited visibility in heavy rain squalls, and a strong, gusting, northeasterly wind. Flying had been abandoned for the day.

Flight Lieutenant Gardiner called the room to attention. All stood as the panel members entered, led by the wing commander. They settled themselves at the long wooden table placed at the head of the room for their use, Bland shuffling his papers importantly.

'Please sit,' said Gardiner, before beginning the hearing by outlining its purpose. 'This is a panel convened to consider the circumstances of a fatal aircraft accident in which Pilot Officer Jack Peters died when his Spitfire, fuselage number 7190, crashed in the Pennines during a low-level navigation exercise on Tuesday the fifth of December, 1939, at approximately 1115 hours. Wing Commander Bland presiding.' He nodded to Squadron Leader Sidey to begin.

Sidey stood to address the panel. 'May it please members, I am going to present matters to you regarding the accident to assist you in forming a view as to what happened, and why.'

'Go ahead, Squadron Leader,' Bland prompted.

Sidey nodded. 'The accident occurred at an elevation of approximately fourteen hundred feet in the Stainmore Gap, a pass through the Pennines. Two of the Squadron's Spitfires were on a low-level navigational training exercise, flying a planned cross-country route.

'The flight was Catterick to Pickering, a town about fifty miles to the southeast. From Pickering, the route went northeast to the coast at Whitby, and then north up the coast to Hartlepool. Once at Hartlepool, the aircraft were to fly west, following the Tyne River Valley to Carlisle, then south to Penrith. After crossing Penrith, the flight was to return to Catterick. The Penrith to Catterick sector was via the Stainmore Gap, a valley through the Pennines, and Pilot Officer Peters was leading the flight of two aircraft at that time. Pilot Officer Laing had led for the first part of the exercise, Catterick to Carlisle. Pilot Officer Peters had assumed the lead from Carlisle. That was pre-arranged by the two pilots.'

'The aircraft became separated in conditions of low visibility as they passed through the Stainmore Gap area. Pilot Officer Laing landed back at Catterick at approximately eleven thirty hours. Pilot Officer Peters did not return. The wreckage of his aircraft was found by a farmer in the Stainmore Gap, who had heard the crash. It appears that Pilot Officer Peters' Spitfire clipped an elevated outcrop before crashing some eighty yards beyond that point. The aircraft structure was found to be severely deformed, indicating that final impact with the ground was at high velocity. There was a post-crash fire.

'The site of the main wreckage was at an elevation of one thousand three hundred and sixty feet above mean sea level. The aircraft's initial collision with a rock outcrop, evidenced by witness marks and a small section of wingtip left there, was some one hundred feet higher, at one thousand four hundred and fifty feet above mean sea level.

'A scene examination revealed that the terrain rose steadily towards the southeast from a point about five miles northwest of the crash site, the direction from which Pilot Officer Peters' aircraft would have approached. In his evidence, Pilot Officer Laing will confirm that because of rising terrain, the available height between the cloud base and the ground was limited. As a consequence of the forces involved, as well as the intense fire, this accident was not survivable.'

'Thank you, Squadron Leader. Let's hear now from those involved, please,' said Bland.

Gardiner called Derek Laing forward to speak. Derek stood in the middle of the open area of floor immediately in front of the panel.

'Pilot Officer Laing, in your statement, when referring to the events of that day, you said you had been briefed by Pilot Officer Noble, the officer who tasked you with the exercise,' said Sidey.

'Correct, sir.'

'Please tell the panel what your briefing comprised.'

'Pilot Officer Noble told us our exercise was a low-level navigation flight, following the route you outlined to the panel a moment ago, sir.'

'Were you instructed on the height at which you were to fly?'

'Yes, sir. Pilot Officer Noble told us we should operate at three hundred feet above ground level. It was a low-level cross-country navigation exercise.'

'What preparation did you undertake?'

'Well, obviously we checked the weather forecast for the route planned, and studied the topographic charts to identify points en route and the required routes and altitudes. After flying from Catterick to Whitby, we flew along the coast to Hartlepool. That was a relatively simple low-flying exercise.

Similarly, there was no problem following the Tyne River Valley at low level to Carlisle. We knew the Stainmore Gap would require care. The margin for safe passage can become limited in certain conditions.'

'By that do you mean low cloud in and around the Gap?'

'Yes, sir, but visibility can be an issue too, not just the cloud base.'

'Did you expect any adverse conditions on this exercise?'

'As I noted, we checked the weather with met, and no low cloud was forecast for our route There was some higher cloud mentioned, broken cumulus with bases at three thousand feet. There was a risk of low stratus noted for the valleys and passes in areas of higher terrain.'

'Did you consider that stratus could have affected areas such as the Stainmore Gap?' Bland interjected.

'Yes, sir, that's one of the places where we expected we may encounter it if the forecast risk came to fruition, and as it turned out, we did meet low stratus there.'

'Did you tell Pilot Officer Noble there was a risk of poor conditions in the Gap?' continued Bland.

'We didn't need to. He had already reviewed the same met briefing we got, so he knew.'

'So, if he knew, did he suggest an alternate route?' Bland pressed.

'No, sir. The stratus was only a forecast possibility, not a known factor. He briefed us that if we could not maintain at least three hundred feet above the terrain, or if our in-flight visibility dropped below three thousand yards at any point, we were to divert or turn around.'

Bland sat back in his chair, and Sidey resumed putting questions to Derek.

'You had been warned of the possibility of low stratus forming, and you said that you were aware that could be an issue if it formed in the Stainmore Gap, which, as it turned out, it did.'

'Yes, sir.'

'And Pilot Officer Noble had briefed you on applicable minima. Three hundred feet and three thousand yards, I think you said.'

'That is correct, sir,' Derek responded.

'So, when you encountered low cloud in the Stainmore Gap, what did you do?'

'Well, I was about one hundred yards behind Pilot Officer Peters' aircraft. It was his turn to lead. I could see that the cloud ahead may affect us, so I waited for him to call and indicate his plan to deal with it.'

'And when he called you on the radio, what did he say?'

'He didn't call.'

'He didn't call you?'

'No, sir, and because I could see conditions were getting worse, I called him. I asked if we should turn or climb out.'

'What was his response to your call?'

'He thought we could manage the conditions. At that stage, we were weaving to stay clear of some areas of low cloud, and they were becoming more frequent and more extensive as we flew on. We sometimes flew through bits of cloud we couldn't avoid.'

'Were you happy with that?'

'No, I could see it was getting worse. On the occasions we flew through patches, we momentarily lost all outside visual reference. Flying blind at three hundred feet above the ground is not advisable, even if it's just for a few seconds.'

'I understand. So, what did you do?'

'If we weren't going to vacate by climbing or turning, I suggested to Pilot Officer Peters that we at least reduce our aircraft speed for the conditions.'

'Did that comply with your instructions from Pilot Officer Noble? I understood from what you said a moment ago that he had specified the minimum heights and visibility at which you were required to turn or climb out.'

'Correct, sir, but at that stage, while I could see conditions ahead were marginal, it was not clear that we could not pass through without breaching our three-hundred foot minimum. Pilot Officer Noble encourages us to be flexible, and to adapt to conditions encountered where appropriate. We were at the limits he had set, but if the cloud had not got much worse and we had proceeded at a reduced speed for poor visibility conditions, I thought we had a good chance of getting through at low level without undue risk and not breaching our minimum height. That would ensure we achieved the exercise's objective.'

'Are you saying that despite setting minima, Pilot Officer Noble would be happy with you continuing when conditions are close to, if not below, those minima, so long as you adapt your flying technique?' asked Bland pointedly.

Gardiner glanced at the wing commander. Richard frowned.

'I don't know what he would think, sir,' Derek replied, 'but I do agree with him that pilots must use judgment and flexibility when faced with different situations, particularly in wartime, and it was not certain at that point that minima would be breached.'

'But there was no war condition affecting you on that day, so that was an unnecessary risk, was it not?'

Derek looked confused. 'Well, we are at war, sir, and we were training for war operations. It was marginal, but we might have been able to continue safely. Certainly, if we had slowed up we would have had a better opportunity to assess as we proceeded.'

'But you didn't reduce your airspeed, so your safety was questionable as you pushed the limitations specified?' Bland asked.

'If we had followed the requirements established by Pilot Officer Noble, the accident would not have occurred, sir. I suggested to Pilot Officer Peters that we turn back. When he declined to do that, I suggested we slow our aircraft to make it less dangerous. He declined to do that, so I pulled up and climbed out, having regard to the minima we had been set and the risks I could see with the cloud base. He could have done either of those things himself, and in that case he would not have crashed.'

Nothing was said for about ten seconds.

'Well, Pilot Officer Laing,' Bland finally said, 'you seem to hold the view that this was a pilot error, pure and simple, and no-one else had any responsibility at all. Not even the officer in charge of the exercise, Pilot Officer Noble.'

John saw both Sidey and Richard look at Bland when he made that latter comment.

'There are some other factors around this training sortie that may be relevant, sir,' Derek said. 'I think these factors indicate the way Pilot Officer Peters was thinking, and are reflected in his decision-making during the exercise. First, when we were pre-flight planning, Pilot Officer Peters refused to use the usual training flight call signs. He insisted on red one and red two, instead of the usual training one and training two.'

'I don't see an issue affecting flight safety in that, Pilot Officer,' Bland interrupted.

'The reason he gave for wanting those call signs, sir, was that he didn't want to be seen as a pilot undergoing training. That's what he told me. I think it indicates a risk that his airborne decision-making could have been adversely affected by ego.'

'You draw a long bow there, I think,' Bland replied.

Derek continued, unperturbed. 'Second, on the Whitby to Hartlepool sector, Pilot Officer Peters left his trailing position some one hundred yards behind me without any warning. He accelerated close past me and dived to wave-top height to make a mock strafing attack on a fishing boat about six hundred yards off the coast. I was caught by surprise, and it was a serious breach of flying discipline.'

No-one said anything.

'Third, as I have already outlined, Pilot Officer Peters made no decision regarding the deteriorating conditions we could see ahead of us in the Stainmore Gap. He declined to take any actions in response to my warning about the risk of minima infringement. Nor did he take any action when I suggested we slow up, to help us deal with the low cloud. In the end I made my own decision, told him what I was doing, and climbed out. He chose not to follow and appears to have crashed moments later.'

'You made it clear to Pilot Officer Peters that you were pulling out, and why?' asked Sidey.

'Yes, sir.'

'How can you be certain he heard you?'

'He responded on the radio in a way that made it clear to me that he had heard my call and knew I was not going to proceed at low-level.'

'You are sure about that, are you?' Bland asked, intervening in the exchange.

Derek hesitated, but then said, 'Yes, sir, quite sure.'

'Quite sure?' Bland queried. 'You don't think he may not have understood you had unilaterally decided conditions were no good and you were leaving him to proceed on his own?' Bland continued. 'How can you be so confident he knew what you were doing, and why you were doing it?'

Derek hesitated before he spoke.

'I had called him several times with my concerns. He knew my view about continuing the low-level passage he was leading. When I told him I was climbing out, he responded by calling me an overcautious wimp.'

The room was silent for some seconds, then Flying Officer Cowles spoke. 'Wing Commander, if you have no further questions, I have heard sufficient to form a view about this. I don't think we need to hear from Pilot Office Noble. I suggest we retire to consider matters.'

'Very well, I agree,' said Bland. 'The panel will withdraw.'

'All stand,' called Gardiner, and the officers comprising the hearing panel left the room.

CHAPTER THIRTEEN

When the panel hearing ended, John left the room quickly, without a word to anyone other than a brief thank you to his assigned Hearing Friend, Tony Smallbone.

Lying on his bed, John found himself going over, yet again, what had happened on the day that Jack had crashed.

The conditions were clearly not good enough in the Stainmore Gap for the task I had briefed, so why did Jack continue? he asked himself. *I was clear about requirements. Not below three hundred and not less three thousand yards. What more could I have said to make things clearer? Should I have gone further and discussed how they might react to any low cloud encountered? I saw the possibility of stratus in the met report and talked about them having to make a one-eighty. Should I have said something else?*

While John knew Jack had been described in the past as "very" confident in his flying abilities, Derek's evidence to the panel had been a surprise. Maybe, as Derek supposed, Jack's inflated ego had interfered with his decision-making on this occasion — with fatal results. Certainly, what Derek had said to the panel about Jack's behaviour during the flight had provided John with answers to the questions he had. It seemed reasonably clear that Jack had exercised poor judgment, ignored set minima, and had failed to react to what was happening outside his aircraft as he had approached the Gap. *I think I know why he crashed, but let's see what the panel says,* John concluded.

There was a quiet knock at John's door. It was Tony Smallbone.

'Pilot Officer Noble, I've just been told the panel is coming back in thirty minutes. They will be delivering their findings. See you there in twenty,' he said.

'Thank you, sir,' John replied.

Flight Lieutenant Gardiner called the room to order, and those present all stood as the members of the panel entered.

Wing Commander Bland began speaking. 'We have considered the circumstances of the accident in which Pilot Officer Peters was killed. We have reviewed the weather briefing provided by our meteorological unit, the operational briefing provided by Pilot Officer Noble, the nature of the exercise to be undertaken, and the evidence of Pilot Officer Derek Laing. Our findings are as follows.'

John leant forward in his seat. *Will Bland place blame on me?* he wondered.

'The training exercise was appropriate for the experience and qualification of the two pilots involved. A weather briefing was obtained and indicated no conditions of sufficient concern to cancel or vary the exercise. The operational briefing by the officer in charge of the exercise, Pilot Officer Noble, established weather minima that were acceptable.' Bland paused and looked up from the paper he was reading, staring directly at John. 'We find that the accident was caused by the failure of Pilot Officer Peters to observe the weather minima set for the exercise, and by his associated failure to operate in a way that would have made continuation safer when he encountered weather conditions affecting his ability to safely navigate the Stainmore Gap at low level. He did not reverse course when he could see minima were at risk of being infringed, nor did he reduce his speed when deciding to proceed in the deteriorating flying conditions. This is despite Pilot Officer Laing, flying as number two, suggesting both a speed reduction and abandonment of their low-level passage through the Gap.

'There was a suggestion that Pilot Officer Peters' judgment may have been affected by a particular attitude he is said to have had, and we accept that may have been a contributing factor in this accident. There is a constant need for aircrew to be alert to, and conscious of matters that may adversely affect decision-making in the air. There is no place for overconfidence, or lack of flying discipline, in operations.

'We find no contributory fault elsewhere. Others involved, the met briefers, the officer in charge of the exercise, Pilot Officer Noble, and the other pilot participating in the flight, Pilot Officer Laing, may all be satisfied that they properly observed and performed the various duties incumbent on them.

'Pilot Officer Peters made an error of judgment. That error was to continue flying towards rising terrain at low level when in-flight conditions were deteriorating and affecting visibility. We accept he was not an experienced pilot, but his continuation was contrary to the specific instructions he had been given regarding in-flight minima, and he ignored warnings being sounded by his number two on the exercise, Pilot Officer Laing.

'As a direct result of his decision to continue, Pilot Officer Peters' aircraft collided, while in controlled flight, with terrain he either did not see, or which he saw but was unable to avoid. The impact destroyed the aircraft concerned, and was of such a nature that it was not survivable. The official record will state that the primary cause of this accident was error of judgment by Pilot Officer Peters. That concludes this hearing.'

Everyone filed out, and John again retreated to the privacy of his room. Now he had been formally cleared of any responsibility for the accident, he felt enormous relief, but also a deep sense of loss. He had been close to Jack. They had told each other about their early lives, family, and experiences. They had talked about their love of flying, and whether that would change when they became directly involved in war operations. Their closeness had even led to Jack taking it upon himself to tell John what he should do to ensure his relationship with Mary went well. Jack had fancied himself as an intimacy counsellor. But now he was dead, killed by a stupid mistake.

John relished his role as a fighter pilot, but he did recognise he sometimes struggled with the air force's command structure. He did not have a problem with the formal RAF hierarchy, the respect, and the saluting, but he was concerned about rigid attitudes to important strategic and tactical issues. He thought that they should be discussed at squadron operational level, at least, but they never were.

He also disliked the fact that individuals could sometimes be promoted beyond their capability. In that regard, he had a particular concern about Wing Commander Christopher Bland. John had heard from some of the other pilots who had flown with Bland that his leadership skills and tactical ability were non-existent. His poor decision-making had affected the whole squadron in the past when on advanced training operation — it was just as well that he was not an active pilot at present, because he had no medical clearance. John had no doubt that if Bland was able to fly, and took over leading the squadron on war operations, he would be a real menace.

And why has he got it in for me? John wondered. *He certainly seemed to want me to be found to have some responsibility, at the special hearing he insisted be held, for Jack's accident.*

As John thought about it, he realised he had made it easy for Bland. He had given him several opportunities to record things against him. That had nearly come home to roost at the hearing. *Right*, thought John. *I will change.* He decided there would be no more criticism of air warfare strategy at briefings, no more arguments about patrol tactics, no more beat-ups of anyone's house. He would proceed with care if he was concerned about something, and he would not give Bland any more opportunities to gun for him.

It was five days since the panel hearing, and John had been summoned to Squadron Leader Sidey's office.

'Pilot Officer Noble, you are now back on war operations. What it's going to entail, heaven knows. The so-called phoney war just continues. In the meantime, we shall maintain our patrols, and see what, if anything, develops.'

'Very well, sir,' John replied.

'One other thing, Pilot Officer. You have had your moments in recent times, but I consider those matters closed. I am confident you won't test the squadron's leadership again on operational matters. Is my confidence misplaced?'

'Not at all, sir. I understand quite clearly what is required. You can have confidence that I will do what is needed.'

'Good to hear you say that. We need people with the flying skills you have demonstrated, but I want to be sure that you will always act appropriately. Acting as a team is going to be important, so perhaps not so many challenges to the status quo? When the Germans come, as they will, I want all my pilots to be operating as a tight-knit group, all following the same rules.'

'Yes, sir,' John acknowledged.

'And one further thing, Pilot Officer.'

John waited, wondering what else he might be about to get a lecture on.

'You have now been operational for over six months, and you've been developing your aviation skills well. Your promotion to Flying Officer has come through. Congratulations.'

On 10th May 1940, early in the morning, all the operational station personnel were asked to meet in No. 2 Hangar. It was one of the smaller hangars, but sufficient to hold a meeting of everyone who was considered operational. That encompassed those who were pilots, flight engineers, armourers, controllers, refuellers, air-defence gunners, and similar.

Wing Commander Bland walked in and moved to the front of the hangar. A hush fell over the crowd. He stepped up onto some wooden cases normally used to store fire-extinguishing equipment and turned to face his audience. He looked tired as he began to speak.

'Many of you will no doubt already have heard this on the radio, but the German war machine has swung into action again. Early this morning, it invaded the Low Countries. Belgium, Holland, and Luxembourg have been attacked by German air and ground forces.

'We have been expecting something like this since Germany invaded Poland last year. If anything, it's a surprise how long it has taken for them to continue military activities. But one thing is certain: you can consider the phoney war over. The officers in charge of the various station activities have been briefed about what this may now mean for you. Ground personnel should withdraw to meet your officer in charge in your normal briefing areas. Pilots should remain here to listen to what Squadron Leader Sidey has to say to you. Thank you.'

Ground-based crews began leaving. The pilots, who had been scattered around the hangar, now all came forward to sit at the front of the area where Bland was standing.

'Gentlemen,' Sidey began, 'your training, skill, and dedication will soon be tested. I don't want to sound overdramatic, but the fact of the matter is that the Germans are coming. As the wing commander has noted, German forces are moving into the Low Countries. Paratroop landings are being reported from Holland. German tanks have emerged from the Ardennes Forest. The focus of the current ground invasion appears, at this stage, to be southeast Belgium and northern Luxembourg. In themselves those areas are not thought to be strategically important, but as a way to attack France, bypassing the Maginot Line, it's a telling move. As I speak, French forces, together with our Expeditionary Force, are moving northwest to meet the Germans. We are hopeful they will be able to halt the German thrust.

'You will be wondering what this means for us, here at four-one-five squadron. The answer is, at least for the time being, nothing much. We have been asked to lift our readiness levels, but current engagement rules remain operative. The number of patrols we undertake will be increased, effective immediately, but nothing else changes for now. Does anyone have a question?'

Greg put up his hand.

'Yes, Flying Officer Somerville?'

'Current engagement rules prevent us crossing the coastline and entering European airspace. And that's even if we are in hot pursuit of an enemy aircraft. Is that to continue, now the Germans are on their way west?'

'As I said, current engagement rules remain in place. Currently, you do not have authority to cross the coast.'

Greg nodded his acknowledgement.

'Anything else?'

John resisted the urge to engage with the squadron leader on the merits or otherwise of the policy just outlined to Greg.

'All right, thank you, gentlemen. This will no doubt evolve quickly, and I will keep you briefed. The only thing I am happy about at present is that the period of war inactivity to date has given us time to re-equip our fighter fleet and get our pilots better prepared. When the time comes, I am confident we will acquit ourselves well.'

In the mess that evening, everyone had an opinion.

'I can't believe we're still forbidden to pursue any aircraft into Europe,' said Greg. 'There are going to be Germans all over the sky in Holland now, and we aren't allowed near them? Madness!'

'If the British Expeditionary Force is going to move north to meet the Nazis, they will risk air attack from the Luftwaffe,' Roger added. 'We only have a small number of aircraft in France supporting the force's commitment, so wouldn't it be sensible to allow us over the coastline to help with air cover in the circumstances?'

There were nods and murmurs of agreement around the table.

'Look, chaps, you know the reason for the restriction,' said Richard. 'The powers that be don't want to risk losing fighter aircraft beyond what Britain has already committed to the Expeditionary Force. The French have a reasonable fighter capability, so that, coupled with what we have there to date, should be sufficient. If the Expeditionary Force and French army stop Adolf in his tank-tracks, I doubt a policy change is needed. On the other hand, if Herr Hitler gets through

Belgium and Luxembourg, and into France, maybe those in charge will change the policy. I think we should wait and see before criticising too much.'

'Actually, Richard, despite being critical of this particular rule in the past, I've now changed my view and agree with what you're saying,' John said. 'Over the next few weeks, if not days, we will get a measure of how good the German army is. If our forces in France can stop them, there is no need to risk more aircraft by sending them over there at present. If they can't stop them, then home defence will loom large, and every aircraft we have should be kept here for that battle.'

Derek Laing, who had just joined them, had been quiet and introspective in recent months. Everyone knew why. He had lost a close friend, and if not for his own initiative and good airmanship, he might have crashed himself. So, when he spoke, everybody listened. 'What happens to our Expeditionary Force if they and the French are overwhelmed? We don't just lose any aircraft we have over there in that case. We lose a large part of our army. Then how the hell do we stop Jerry coming across the Channel in landing craft and walking up our beaches?'

The group stayed quiet. No-one had thought of it from that angle.

'Dinner is served!'

The call from the head steward broke the silence. Derek's question remained unanswered as they made their way through to the dining room.

Over the next two weeks, little changed in the daily activities of the Spitfire pilots of 415 Squadron. They continued their patrols out over the sea towards the Dutch coast, but there were no Luftwaffe aircraft to be seen. However, everyone was aware the land battle against the Germans in Europe was not going well.

The Wehrmacht had entered France. Parts of the French army, and the British Expeditionary Force, were being pushed back towards the coast. Holland and Belgium had surrendered and were firmly in the hands of their German occupiers. The mood was becoming more sombre by the day in the officers' mess at RAF Catterick. The Germans appeared to be unstoppable.

Then, on the afternoon of 24th May, 415 Squadron's pilots were summoned to the briefing room.

As soon as everyone was seated, Wing Commander Bland began to speak. 'Britain has made the decision to evacuate all its troops from Europe. There is a risk they could be completely overrun at any time. To preserve army manpower, it's imperative that we successfully extract our forces. We must get them back home to fight another day. As a consequence, the government has instructed the Royal Navy, assisted by the Royal Air Force, to mount a rescue mission. Our troops are holding the Germans at a defensive perimeter at present, near the French town of Dunkirk. That's not a long-term solution, the force in opposition is so large.

'The plan is to lift our soldiers from the port area of the town. The Royal Navy is putting a lot of vessels together to use for the evacuation. The role of the RAF is to provide air cover. The Luftwaffe is using both conventional bombers and Stuka dive-bombers against our boys' ground positions. In addition, there have been reports of fighters making strafing runs at human targets on the beaches, where our soldiers have no cover.'

John heard the ripple of angry comments around the room.

'I will leave you in the hands of Squadron Leader Sidey to brief you on the detail of the operations we propose for this squadron. All I will say at this point is that this is a crucial time for Britain. If we can't get our forces out of Europe, our overall strength will be substantially weakened. So, what we do, and how well we do it, will be critical to the course of this war. Good luck to you all.' Bland paused. 'And just so you know, this operation has been given a name by military command. It is to be known as Operation Dynamo.'

David Sidey then spoke. 'Gentlemen, we are one of several squadrons being temporarily relocated to Hornchurch to participate in Dynamo. We are going down tomorrow, with departure from here planned for ten hundred hours. The evacuation from Dunkirk is scheduled to begin on the twenty-seventh.

'With other squadrons being positioned to Hornchurch, it will be busy down there. You will all need to ensure you keep a good lookout when operating in the vicinity of the aerodrome. For your information, we are also arranging for our ground crews to go down. That is to ensure our repair and maintenance needs are well met while we are stationed there.

'Operations will be briefed each day at Hornchurch, but I can tell you all that the bottom line will be keeping Jerry bombers away from the beaches at Dunkirk. The troops waiting there to embark will be vulnerable. You should also be aware that there is a possibility we will be flying war ops as part of a big wing, with up to four or five squadrons operating together.'

John screwed up his face when he heard that, and exchanged glances with Richard and Greg. While John appreciated the fire power and presence of forty or fifty Spitfires acting together, he also saw the pitfalls. He and the other pilots had discussed the big wing concept previously, when they had first heard about the strategy. His view was that it risked delay, as various squadrons sought to rendezvous with each other in the air. That delay would affect the time they could spend over Dunkirk before fuel became an issue. He also thought it less than satisfactory that the airborne leader of a big wing would be unfamiliar with many of the pilots flying in the enlarged group. It did not seem to John to be a good idea that the leader would not know the capabilities of pilots he was leading into battle.

Despite his resolution to keep his head down at operational briefings, John decided to ask the questions on his mind, and raised his hand. This was important, he thought.

'Yes?' Sidey asked.

'Our endurance will be affected if we take some time to locate other squadrons with which we have to join up, to form a big wing. Has there been any thought about that?' John asked.

'We are confident the new Chain Home system will ensure squadrons are able to locate each other in the air as required, even where they originate from different aerodromes. The control and command systems developed for Chain Home are very effective.'

John nodded his acknowledgement. That seemed reasonable, but the proof will be in the pudding, he thought. Then John decided he would ask the second question he had on his mind.

'The big wing leader will not be familiar with many of his pilots, as they will be from other squadrons. Will that be a disadvantage when he is ordering different parts of the wing to take some action? He will be unsure of the capability of those he doesn't know.'

'Any lack of familiarity with some doesn't matter. We have all studied and rehearsed Fighter Command's air attack plans. If they are followed by pilots as they fly into action, everyone knows what they must do, and how they should go about it.'

John did not like that answer. He thought inflexible pre-ordained air attack plans were a recipe for disaster in the dynamic environment of aerial warfare, but he decided to say nothing further about that. He was not going to risk any confrontation with the squadron leadership.

'Thank you,' John said. 'One last question. If most aircraft are committed to go up and form big wings, does that mean there could be times when there is no ability to maintain some aircraft in reserve?'

'That is something considered by Fighter Command strategists. Their view is that it will depend on circumstances at the time, and reserves will be kept available, where thought necessary.'

John realised that response from Sidey did not answer his question, but he also knew there was no point in pushing on with his line of questioning. If he did, he would probably meet some resistance from Sidey, and John had decided to be careful.

'Thank you, sir,' was all he said.

CHAPTER FOURTEEN

After being told that they were being relocated to RAF Hornchurch, to be closer to Dunkirk, John decided to call Mary. Since Mary was only free from her hospital duties between midday and three, they arranged to meet for a picnic beside the Northallerton Cricket Club grounds.

Mary brought along sandwiches and a thermos flask of tea, and they sat together beneath some oak trees to eat.

'That would have to be one of the best mutton sandwiches I have ever had,' John enthused. 'I'm sorry we won't get to do this again for a while.'

'Where are you going, John?' Mary enquired.

John paused. He knew he should not say, but he could not help trusting Mary. 'We are being sent to a station that will put us nearer Dunkirk, in France, to provide air cover for the troops on the ground there. But that is for your ears only. Don't share it with anyone, please. Strictly speaking, I shouldn't be telling you.'

'Of course, John. It's probably the same thing I heard Father talking about last night. Squadrons are moving south to bases better placed to provide protection for some evacuating troops.'

John felt better. He had not given away anything that Mary did not already know.

The time they had allowed themselves for their picnic was soon over. John had to get back to Catterick, and Mary was due to restart her shift at the hospital in Thirsk. As they packed up, John decided he wanted Mary to know how he felt about her. *Who knows?* he thought. *I may not come back if some bloody German flies better than I do over the coming weeks.*

'Mary, thanks for coming today. I don't know when I will next see you,' he said, starting to feel slightly awkward, 'but I wanted to tell you that I think about you a lot.'

'Oh, thank you, John. That's so nice to hear. I think about you too.'

Before he realised what was happening, Mary stepped forward and kissed him. Her lips were soft on his, and the kiss seemed to last for a long time.

'I'm looking forward to having a lot more time with my favourite Spitfire pilot soon,' Mary said, smiling at John as she stepped back.

John was flustered, but he managed to reply, 'Great. I will contact you as soon as I am back. We could do this again. The sandwiches make it well worth it.' He laughed, and so did Mary.

In the mess that evening, before dinner, some of the pilots were talking about developments in Europe and the rapid German advances.

'I understand we have over three hundred thousand troops at Dunkirk. How do you pull that many out from under the noses of the Germans?' Roger asked.

'Not easily,' said Richard.

'Air cover will be important,' John said, 'not just for the troops, but for any vessels being used to extract the troops.'

'Well, you can bet the first thing the Jerries will do is destroy wharves and docks in the area. How do you load thousands of soldiers onto boats to get them home then?' Richard said. 'And if there are in fact as many troops as we think being threatened by the German advances, and they can't get out, what sort of hole does that make in our ability to face Hitler?'

'Agreed — if he sends his soldiers across the Channel soon and doesn't stop at the French coast, we are in trouble. They keep coming, and we've already lost an army. It's the same point Derek raised the other evening,' Roger replied.

'The plan is to get them out and back to Britain to fight another day,' Richard said, 'and we will damn well be there to help them and make sure that succeeds.'

As he listened to the talk amongst his fellow pilots, John recognised how rapidly things were changing. Three weeks ago, they had been complaining about insufficient opportunity to engage with the enemy. Now, they were wondering about their ability to withstand the sudden onslaught unleashed in Europe, rapidly coming their way.

The next morning, all the squadron pilots were gathered in the briefing room. There were sixteen of them, though the squadron only had to stand up twelve Spitfires for any war operations. The additional four pilots were to cover unexpected absences that might occur due to sickness, emergency leave, or commitment to some training agenda. And, while no-one said so, when the squadron started suffering losses, there had to be some reserves to cover deaths. They were also taking two additional aircraft down to Hornchurch, as spares to cover damaged machines.

'Yesterday, I briefed you on our involvement in Operation Dynamo,' Squadron Leader Sidey said to the gathered pilots. 'As you heard, Hornchurch is to be our base for missions across the Channel to France. The move is not permanent, of course, but it will be for as long as is required for our participation in the evacuation of Dunkirk.

'Our role will be to intercept bombers attempting to attack our forces and the infrastructure at Dunkirk. The Germans have already destroyed much of the town itself. The port's wharves have been damaged so badly that they are now unusable by any ship of reasonable size. The mole there is still available, but that is not likely to be the case for long, as Jerry hammers the port area. They want to prevent any evacuation by sea. Troops are on the beaches behind the town.

'The evacuation will involve smaller boats coming in and ferrying soldiers out to larger vessels waiting offshore. The planners expect large numbers of Luftwaffe aircraft to be used. The Germans will have seen the opportunity they have here to capture hundreds of thousands of our soldiers trapped between their forces and the sea. To maximise our presence, we are, as I told you, going to be operating together with three or four other squadrons as big wings. We will assemble airborne this side of the Channel, and then make our way to the Dunkirk area as one large group.

'Our prime targets will be the bombers, but you will have to deal with their fighter escorts as well. As a general principle, the tactics are to arrive *en masse* over the target area at a relatively high altitude. We expect the bombers to come in at about eighteen to twenty thousand feet. If we are at twenty-three, that will give us some initial advantage. There may be some bombers lower, especially if Jerry uses Stukas. You can expect to encounter them at about ten thousand feet as they prepare to attack.'

The pilots had all heard about the Ju 87, the Stuka — an aircraft that delivered its deadly payload from a dive. Stukas had a siren-like device that gave a very loud and ominous scream as the aircraft plummeted out of the sky towards its target. Psychological warfare, really, some were thinking.

'Height is our priority,' Sidey continued. 'We want to arrive at a level that has a height margin over the enemy's bombers. I accept that after contact you may end up lower, but avoid remaining down there and scudding around at low level. Get back up to the initial attack altitude as soon as you can. That's what the strategists at Fighter Command want us to do.

'On each occasion, we will use one of Command's designated air attack plans, which you have been practising. The plan will be called by the formation leader when he has assessed the situation.

'Any questions before I hand over to the flight commanders, who will talk about detailed operational issues and take you through some of the specific tactics we think should be used?'

There were no questions, although John did have some thoughts racing through his mind. He understood the importance of stopping the bombers hitting their targets. They were the priority, but he had some operational concerns. Quite apart from trying to organise a mass airborne rendezvous of aircraft for a big wing, and the wing leader's lack of familiarity with all the pilots under his command, John wondered if the requirement to stay high after the initial engagement was appropriate. It would be better if they could then simply fly at the level best suited to the circumstances.

John knew that once they engaged, there would be a swirling mass of ducking and diving aircraft — bombers defending, fighters attacking. In that situation, he felt the pilots should be able to react to the situation as it developed, rather than following rigid plans. Having to choose one of the six common attack methods formulated by the planners at Fighter Command might not be optimum.

Despite his concerns, John kept quiet. He had asked some questions at yesterday's briefing. That was enough. He had taken all the criticism he wanted, and now he was steadfastly maintaining his silence, despite his concern about the proposed engagement tactics.

'All right. The flight commanders will now take you through how we plan to use the various attack scenarios,' said Sidey.

That evening, John talked with Richard about what was soon to happen with the squadron. He always found Richard to be insightful when giving his views on operational issues.

'I wasn't going to say anything more today, Richard,' John said, 'but I am worried about how effective we are going to be as we hang around forming ourselves into a multi-squadron wing. That could waste valuable time and fuel. And what about this requirement to always operate at higher altitudes, and the use of agreed, but inflexible in my view, air attack plans? I would have thought we should be free to adapt and respond to whatever we end up facing, patrol to patrol. And how the hell do you keep a big wing operating together anyway, once the enemy is engaged? People should be able to operate as they see fit at that point, rather than looking to reform at altitude.'

'John, don't worry about it. It's just bureaucratic planning. If it doesn't work well, things will change, quickly, I think. In fact, my guess is that pilots will just do what they think is best in the situation they find themselves in from time to time anyway. Usually that won't involve climbing back to try to reform in a big wing once engagement has begun.'

John was surprised that Richard, who was so clear that the plans outlined were not likely to be effective, had said nothing in the briefing. 'But you didn't say anything to Sidey. I thought you agreed with him.'

'John, you'll soon learn when it is worthwhile speaking up and when it is better not to bother. Today was the latter case for me. I don't want disagreement and angst among the squadron's leaders as we approach our real-war baptism. Anything I said was not going to cause a change of tactics. For me, the main thing is that everyone feels comfortable we are on the same team, doing what needs to be done. Fighter Command will see soon enough if their planned tactics are not the best, so there will be a change. In the meantime, once engaged with Jerry, I know the lads will fly intuitively, so I'm not concerned with textbook attack profiles being offered. They will do what they need to do to survive and, hopefully, succeed in their individual air battles.'

'Fair enough,' John replied, impressed by Richard's measured response, as well as his logic and analysis.

CHAPTER FIFTEEN

As the squadron prepared to depart for Hornchurch, John felt a great sense of pride as he sat in his Spitfire looking at the other aircraft parked around him, engines running. They were all waiting for the signal that would tell them they could take off.

The mass of Merlin engines created a deep throbbing sound as they idled. Soon that would turn into a roar as the aircraft accelerated for take-off. Then their wings would generate the lift that would enable them to fly, and the fourteen Spitfires would climb into the sky together.

Aircraft cockpit canopies were open, and leather-helmeted heads were either down, completing last-minute checks, or up, looking out, with smiles to adjacent pilots. John could sense the anticipation.

Greg was on one side of him, and Richard on the other. They were both looking around, having completed their checks. For today's positioning flight to Hornchurch, Greg was leading red section, with John as red two and Derek Laing as red three. Richard was leading yellow section.

A green flare went up from the control cab. John could see the airman who had launched it, awkwardly hanging out of the cab's first-floor window.

'Take-off approved. In ground-assembled order, sections go,' John heard on his radio.

Soon all the aircraft were airborne, climbing to the south towards Hornchurch. The weather was fine, and after about an hour the Spitfires of 415 Squadron were positioning to land at

Hornchurch. As red section was crossing the airfield boundary to land, there was an unexpected call on the radio.

'Red three, go around. Abort your landing.'

The call came from Richard, the leader of yellow section. Approaching to land immediately behind red section, Richard had noticed red three's left-hand undercarriage leg had not fully deployed. It would collapse on touchdown, risking the aircraft's port wing hitting the ground. If the wing dug in, it could cause the Spitfire to cartwheel.

Red three, Derek Laing, responded immediately, without questioning why he had been told to go around. The sign of a well-trained pilot, John confirmed to himself as he saw Derek climbing away under full power. Derek's reaction to the urgent radio call must have been quick, he thought, to be able to stop his Spitfire's descent from just feet above the ground.

'I will hold at one thousand east of the field,' Derek called.

'Roger,' Richard acknowledged, now close to touchdown himself.

'What's planned?' the airfield controller asked Greg, as he and John came into the tower cab at Hornchurch. 'I've got one of your lot holding to the east. Undercarriage issue?'

'Yes, that's correct. May I have the mic?' Greg asked. After a moment's hesitation, the controller handed it over, and Greg addressed Derek. 'Red three, this is red leader in the tower cab. Do you read, over?'

'Read you loud and clear, red leader.'

'Did you retract your gear when you climbed out from the aborted landing?'

'I tried, but I don't think both the wheels came up, or at least that's what I'm seeing looking at the port wing indicator. Right gear looks to be up. I can feel some drag, so something's definitely hanging out.'

'Roger. I want to see what I can of the undercarriage's position, so complete a slow fly-by of the tower, please. Two hundred feet would be fine, and we will have a look as you go over.'

'Wilco, positioning for the low and slow this time,' Derek responded.

Those in the cab watched as Derek's Spitfire slowly turned on to a long approach and flew directly towards them. As it got closer, Greg went out onto the balcony and peered through the binoculars he had borrowed from the controller.

When he came back, John asked, 'What did you see?'

'The right-hand undercarriage leg is up. The left-hand leg is hanging down a bit,' said Greg. 'By the look of it, it may have failed at the attachment point. Little wonder it wouldn't retract fully when Derek tried to raise it.' He seized the mic again. 'Red three, this is red leader.'

'Go ahead, red leader.'

'Your port undercarriage leg has not retracted and appears to have suffered a structural malfunction.'

'Oh. I might try recycling the landing gear,' Derek responded, 'to see what that does.'

'No, don't do that. Your starboard leg is up at present, and you certainly won't be able to get the damaged port leg up. It will probably fail on landing. Better in that case that the starboard side remains up, in case you can't retract it again after you recycle. Better that you ensure the aircraft is able to settle on its belly when the port gear collapses.'

'All right, I will leave the undercarriage as is and treat the landing as a wheels-up arrival,' Derek responded. His voice sounded calm and professional, though he was about to commit to crash-landing his Spitfire.

'Go ahead in your own time, Derek. We have the wagon out.'

Greg had dropped the call signs from his interchange with Derek. Less formality seemed appropriate, given that he was telling a friend to go ahead and crash-land.

'Wilco, positioning now,' Derek responded.

'Go well, chap,' said Greg, who then left the cab and made his way down to the landing field, closely followed by John.

Once outside, they saw that Derek was flying the normal, slightly curved approach. That ensured he could keep his touchdown point in view, not hidden by the Spitfire's long nose. The wind was blowing at twenty-five miles per hour down the grassed area he intended to use for his landing. John knew the wind would reduce touchdown speed, and hopefully lessen the force of impact.

There was an ambulance out to the left of the landing area, about halfway along, and near that, the crash-wagon.

'I expect the damaged left hand gear leg to be ripped off on touch down,' Greg said to John. 'Derek will be fine if he can ensure the Spit doesn't bury its nose.'

'What a sod awful start to our ops,' John said. He knew war operations would cause their own problems, with aircraft and personnel losses expected, but to have a prang at this stage due to some technical malfunction seemed very unfair.

They watched in silence as Derek continued his approach. They could hear his engine's exhausts popping occasionally, indicating that he was throttling back as much as he safely could, to land as slowly as possible without letting his sink-rate get too high.

Derek's aircraft came in low over the boundary hedge and started sinking quickly towards the surface of the grass on which it was about to touch down. He was sinking too quickly, John thought, but then he heard Derek apply a trickle of power. The aircraft was now flying level, close to the surface of the airfield. John thought he was about six feet above the grass. Then all engine power was cut and the Spitfire started to drop towards the grass, but relatively slowly. Derek was applying back-pressure on the control stick to keep the aircraft's nose up.

Go easy, Derek, don't let the tail touch first, John thought. He knew that if the aircraft was too nose-high, there was a risk the tail would strike the ground first. If that happened, it would cause a violent pitch down. That risked the Spitfire flipping over. But John need not have worried. Derek, clearly sensing the position of his tail close to the ground during his touchdown flare, checked the stick slightly forward, and the entire underside of the aircraft made contact with the ground at the same moment, sliding to a halt after only eighty yards. The dangling port leg had caught the ground and ripped itself free in an instant.

'Well done, Derek,' Greg said aloud, as he saw Derek climbing out of his aircraft once it had stopped. 'Always a good crash-landing when neither the ambulance nor the crash wagon are required,' he grinned at John.

John looked at him, smiling. 'Question is, Greg, who buys the celebratory beer tonight? Derek, because he's happy he pulled it off without hurting himself or badly damaging his aircraft? Or us, recognising his excellent efforts?'

'Ha, I think we buy for Derek, and probably also for Richard, who spotted the problem and warned him just in time.'

The day before the beginning of the planned evacuation of Dunkirk, Squadron Leader Sidey gathered the pilots in the large sitting room at the back of the Hornchurch officers' mess.

'Tomorrow morning, we are to be airborne at o-four-forty hours,' he told them. 'We are to rendezvous with other squadrons over Margate, not below fifteen thousand feet. Actual height will be confirmed by control when we are airborne. Our task is offensive patrol, looking for Jerry bombers as they approach Dunkirk. I have been told we will probably be directed to penetrate at least forty miles into France.

'Early breakfast, gentlemen, and be ready for take-off at the appointed time. The day's weather brief will be put on the dispersal hut noticeboard first thing, but at this stage it's looking all right. I suggest you get an early night. Thank you. That is all.'

There was a scraping and scuffing of chairs around the room as the pilots of 415 Squadron got up and made their way to the door.

As John walked towards his aircraft early the next morning, he could see pinpricks of light moving around the dispersal area. In the pre-dawn twilight it looked ghostly, but as he got closer, he saw the solid shapes of people and planes. The ground crews were moving around, using torches to complete their pre-flight inspections of the Spitfires.

'All good to go, sir,' the ground crew chief, Bertie Smith, called to John as he approached his aircraft. 'Full fuel. Fully armed, and, if I may say so, sir, in immaculate condition, as always.'

John laughed. He knew Bertie was proud of the condition in which he kept the squadron's Spitfires.

'Thanks. I'm sure it is,' John replied. With that, he climbed up onto the inboard section of the port wing and stepped down into the cockpit. He was soon strapped in, with the Spitfire's Merlin engine murmuring contentedly in front of him. A green from the tower cab, followed by Sidey's call to roll, would soon have the squadron in the air.

As he pushed the throttle lever forward on his aircraft, John quickly glanced across at the windsock. It was limp — no wind at all. That matched what had been said in the met brief pinned to the noticeboard John had read earlier, although it had also noted that windy and cloudy conditions should be expected over France.

Climbing towards the English Channel to complete the rendezvous over Margate, John was enjoying the flying conditions. The air was smooth and clear, and he was pleased that they could watch the sun rising ahead of them as they flew east.

After linking up with two other Spitfire squadrons over Margate, all the aircraft continued climbing together. They had been instructed to patrol at twenty-two thousand feet. As they got closer to the French coast, John could see huge columns of thick black smoke rising from the area where the town and port of Dunkirk were situated. He was not sure if it was the result of ground warfare, or attacks by the Luftwaffe.

'Margate wing,' John heard on his radio, 'maintain angels twenty-two, and eyes peeled for hostiles, please.'

Margate wing was the call sign allocated to the group of Spitfires formed when the three squadrons had met and joined up over Margate. *There are thirty-six Spitfires in this wing*, John thought, *so I hope we meet Jerry, otherwise it's a bit of a waste.*

'Bandits, twenty plus, ten o'clock. Tracking west, towards Dunkirk. Estimate angels eighteen.'

John saw them immediately, lower and to the left. He thought they were Dornier 17s.

'Tally-ho,' called the commander of the wing, someone unknown to the pilots of 415 Squadron — one of the issues with these big wings.

'Select your targets, working back from lead Jerry using attack wave sequences.'

John recognised air attack method two. The first Spitfires to attack would go in line astern, aiming for the aircraft in the first two rows of the enemy formation. The next to arrive would aim for the centre of the enemy formation, and the final group would attack the Luftwaffe aircraft flying at the rear.

The lead Spitfires in the wing were peeling away and diving towards the Germans. Others were setting up to follow them down. Half of the wing had rolled into a diving turn to attack the enemy formation when John saw a glint high in the sky, about five miles behind the formation. *Fighter cover*, he thought, as he called a warning.

'Margate wing leader. Alert. Fighters above and five miles behind the bombers. Multiple hostiles.'

There was no reply from the wing leader. *Maybe he's too intent on his attack, or maybe he didn't hear my call*, John thought, his mind racing. He repeated his warning. Still no reply. Then the reassuring voice of David Sidey came through.

'E flight, F flight, with me, climbing to intercept fighters.'

E and F flights were the last twelve aircraft in the large formation known as Margate wing. They were, in fact, all the 415 Squadron Spitfires.

The noses of the twelve Spitfires rose in unison, as full power was applied and they climbed towards the fighters John had spotted. The remainder of the big wing continued down to attack the bombers headed to Dunkirk. John could feel his heart thumping. He knew that very soon he would find out what it was like to be in a dogfight with a young man from another country, whose sole aim in life at that point would be to shoot him down.

'Split into pairs.'

That instruction from Sidey required them to operate in sections of two aircraft each — a leader with his wingman, who would protect the leader's tail. It was a technique John had suggested some time ago, in place of using an approved Fighter Command method. He had not expected Sidey to adopt it.

John manoeuvred his aircraft to trail Greg's Spitfire, which was to be John's lead aircraft. He could see the German fighters were Me 109s — formidable opponents.

As they closed with the oncoming German fighters, John momentarily thought his life as a fighter pilot was going to end before it had properly started. It looked as if a head-on collision was going to occur. One of the Me 109s held a heading that took it straight towards Greg and John. It was not deviating. John saw the flickering of gunfire along the leading edge of its wings, and realised that for the first time in his life, someone was shooting at him. At the last moment, the Me 109 rolled steeply to the left and flashed by, less than fifty yards from John's starboard wing. Greg was already hard into a right-hand turn, after the German. John followed.

Greg had got on to the 109's tail, and John could see he was shooting at the enemy aircraft. Lazy tracer showed the path of Greg's fire. It was like watching an arc of water from a garden hose. *Come on, get him,* John silently urged. His focus was suddenly interrupted by bullets and cannon fire exploding across his port wing. He felt, rather than heard, their impact. He saw that a row of holes, some quite large, had appeared across the wing's surface, in a neat and straight line. The yellow spinner of the Me 109 that had just hit him filled his rear-view mirror.

Reacting quickly, and angry with himself for being caught out, John rolled his Spitfire violently to the right and hauled back hard on the stick. The German did not follow and instead continued after Greg. John called a warning.

'Red one, bandit behind you, break left.'

Greg reacted instantly, rolling his Spitfire into a steep turn to the left. As he did that, tracer from the pursuing Me 109 slid past him on his right.

The high speed of the 109 in its diving attack caused it to streak past Greg, who immediately set off, diving in pursuit of the German. The pilot of the Luftwaffe aircraft must have decided he had had enough, because he made for a nearby cloud mass and disappeared. Greg pulled up and resumed level flight, weaving carefully. A few moments later, John managed to resume his wingman's position.

'Thanks for that,' Greg called.

As they continued, it felt as if it was just the two of them flying this morning. Despite their big wing and the many German aircraft, they knew were somewhere in the area, there was no-one else to be seen at present.

'Back to base I think, John,' said Greg. 'Don't know about you, but I'm down to forty minutes' of fuel, and I don't want a swim in the Channel.'

'Agreed. Set heading and I'm right behind you,' John replied.

The two Spitfires turned on to a course that would take them back to Hornchurch.

CHAPTER SIXTEEN

'Thanks, your call saved my bacon,' Greg said to John when they were back at Hornchurch, sitting in the mess. 'Much appreciated.'

'Glad I was there as your cover and able to help,' John replied. 'You would have done the same for me.'

'We had no losses at all,' Roger chipped in. 'Everyone got home. Bloody good.'

'Did the squadron score any kills?' Charlie asked.

'A probable, courtesy of a long-range deflection shot by Richard, so I hear from the intelligence officer,' said Squadron Leader Howarth.

'Very good,' Charlie replied.

'The local boys from five-four-four lost two of theirs today, apparently,' Howarth went on in a lower voice.

'Bugger,' Charlie muttered.

'Let's toast four-one-five squadron's first day results,' Roger said enthusiastically after a brief pause in the conversation. 'Today we got an initial kill, even if it was only a probable, and we all returned safely. That's worth a drink.'

Howarth nodded towards a group of 544 Squadron pilots sitting on the far side of the room. 'They are down. They lost some today. It's not appropriate, I think, for us to be loud and celebratory right now.'

'Of course, you are right. That was unfeeling of me. Sorry, chaps,' said Roger humbly.

'The big wing experiment seemed to work all right, at least initially,' John put in, breaking the awkward silence. 'The rendezvous went well and was on time. Having a large group of aircraft gave us the ability to attack both the bombers and defend against the fighters. We had thirty-six Spitfires. I would've felt threatened if I was a Jerry looking at that many Spitfires coming towards me.'

'I agree,' said Richard, who had just joined them. 'But, having said that, I do query the effectiveness of in-air command and control. The wing was being led by someone who knew very little about the character and capabilities of two thirds of the force he was leading.'

'Yes,' Greg added, 'and it was Squadron Leader Sidey who made the call to intercept the fighters, not the formation leader. To me, that highlights a potential problem with big wings. What would have happened if Sidey hadn't exercised his initiative? I'm sure action would have been ordered at some point, but not as quickly. As well as not being so timely, it couldn't ever have been based on capability knowledge. The leader of a big wing doesn't know who his pilots are, let alone how well they fly and what experience they have.'

'I suppose the more we operate together as one large wing, the more familiar we will become with one another,' Charlie ventured. 'Every leader needs time get to know his pilots, so this is just a normal process, isn't it?'

The others were all silent for a moment as they thought about Charlie's proposition.

'You could be right there, Charles,' said Richard, who never used Charlie's nickname. 'Moving on, any lessons for us from today, and our first serious encounter with the self-proclaimed mighty Luftwaffe?'

'I think using pairs for attack was good,' John volunteered. 'I was pleased Sidey called it, because it means we can be nimble in our attack. It allows flexibility in positioning a lot of aircraft in different parts of the sky as we close with the enemy. Also, flying tail protection for the lead aircraft of a pair works well. It allows the leader to focus on getting the enemy into his sights, knowing his wingman has his back.'

'Very eloquent, John,' said Richard with a laugh. 'That sums it up nicely.'

'And very true,' Greg chimed in. 'I'm conscious that pairing is the result of John pushing, and taking some criticism as a result, but it clearly works well. I say that as a beneficiary of the system today. John's call as my wingman saved me.'

'I see we have another dawn take-off tomorrow. That calls for another early night. Dinner and bed for me,' said Richard.

The others nodded and followed suit.

When they woke the next morning, the pilots of 415 Squadron guessed they would not be flying. Mist and drizzle lay across Hornchurch, so low it obscured the tops of nearby trees. The wind was getting up too, but instead of clearing the conditions, as it often did, it was just causing thick sheets of rain to drift over the airfield.

Some of the pilots wondered why a mess orderly was knocking on their doors to wake them so early, since no flying operations were possible due to the conditions. They were all still being summoned to the briefing room.

Squadron Leader Sidey was waiting to address them. 'Gentlemen, no ops this morning. You can see why — effectively no visibility and a low ceiling. And the met people say it is bad over the Channel too. That means the Luftwaffe will be grounded as well, so that's a relief. At this stage met is predicting a clearance here by midday. They are not so sure about the Dunkirk area, but they are forecasting some improvement there. We are going to mount an offensive patrol as soon as the weather improves sufficiently, so consider yourself on weather standby this morning.'

No-one liked weather standby. It required the pilots to be in their flying kit, parachute handy, ready to be airborne within ten minutes of a call — a call that would be made as soon as the met officers saw an improvement in the weather. It required them to sit in the dispersal hut, small and cramped as it was, waiting. It was boring and it stretched the nerves. They would much rather have been airborne and in action than sitting around, wondering when the call would come and what the action would involve. The only saving grace was that as they sat around grappling with their own thoughts, the occasional wag would tell a story. Sometimes about flying, but more often about some wonderful woman he had met, or would like to meet. It helped pass the time and keep the minds of the young men off the serious business of war.

A few hours later, the telephone in the dispersal hut rang. Charlie was closest to it, so he picked it up. He listened to what was being said, with everyone in the hut watching him.

'We're on,' he announced at last. 'Airborne soonest, rendezvous over Margate, height to be advised.'

There was a clatter of chairs and the thud of feet hitting the timber floor as the members of the squadron got up, grabbed their parachute bags, and made their way to the door. Outside, the mist and drizzle were not as bad as earlier. Some light rain was falling from what looked to be an eight-hundred-foot cloud base. The wind had reduced too, to about fifteen miles per hour, John thought.

Once he was in his Spitfire and climbing away from the airfield, John heard Squadron Leader Sidey call their instructions.

'We are to position ourselves over Margate at twelve thousand feet. Once there, we will join up with three other squadrons and proceed to Dunkirk as one wing of forty-eight aircraft. Flight commanders, maintain squadron Vic formations on my lead.'

As the squadron approached the rendezvous area, in-flight visibility began to deteriorate. As well as the cloud below them, some of which had billowed up through the squadron's current altitude in places, heavy rain was starting to fall from a layer of dark cloud above them.

Sidey radioed sector control. 'Control, this is Eely red one,' he called, using the radio code allocated to 415 Squadron for this operation.

'Eely red one, Control, go ahead.'

'The cloud conditions in the rendezvous area are affecting our ability to locate the other squadrons. Can you confirm their position and height, and assist with vectors towards them?'

'Eely red one. Your friendlies are at your eleven o'clock, angels ten, climbing twenty-two. Their heading is currently passing through three one zero. They are in a left-hand climbing turn. Twenty-four of them.'

That meant that two squadrons had already joined up as part of today's big wing, but they were still not visible to 415 Squadron, something not helped by the conditions. John understood the difficulty in finding the other squadrons with which they were to form a big wing, as he looked at what was effectively a valley formed by towering formations of cloud on each side of them

After a few more minutes, John heard Sidey call on his radio.

'Control, Eely red one, we are unable to locate rendezvous squadrons, there is too much cloud,' said Sidey. 'Proceeding independently to the target area, climbing angels twenty-two.'

'Roger, Eely red one,' was all the response he got.

'Eely squadron, you will have copied that,' Sidey called over the radio. 'I will lead, climbing angels twenty-two this time.' He swung his aircraft right, heading for twenty-two thousand feet. Behind him, the other Spitfires of 415 Squadron followed.

They soon reached their target altitude and were flying in clear air above the cloud tops. There was an occasional break in the cloud cover below them that allowed some glimpses of the ground. John was able to see they were over the port area at Dunkirk. It was showing the effects of constant bombardment.

'Bandits, twenty plus, two o'clock high, estimate angels twenty-five.'

The call from Sidey brought John's attention back to the sky. He looked up and to the right, and there they were — Me 109s. He could not see any bombers in the area that they may have been escorting.

'Attack independently, in your pairs,' ordered Sidey.

Dutifully, the twelve Spitfires he was leading formed into six pairs and turned towards the German fighters.

The Me 109s responded as the Spitfires climbed towards them. Half of the Luftwaffe aircraft moved to the left and half moved to the right, so they were in two groups separated by what John reckoned was about one thousand yards. *Planning an attack from two quarters*, John thought as the Germans dived towards his squadron.

Sidey had noted the movement of the Me 109s as well. 'Red and yellow sections, go left to intercept. Blue and green, right to intercept those approaching from that quarter,' he said.

John turned right, following his lead aircraft flown by Greg, blue one today. They were now climbing directly towards the oncoming Luftwaffe fighters. As they closed in, Greg was head-to-head with an Me 109. They started shooting at each other, with the Spitfire's tracer painting an arc over the top of the German aircraft. Bits flew off the left wing of the Messerschmitt as Greg managed to lower his line of fire and score a hit. The German pilot immediately pulled into a steep left turn, away from Greg's approaching Spitfire. Greg banked right to pursue his quarry.

John swivelled his head back and forth as he followed Greg. He was searching for any aircraft that might be trying to get behind them to attack.

Greg fired and hit the Messerschmitt again. This time, his guns raked its fuselage, from near the cockpit to the tail area. Then there was an explosion. A tracer round had penetrated a fuel tank. The 109 rolled onto its back and plunged vertically into the cloud below, leaving a trail of oily smoke to mark its path.

That's a kill, John thought. *Good work, Greg.*

As he continued to search for other enemy aircraft above and behind them, John saw movement as he looked towards the sun. He was about to call a warning when his Spitfire shuddered with the impact of multiple rounds hitting his aircraft. They struck just behind where John was sitting in his cockpit.

'Jesus!' John exclaimed. He had been warned about the Hun in the sun, and now it was coming for him.

Instinctively, he hauled back on the control stick to come out of the dive he had been in and began climbing steeply. At the same time, he rolled his aircraft to the right, stopping the roll when he had gone through 120 degrees. Now he was almost inverted. He pulled harder on the control stick, causing his Spitfire to angle off into a dive. While he was doing so, he called a warning on the radio. 'Blue one, a one-o-nine behind us.'

John was not hit again, and his escape manoeuvre appeared to have been successful. He couldn't see the Me 109 anymore. Looking down, he saw a Spitfire in a dive, being pursued by a 109. *Bet that's the bastard who shot at me,* John thought. *Time to even the score.* He set off in pursuit. As he got closer, he saw it was Greg being chased. He called him.

'Closing in on your bandit from behind, blue one. I want him to turn left, so on the count of three make a hard turn left. He will follow you. One, two, three, go.'

Greg banked steeply to the left as John called go. The German followed, and flew into the hailstorm of fire John had just loosed off in anticipation of the Messerschmitt's turn. The Me 109 began smoking from its engine and entered a steep dive, rotating as it went, clearly no longer being controlled by its pilot.

John saw the Germans were now breaking off and vacating the area, heading east. *Time we went back to base too,* John thought, and was pleased to hear Sidey confirm that thought with a call to set a heading for Hornchurch.

After they had landed, Greg came up to John, smiling widely.

'You are making a habit of this. Thank you for getting that bloody Jerry off me!' Greg said.

'Well, I'm just sorry I didn't spot him sooner. He was against the sun, and I only saw him moments before he shot at me.'

'You got a probable there, John. He paid the ultimate price of tangling with four-one-five squadron,' Greg said, with just a little too much bravado, John thought. But he understood. Greg had come close to being shot down, and was probably just showing how happy he was to be back. He might have done the same, if their roles had been reversed, John acknowledged to himself.

CHAPTER SEVENTEEN

After leaving Greg, John went back to his room to freshen up. Then he made his way to the mess lounge. Sidey had indicated no further operation involving 415 Squadron was planned that afternoon. None of John's friends were there, so he opted to sit quietly, and read the newspaper.

Nearby, Squadron Leaders Bayliss, Smallbone and Sidey were sitting at a table, talking between themselves. They didn't seem to notice that John had come in. Taking advantage of the situation, John decided to subtly eavesdrop.

'So, the CO has been medically cleared to fly again,' said Smallbone with a sigh. 'And now he wants to join us in the air, even though he has no experience of flying in war operations.'

'How do we accommodate him?' asked Sidey, sounding rather desperate.

'This is what I suggest we do, chaps,' said Bayliss. 'We operate in three formations of four aircraft each.'

'Like the *Schwarm*?' asked Smallbone.

John knew he was referring to the flight formation the Luftwaffe had been known to use, which they had developed while supporting Franco's Nationalists in the Spanish Civil War.

'Yes, exactly, Tony,' said Bayliss. 'I think it's an efficient patrol formation. And, if we use it now, I can put three aircraft with the boss, seeing as he's insisting on being involved. More eyes, more cover.'

'Are you going to put our more experienced pilots with the wing commander?' asked Sidey.

'Yes, I think there would be value in that, Dave. I'll lead, the CO will be number two, and Flying Officers Somerville and Noble will be numbers three and four.'

The other two squadron leaders murmured their agreement.

'Good, that's settled then,' Bayliss continued. 'We will use the *schwarm* formation. The CO has come down from Catterick to get his re-currency flying with me underway. I will monitor that and talk him through some of the battle tactics we have been using and the emerging engagement trends we have seen. Everyone happy?'

'Not really,' Sidey replied, 'but it is what it is. We will just have to do what we can to assist the boss through this.'

'He will have to learn bloody quickly,' said Smallbone.

Just as the squadron leaders were leaving the mess bar, some of John's fellow pilots walked in. John waved and they came to join him.

'I hear we are up early again tomorrow,' said Greg, taking a seat.

'Indeed we are, old chap,' replied Richard. 'O-four hundred take-off.'

'And it's a big wing again, but no in-flight rendezvous is required,' said Derek. 'All the squadrons from here are departing together.'

'Just as well. Those airborne assemblies are bloody hopeless in poor weather. If we can't see much, looking for the squadrons we are meant to link up with is damn near impossible,' said Greg.

John decided to divulge the news he had just overheard. 'Apparently, we are going to fly in fours, and Wing Commander Bland has been medically re-cleared for flying. He will be joining us on ops as soon as he has had a quick recurrency session with Bayliss. That could be happening later today, so he could be operational tomorrow.'

The news was greeted with a mixture of gasps and uneasy murmurs.

'Well, I hope he's a quick learner,' said Richard. 'Quite apart from lacking currency after an extended grounding, this will be his first exposure to serious air warfare manoeuvring. A literal baptism of fire for him.'

'Alastair Bayliss has put together a special team for this. It's the main reason we are going to fly in fours. He is going to lead the section in which Bland will fly. The CO will be number two, Greg will be number three, and I'll be number four. Babysitting is too harsh a term, but I think we'll be expected to look out for him as he goes into his first encounter with Jerry,' said John.

'Quite a responsibility,' Richard observed.

'Got to look after the boss,' said Greg with a tight smile.

'I also heard Tony Smallbone talking about Luftwaffe tactics at Dunkirk. Someone at Fighter Command had told him that when the weather is too bad to allow the bombers to see their target on the ground, Jerry is running an alternative plan,' John said.

'Oh, what's that?' Greg asked.

'Command thinks Jerry is sending in fighters when conditions are no good for their bombers. They think the Luftwaffe commanders are doing that to reinforce the air superiority they consider they have over Dunkirk, and to ensure their fighters get a chance to engage with ours every day. No let up for us just because Luftwaffe bombing operations are suspended due to the weather, is what Bentley Priory thinks the Luftwaffe has in mind. Constant pressure on us because they know we are outnumbered, so attrition is their aim.'

'Damn them. That just makes me more determined,' Greg replied, grimacing.

Early the next morning, cruising at eighteen thousand feet, the aircraft of 415 Squadron were positioned at the rear of the big wing formation. Some miles behind the big wing, and five thousand feet above, there were more Spitfires. A squadron from Biggin Hill had been separately positioned to intercept the fighter escort that any German bombers were expected to have as company.

The conditions in the Dunkirk area were poor. There was a lot of cloud, and rain showers had reduced visibility. There was no sign of any Luftwaffe aircraft. *The Germans must have decided it isn't a good morning for an air-raid*, John decided.

After patrolling for thirty minutes, with no Luftwaffe activity seen, not even the fighters that John had heard Tony Smallbone talking about, the big wing turned back across the Channel, to England.

After they had landed, Squadron Leader Sidey talked to the 415 Squadron pilots in the mess sitting room.

'The weather kept all Jerry aircraft away this morning, but the met office says the weather over Dunkirk will improve, so we will run another patrol later. Time to be confirmed, but it's looking like we are to be airborne at thirteen hundred hours. This morning was a good rehearsal for our new four-aircraft formation, which we are calling finger-four. I was happy that it freed up more eyes to look out, and, if we engage, I think it will assist us in both attack and defence. Also, when we get into airspace where we are likely to meet the enemy, open your positions to, say, fifty yards between aircraft.'

John nodded to himself. He knew the extra space would make it easier for them to scan the sky for hostile aircraft. It would also reduce the risk of any collision between formation members when it all got a bit frantic.

'The thinking at Command is that whenever the weather is suitable the Germans are likely to intensify their attacks on the troops at Dunkirk,' Sidey continued. 'Their intelligence assessment is that the Germans will use Dorniers and Heinkels to carpet bomb the town and dock area, with Stuka dive-bombers attacking the ships and boats waiting to pick up those evacuating. Ten thousand is the best height for positioning to attack the Stukas. Higher for the Dorniers and Heinkels. Depending on cloud height and position, they will most likely bomb from the high teens. Above them, of course, there will be their fighter protection.'

At that point, Wing Commander Bland interrupted. 'As you all know, I have been out of the air for some time, and I'm pleased to be back. Observing this morning's operation, from take-off to return, I noted two things I want to comment on. First, it seemed to me that you all had a very clear idea of the patrol plan, from its intent to its execution. I know nothing happened today, but I was impressed by your professionalism and preparation. So good work there. Second, I got the impression that some of you felt we should be more aggressive on patrol — that we should be moving further inland, past the German front line, looking for ground targets if no hostile aircraft are seen. I want to be clear about this: Command doesn't want us down at low level looking for ground targets. Even if no enemy aircraft are seen, we are not to go looking for alternative targets of opportunity. They want us to stay at altitude, at all times.'

John, despite recalling Sidey's comment from some months ago: *Do not get involved in an open disagreement with a senior officer at a briefing*, could not help putting forward a question. 'If there are no enemy aircraft at altitude, as was the case this morning, wouldn't it help the troops trapped in the town and on the beaches if we were to go down and have a crack at some enemy ground targets?' he asked.

'Command's view, Flying Officer Noble, is based on its risk versus reward assessment,' said Bland, his tone abrupt. 'There is an increased risk to our aircraft when low, but there are only targets of lesser value available to attack down there. Consequently, there are to be no low-level operations over the Dunkirk area. Any other questions?'

John spoke up again. 'What about a situation where pursuit of an engaged enemy aircraft diving to escape is required? Can we follow it down?'

'Of course, Flying Officer, but as soon as that engagement is over, you must climb back to altitude to re-join your section. That is the operational requirement.'

John was not impressed by the inflexibility of what was being suggested. Climbing back up may or may not be the better course of action. It would always depend on the circumstances. 'When we climb back up, it might be difficult to re-establish contact with elements of the squadron, sir,' he said. 'Everyone breaks off, normally in pairs and sometimes even in threes or fours, when an attack is made. It can be a confusing melee of aircraft. Flight as a squadron is gone at that point.'

'You must get back up there to try, Flying Officer, and look to reform with other elements of the squadron. That's the requirement placed on you. No scudding around at low altitude on your own.'

'Yes, sir,' said John, grudgingly acknowledging what Bland had said.

Squadron Leader Sidey resumed control of the briefing. 'One last thing before we finish. We have been breaking into pairs when attacking, with number two acting as wingman, a rearguard. For the present, we are going to stay with spaced fours as we attack.'

John decided the reason for that approach was that Sidey thought fours would better protect their inexperienced commanding officer. *Bland's presence already making its mark,* he thought.

'All right. That's it, thank you, gentlemen. Plan to be airborne at thirteen hundred, unless you hear anything to the contrary,' said Sidey.

The pilots pushed back their chairs, stood, and left, saying very little.

The big wing was flying towards the French coast. This afternoon they were briefed to complete a sweep for any enemy aircraft that may be bound for the Dunkirk area from the southeast. At twenty thousand feet, apart from the occasional area of cumulus build-ups, the day was clear over France. There did not appear to be any other aircraft in the sky at present.

As they flew by, south of Dunkirk, they could see a lot of small boats, busy ferrying people between the beach and larger vessels lying further offshore. The dock area had been destroyed, but there was some activity on the mole adjacent to the harbour entrance. *At least a small part of the port area still has some use,* John thought, as he looked. He saw a destroyer lying on its side, half submerged, at the harbour entrance. It appeared that its bow had been blown off. *Bomber or naval mine?*

John wondered. There was a line of trucks on the beach close to the mole, parked nose to tail. The trucks extended out into the sea, about a hundred yards, he guessed. The troops on the ground appeared to be trying to create some sort of artificial wharf to assist the smaller boats coming in.

A radio call from the leader of the big wing interrupted John's thoughts.

'Thirty plus bombers. Nine o'clock, low, estimate angels sixteen. Eely squadron,' he said, using the code allocated to 415 Squadron, 'stay here and deal with any fighter cover. Everyone else, follow me down.'

The other three squadrons making up the big wing swung left and dived to attack the oncoming bombers. The Spitfires of 415 Squadron continued at twenty thousand feet, scanning above the approaching bombers, looking for their fighter escort. Squadron Leader Bayliss saw them first.

'Me 109's, twenty plus, eleven o'clock, high,' he radioed. 'Maintain fours and increase spacing.'

Looking down, John could see the remainder of the big wing was engaging the bombers, which had broken their formation. Some of the enemy aircraft appeared to be trying to reach adjacent cloud cover, and some were diving to escape, while others were simply flying in erratic patterns to make shooting at them more difficult. The Spitfires attacking the bombers below broke formation as they selected and followed individual targets. John turned his attention to the approaching Messerschmitt fighters. They were head-on with 415 Squadron's Spitfires, at a range of three miles and closing rapidly. When the Germans were down to what John thought was about two thousand yards, their formation suddenly split into two. Half of them banked left, and the others banked right. This seems to be becoming a standard Luftwaffe tactic, he thought.

As he continued to watch, the Me 109s on each side rolled back towards the Spitfires. Now the enemy aircraft were approaching 415 Squadron at an angle of forty degrees, from both the left and right, a bit like a pincer-movement.

'Eely squadron, this is red leader,' Bayliss radioed. 'Red section going left to intercept. Yellow section, go right for your attack. Blue section, take targets of opportunity. Go.'

The four aircraft of red section had opened their spacing as required and were now flying about fifty yards apart. John, as red four, saw that Bayliss had one of the leading Me 109s in his sights. The squadron leader fired a quick burst, and the German rolled onto his back and dived away. Bayliss pursued him, clearly trying to get into a position where he could take another shot at the fleeing target. Behind Bayliss, as red two, Wing Commander Bland followed, steadfastly keeping his position. Greg, as red three, came after him, with John bringing up the rear.

As they descended, Greg was attacked by an Me 109 that had turned to follow the diving section of Spitfires. As tracer flew past his cockpit, he banked steeply to the right. The Me 109 followed him into the turn. John, coming up behind Greg, was able to manoeuvre his aircraft into a position where he could take a shot. He fired a burst and saw puffs on the left wing of the Me 109 as it was hit. The German went into a steep dive. For a moment John thought he had shot him down, but then he realised the damaged aircraft was heading towards some adjacent cloud, seeking to escape John's attack. He followed, firing another quick burst. He saw pieces fly off the aircraft's tail just as it entered the cloud. Pursuit was a waste of time.

Seeing him through the cloud was impossible. John turned back in the direction Greg had been heading.

He could not see Greg's aircraft, or any of red section. In fact, he could not see an aircraft anywhere, German or British. It was one of the strange things John had experienced before. One moment the air would be full of aircraft diving, rolling, climbing, and turning as they fought their individual dogfights. Next moment, everyone would disappear.

John continued flying a large orbit around the area, looking for other aircraft. After a few minutes, he saw two Spitfires far beneath the height at which he was flying. They were very low above the sea, so low he could see their shadows flitting across the surface of the water. John peeled over into a dive to follow them. They appeared to be going home, back across the Channel. With the additional speed he could build in his dive from altitude, John soon caught up. Now he was closer, he could see one of the Spitfires was trailing smoke from the area around its engine. The other Spitfire was flying protective cover behind it, slightly higher and weaving from side to side to look out for enemy aircraft. The weaving also ensured it did not overtake the slower damaged aircraft.

As he closed in on the two Spitfires, John could see the aircraft suffering the damage was the one being flown by Bayliss. The weaving escort was Bland.

John thumbed his radio button. 'Red one, this is red four.'

There was no reply from Bayliss to John's call.

'Red four, this is red two,' Bland called. 'Red one has been badly damaged and Squadron Leader Bayliss appears injured. He's not saying anything.'

'Roger,' John responded.

'We haven't seen any enemy aircraft in the last few minutes,' Bland continued. 'Another twenty minutes and we will be landing, but I suspect red one may have suffered incapacitating injuries.'

'I will move up alongside to see what I can,' John replied, gently increasing power and easing alongside Bayliss's aircraft.

He could see the squadron leader's head was down, and it lolled about when the aircraft encountered light turbulence from time to time. John tried to call him again.

'Red one, this is red four. Do you read me?'

No response. John peered in, moving as close as he dared. Was it an injury or a radio problem that was preventing Bayliss's response? John could see the squadron leader's fuselage was riddled with bullet holes, and there were also some large holes, there and in his left wing. *Cannon*, he thought. As he watched, John thought he saw Bayliss's head move slightly.

Approaching the English coastline, descending slowly as they flew westwards, John decided Bayliss must have some level of consciousness. His aircraft was not so perfectly balanced that it would fly as it was without any control inputs. He must be using his blind-flying panel to keep the aircraft the right way up, since he did not appear to be able to lift his head and look out of his cockpit, John concluded.

'Red one, if you hear this, lower your port wing slightly.'

After what seemed too long a time, John eventually saw the left wing of Bayliss's aircraft dip very slightly, and then resume its previous level. It looked too precise to be a turbulence-induced wobble. *Bayliss can hear and respond*, John thought, very pleased. *But how's he going to land if he has injuries preventing him from lifting his head up and looking out?*

John thought about his question for a moment. He would have to escort Alastair all the way down, talking him through what he could not readily see for himself because of his apparent inability to raise his head.

'Red two, red four. Red one is responding but appears to have some incapacitation. I'm going to escort him in and act as his landing guide,' John called to Bland, who was still providing cover above and behind.

'Roger, red four, if you think that's possible, good luck to you both.'

'It's all we can do,' John responded.

'Red four, red two is proceeding to Manston — it's closest. That's where we should go. I'll alert them to the situation. See you on the ground. We're now well clear of any risk from hostiles. All the best.' With that, the CO opened his throttle and flew on, leaving John to accompany Bayliss.

Fifteen minutes later, as the two Spitfires flown by Bayliss and John turned on to a long final approach to land at Manston airfield, John called on his radio.

'Manston, this is Eely squadron Spitfire, red four, accompanying Spitfire red one. The pilot of red one has been injured and has no ability to look out from his cockpit. I am going to pair with him and guide him down to a landing.'

'Roger, red four, we have just been briefed by your CO, who landed a few minutes ago. Proceed as required. Wind is calm.'

John flew as close to Bayliss's port wing as he dared. The squadron leader's head was still down.

'Red one, if you can still hear me, dip your port wing again.'

The wing dipped slightly in response.

'You probably heard my plan when I talked to Manston, but to be clear, I will sit off your wing, guide you in, and call out when you need to make inputs to be able to land. Just do what

I say. We can get you down.' John paused and glanced down at the landscape rushing by beneath them. 'All right, here we go. We are two miles out.'

Every few moments, he gave Bayliss a new instruction:

'Reduce your power.'

'Flaps, now.'

'Lower your undercarriage.'

John was very happy to see the squadron leader responding.

'Good. I can confirm your flaps and gear. We are one mile out.' After a moment, John went on, 'You are drifting right of our line of approach. Very small turn left. Start it, no more than a rate one, and I will tell you when to stop.' After five seconds of a slight turn left, John was satisfied with the track of Bayliss's approach. 'Level your wings. Stop your turn, now. Speed back to one hundred.'

John was alternating between looking ahead towards the landing area at Manston, and watching how Alastair's aircraft was replicating his approach. He could see a fire engine waiting near the threshold, and next to it, the station ambulance. John was briefly side-slipping his aircraft from time to time, to enable him to see more clearly where they were going to land. His usual curved approach was not going to work while he was shepherding Bayliss in like this.

'I will call heights so you can flare your aircraft, red one, and I will also call for you to chop the throttle when you are close to touchdown.'

John knew Bayliss's landing would be rough, but he hoped it would not be so bad as to hurt him or badly damage his aircraft.

'Start bringing your speed back some more. You just crossed the airfield boundary hedge. The landing area is right in front of you. Plenty of room. Forty feet ... thirty feet ... twenty feet, start a gentle flare ... ten feet ... chop power, hold the stick back.'

Bayliss's Spitfire landed heavily and bounced, but then settled onto the grass surface. John then touched down, slightly behind and forty yards out to the left.

'Bit of left rudder, more — that's it. Slight right rudder now,' John called as he watched Bayliss's aircraft in front of him and called instructions to try to ensure it stayed reasonably straight as it slowed up.

Bayliss's aircraft was swerving left and right. Near the end of its landing roll, its tail swung widely to the right and kept going right around in a ground loop. The pressure on the right undercarriage leg was too much, as the Spitfire went sideways across the surface. The leg collapsed, and the right wing dug into the grass as it fell, spinning the aircraft around. Finally, the Spitfire came to a stop, on its belly and facing the direction from which it had just approached and landed.

Thank goodness it didn't cartwheel, John thought. He brought his own Spitfire to a halt, shut it down, and then got out and ran over to where Bayliss's aircraft had come to rest.

As he ran towards the damaged Spitfire, he knew the crash-landing was not likely to have caused any additional injury. It had not been that bad. More important would be what had happened to Bayliss during his encounter with the enemy.

CHAPTER EIGHTEEN

John jumped up onto the wing of the damaged Spitfire. He saw Bayliss was slumped forward in his seat, unconscious. Wisps of smoke were coming from the engine area.

After turning the release latch on the cockpit hood, John tried to slide the canopy open. It would not move. The smoke was now starting to billow from the nose of the wounded aircraft, thick and black. Fire was clearly taking hold. He bashed the cockpit frame with the side of his closed fist, hoping that would free up whatever was causing the jam.

He pulled at the canopy again, but it remained firmly shut. Normally it would have been opened for landing by the pilot, but that precaution had not been available today, given Bayliss's state. John felt panicked. Flames were now mixed with the smoke. He needed to get Bayliss out quickly. One of the station's rescue firemen appeared at his side. In one hand he held a small axe, in the other a crowbar. He passed the axe to John.

'I will try to lever it open with this,' said the fireman, inserting the crowbar between the top of the cockpit windscreen frame and the sliding canopy. 'If this doesn't work, smash it with the axe,' he went on, as he started to lever away.

There was a bang, and the canopy suddenly freed itself and slid back a few inches. They both grasped the front of the partly opened canopy and pulled hard. The canopy moved back. Now they could pull Bayliss out. Reaching into the cockpit area, the fireman used a cutting implement to slice through Bayliss's harness. That was quicker than fiddling with the straps and buckles and risking a delay in getting him out.

The flames were now moving back along the nose area towards the cockpit. Bayliss needed to be out of the aircraft in seconds, otherwise he was going to be caught by the fire. John was also conscious of the risk of fuel igniting and the catastrophic explosion that would follow.

Grasping Bayliss under his armpits, John and the fire service rescuer hauled him up, only to find that his left foot seemed to be jammed under a rudder pedal. John reached down into the cockpit to see if he could free Bayliss's leg. Gripping him behind his knee, John wrenched hard. In his semiconscious state, Bayliss moaned in pain, but his foot came loose. Now they could pull him out of the cockpit.

Bayliss was soon on a stretcher being carried to the waiting ambulance. Shrapnel from an exploding shell had left him with deep gaping wounds to his upper back and neck. No wonder he had been unable to lift his head and look out, John thought, wondering if Alastair would survive his injuries.

The fire personnel were busy trying to extinguish the flames now covering much of the crashed aircraft. It was a fierce blaze. Realising they could not control it, the firefighters backed away. A wise decision. A few minutes later, the flames reached the fuel tank. The high-octane aviation fuel exploded, and in seconds the damaged Spitfire was a fireball.

When they were all back at Hornchurch and Bayliss was being examined at the hospital, Wing Commander Bland called John into his office.

'You did very well, talking Squadron Leader Bayliss down in that situation,' he said. 'Also, your actions to get him out after he crash-landed were highly commendable. You saved his life, and that is appreciated by us all. Thank you.'

'I did what had to be done,' John replied modestly.

'Very well. I will be commending you in reports. You'd better get back to the mess now. I have told the mess sergeant you don't pay for a drink tonight. My way of saying thank you. That is all.'

What an enigma that man is, John thought as he walked back to his quarters. Bland had flown protective cover for Bayliss on the way back, a sensible manoeuvre, and now he was offering John compliments. Maybe he has turned a corner.

'A few of us are going into town for a late lunch. Want to come?' Greg asked John the following day.

The weather had again prevented any operations that morning, and because it seemed to be getting worse, operations had now been cancelled for the day. Low cloud and poor visibility around Dunkirk meant no-one could fly in that area either, including the Luftwaffe. Conditions were so bad that no standby aircraft were required for the afternoon. It was a welcome respite.

'Yes, lunch in town would make a pleasant change from hanging around the airfield,' said John.

'Good. There will be six of us: you, me, Richard, Roger, Craig, and Charlie. The local boys have lent us their squadron car. It's not big, but we can squeeze in. We'll meet outside the mess at two o'clock. Be there or miss your ride.' With that, Greg moved off down the corridor.

'Has anyone heard how Bayliss is?' Richard asked as they sat down for lunch in the Sutton Arms. Even though there was a war on, the hotel was still able to offer some enticing-looking food.

'Yes,' said Charlie. 'I was talking to the adjutant, and he told me that his injuries are not considered life-threatening, but he won't fly again. He may not even walk again because of damage to his spinal cord from shrapnel.'

'Damn,' said Richard, succinctly summing up how they all felt on hearing that Bayliss's flying days were over. No wonder he had been unable to lift his head and look out of his cockpit.

'I suppose we should be grateful he is alive,' Roger said. 'He was lucky not to be killed by the Me 109 that attacked him, and if there hadn't been someone to guide him down to a relatively safe crash-landing, well…' He trailed off.

'It'll be interesting to see who will be appointed to cover Bayliss's role, where he alternated war ops leadership with Squadron Leader Sidey,' John said.

'I think Tony Smallbone will take it on,' Greg replied.

'He would be a possibility,' Richard said, 'but he can't commit to it. He is likely going to be posted to another squadron to help with the high number of inexperienced pilots there, although that is not definite yet. We shall have to wait and see who takes over. It's in the hands of the CO.'

'Christ, there's no risk Bland himself would try to assume the role, is there?' Roger asked. 'He wouldn't be up to it in terms of war ops exposure, nor leadership capability. Oh, am I able to say that?'

'Of course. It's what we're all thinking anyway,' Richard answered. 'Now, I'm starving. Let's eat.'

Late that afternoon, after returning to RAF Hornchurch following an enjoyable lunch, the pilots received word of a briefing to be held at seventeen-thirty hours. It was just for the pilots of 415 Squadron, not the other Hornchurch-based squadrons.

Wing Commander Bland and Flight Lieutenant Gardiner were waiting to speak to them when they arrived as ordered.

'Welcome,' Bland said, beginning proceedings. 'I want to talk about how we will operate in the absence of Squadron Leader Bayliss. Before I do that, however, I have a brief report on the squadron leader's situation. I am very pleased to be able to tell you that his injuries are not life-threatening. But I am advised it is unlikely he will ever fly again.'

He paused as the assembled pilots, particularly those who had not heard anything about Bayliss's state earlier, exclaimed and sighed.

'I will keep you advised of developments, but that is how things are seen at present by the doctors. What this means is that we need a replacement to lead the squadron on war operations, something that he and Squadron Leader Sidey have been doing to date. I have thought a good deal about this, and after discussing it with the adjutant, I have decided what we will do.' After a pause, he said, 'Squadron Leader Smallbone may not be available to replace Squadron Leader Bayliss, so I will take over the squadron's war operations leadership, working with Squadron Leader Sidey.'

Stunned, John glanced at Gardiner and saw the look of unease on his face. Like the pilots, he clearly did not think Bland was the man to lead them in the air as they battled with the Luftwaffe.

John was surprised when Richard stood up and questioned the decision.

'Sir, with respect, I wonder if there would be some advantage in me being the alternate lead with Squadron Leader Sidey in war operations, in place of Squadron Leader Bayliss? I have the necessary experience in those ops as well as in the aircraft. Unlike some of our recent squadron joiners flying into battle, I don't have to learn on the job.'

John immediately saw what Richard was doing. *Clever tactics*, he thought. The way Richard phrased his question would discreetly remind Bland that the operational leader of the squadron should have experience in air warfare. It also signalled the potential consequences of anyone going into battle with a knowledge deficit. Referring to having to "learn on the job" highlighted the personal risk faced by an inexperienced pilot. But more importantly, it also signalled that such a person should never be charged with leading the squadron's war operations. To do so would simply extend that inexperienced pilot's personal risk to the whole squadron.

'I think Flying Officer Cowles has a point, sir,' Gardiner put in, so quickly that John decided he was seizing the opportunity to push for an alternative solution to the loss of Bayliss, something confirmed in John's mind as the adjutant went on to make the case for Cowles. 'He is experienced in the air, having participated in multiple offensive patrols. Also, war ops leadership should continue to be alternated, as it is at present. It can be too much for one with multiple sorties every day. I would recommend you consider taking him up on his offer, with Squadron Leader Sidey and Flying Officer Cowles alternating as required, and you maintaining a strategic oversight role as the commanding officer.'

After a moment's consideration, Bland agreed. 'Good idea, thank you, Adjutant. Flying Officer Cowles, you take it on as suggested. I will maintain oversight.'

Collective sighs of relief from the 415 Squadron pilots were suppressed to avoid any embarrassment.

Gardiner then brought the briefing to a close, after advising everyone that, yet again, there was to be a pre-dawn wake-up call, with take-off scheduled for o-four-thirty hours. 'More detail in the morning, but you will be forming a big wing with some non-Hornchurch squadrons, assembling over Dover,' he concluded.

The weather had been fine over the southeast of England, but as the big wing approached the French coast, they could see flight conditions around Dunkirk were poor. The pilots were becoming used to the bad weather that seemed to continuously hang around this part of France. The only benefit was that it also made it difficult for the Luftwaffe to accurately bomb those trying to escape back to England.

Some sea mist had rolled in over the beaches and it was foggy for what appeared to be at least five miles inland. The usual smoke rising from the battle areas on the ground had mixed with the fog, making it very dense. After patrolling the area for thirty minutes, with no sign of any enemy aircraft, the leader of the wing ordered a return to base.

Once back at Hornchurch, all of 415 Squadron's Spitfires were refuelled. The pilots grabbed a quick sandwich and a cup of tea, which were brought out to their dispersal area by some of the station's catering staff.

'Thanks, just what I needed,' John said to the woman who had just poured him a cup of tea, to go with the second egg sandwich he was devouring. 'I was damn hungry,' he confirmed to her with a grin.

They had barely finished their food when there was the urgent ringing of an old handbell.

'Scramble!' was the call.

Bugger, John thought as he hurriedly wolfed down the remains of his sandwich, gulped a last mouthful of his tea, and ran to his waiting aircraft.

Engines were being started by ground crews where their pilots had not yet arrived, which enabled the aircraft to get underway more quickly. Within seven minutes of the bell sounding, all the Spitfires of 415 Squadron were airborne and climbing east towards France. Their sector controller wanted them over Dunkirk as soon as possible. There was no big wing link-up this time. The call to fly had come too unexpectedly.

As they approached the French coast, John could see that the weather had improved, and there were puffs of black smoke at around what he estimated to be ten thousand feet. The British forces were putting up anti-aircraft fire, so he realised Jerry must be there somewhere, but he could not see any enemy aircraft. Then he spotted them. Stuka dive-bombers, about thirty, he estimated. At the same time, Richard came on to the radio.

'This is red one. Stukas, twenty plus, eleven o'clock, low. There will be fighter cover somewhere, but we will have a crack at stopping the Stukas bombing the boys on the beach, and deal with the fighters when they arrive. Current priority is the Stukas. Tally-ho, chaps, in we go.'

As they closed, John saw Richard line up the lead Stuka coming almost directly towards him. As Richard fired, the Stuka took multiple hits around its nose and cockpit. It pitched up violently, rolled onto its back, and plunged earthwards in a spin, smoke streaming out behind it.

'Me 109s and 110s coming down from two o'clock,' someone else warned over the radio. 'At least forty of them.'

John looked around and saw three Me 109s coming straight towards Richard, shooting as they approached. Richard rolled hard to the right. The Germans followed, still on his tail, and a line of bullets ripped across his starboard wing. He pulled up into a steep climb, disappearing into the clouds.

After a few minutes, John spotted Richard's aircraft as he came back down, and he and Derek made their way towards him. They positioned themselves at least one hundred yards out from his aircraft, one on his port side and the other on his starboard.

'We need to get back to Hornchurch. Fuel is getting marginal,' John radioed to Richard.

'Agreed,' said Richard, and he turned his aircraft to the west, back to Britain, with Derek and John following.

John continued scanning around him, above and below, as they flew. He saw the German fighters just as they started to dive down towards them.

'Five bandits, coming down on us from nine o'clock. Me 110s,' he radioed.

Richard responded quickly. 'Break, break, break.'

John went left, in the direction of the approaching Germans, but in a dive to avoid them as best he could. Richard continued straight ahead, and Derek went right. John saw the enemy aircraft respond. Two followed Derek, and three peeled off to chase Richard. *They must have decided not to spread themselves too thinly*, John thought, as none of them pursued him.

The Germans started shooting at Richard and Derek, but because they were still quite a distance away their fire was largely ineffectual. They soon got closer and started registering some hits. John could see Richard and Derek were now flying hard avoidance manoeuvres, rolling and diving to avoid their Luftwaffe pursuers. He increased his power to maximum continuous to follow the fighters on Richard's tail. He thought that since Richard was facing three enemy aircraft, he was most needed there. His first burst hit the third Me 110 chasing after Richard. It immediately peeled away and headed back towards France.

Out to his right, he could see Derek was in trouble. The fighters on his tail were close, and one had already damaged his

Spitfire with a burst of fire that had raked the length of his fuselage.

John saw another Me 110 suddenly appear directly behind Derek, and wondered if he could get there in time to help. As he was contemplating that, the Me 110 suddenly disappeared in an exploding fireball. Moments later, a Spitfire flew past him, at the end of a dive that had involved closing with and taking out the Me 110. With a jolt of surprise, he recognised the aircraft as the one being flown by Wing Commander Bland.

Who would have guessed it? John thought, impressed by the airmanship exhibited. *Good for you, boss.*

'Gentlemen, all the hostiles are either down or they have run. Let's get home before we run out of fuel,' Richard called.

The Spitfires headed home. They would be touching down at Hornchurch in twenty minutes. It had been a fraught day, but they were all alive, and they had achieved some success against the Luftwaffe.

CHAPTER NINETEEN

At dawn the next day, the weather was clearly going to be fine. There was no cloud to be seen anywhere, and the sun's first fingers of light were turning the propellor tips pink on the parked Spitfires.

It was the sixth day of the Dunkirk operation. The pilots of 415 Squadron had been operating war patrols on every one of those days, except when grounded by poor weather. Their principal task had been relatively simple: patrol the evacuation area and its eastern approaches, and intercept any German bombers sighted.

Today's weather forecast covering the northern French coast indicated that conditions would be sufficient to allow the Luftwaffe to launch bombing operations against the evacuating troops. It was going to be a busy day for Spitfire pilots. After an unexpected wait, at 0800 hours the squadron was finally ordered to take to the air. Soon, twelve Spitfires were airborne and heading towards France. Richard was in charge, leading red section. He was red one. Behind him, Wing Commander Bland was red two, and Roger followed as red three. John, as red four, flew the last aircraft in red section's four-ship patrol formation.

As they approached the beaches of Dunkirk, Richard called, 'Flak, straight ahead on the other side of the town, estimate sixteen thousand. There must be bandits there somewhere.' He paused. 'Got them now. They look like Heinkels. Twenty plus. Can't see their escort, but they will be there, so watch out for divers coming at you as we attack the bombers. In pairs, please, go.'

The three fours in which the Spitfires of 415 Squadron were flying moved into their favoured fighting formation, pairs. The squadron had learnt that twelve aircraft attacking in six pairs was more effective than three flights of four aircraft. While they had briefly suspended the pairs tactic, to allow Bland and some other inexperienced pilots to have their initial battle engagements as part of a flight of four aircraft, it was now time to fly in twos again. That had been one of Richard's early decisions as a new war operations leader.

Red section led the way, sweeping down towards the Heinkels. Richard was first, with Bland right behind him. Then it was Roger, leading the second pair in red section, with John as his number two. The Spitfires opened fire when they were about three hundred yards from the Luftwaffe bombers.

The German aircraft reacted chaotically, scattering in all directions when they sighted six pairs of Spitfires coming at them. Two even dropped their bombs immediately, nowhere near the British forces, and turned to flee east. Within just a few minutes, five enemy bombers had been shot down by the squadron.

'Got him! This is easy!' someone shouted.

John groaned. *Stay focused and don't get overconfident*, he urged silently.

Then there was a call from Richard. 'Here comes the fighter cover. One-o-nines, lots of them, two o'clock high.'

Moments later, it was the Spitfires' turn to take evasive action. John saw two Me 109s flash past him on his right. They were so fast in their dive, trying to attack the Spitfires before they could do too much damage to the bomber formation, that they overshot their targets. Roger turned and followed them down, with John behind him. Roger fired a long burst at one of the Me 109s. The German rolled quickly left and pulled hard into the turn, trying to get inside the path of Roger's pursuing Spitfire.

As Roger's wingman, John followed, pulling a very tight turn himself. He felt a momentary dizziness, and his vision started to grey out. Not wanting to be blind as he flew, he relaxed back-pressure on his control stick to lower the turn's gravitational load. His vision cleared immediately, but he could not see the German aircraft, nor could he see Roger's Spitfire. *Where the hell are they?* he thought. As he wondered, a hail of fire hit his aircraft.

John was startled, but not afraid. He had no time to think and be scared. He just flew instinctively, rolling hard to the right. When inverted, he stopped his roll and pulled hard on the stick to accelerate into a dive. *No sign of Jerry in my mirror. Have I lost him?* he wondered. He scanned around. There was no sign of any Luftwaffe aircraft anywhere, let alone the one who had been on his tail.

Maintaining a careful lookout, he began climbing back to a higher level. As he passed through thirteen thousand feet, he saw three Spitfires silhouetted against some white cloud out to his left. Flying towards them, he soon got close enough to see that it was red section — Richard, Bland, and Roger. He called on his radio.

'Red one, this is red four, about to re-join you from your three o'clock.'

'Good to hear from you, John,' Richard replied, dropping radio call sign formality. 'When I lost you during the melee, I wasn't sure if you were okay. Bloody pleased you are. We are heading back to base now.'

'Roger, following,' said John.

After they had landed back at Hornchurch, Richard, Bland, Roger, and John climbed out of their respective aircraft and made their way to the dispersal hut.

'Flying Officer Cowles,' Bland said, turning towards Richard as they walked.

'Sir?' said Richard.

'Now I have more time under my belt against Jerry, I have decided I will take over squadron lead for war ops. Thank you for your assistance. I appreciate what you have done.'

Richard did not reply straight away, clearly taken by surprise. John and Roger exchanged uneasy glances.

'Very well, sir, if that's your wish, but I am ready, willing, and able to continue in the role for a little longer if that would be of assistance,' said Richard.

'I'm ready, so no, there will be no need for you to continue in the role, thank you,' Bland replied firmly.

They all recognised that there would be no further discussion. Bland's success in the air appeared to have given him the view that he was ready to lead. It was not even clear if he intended to share ops leadership with Squadron Leader Sidey. The group walked on towards the dispersal hut in what John felt was an awkward silence.

At dinner that night, John raised with Richard the issue of Wing Commander Bland taking over war ops leadership. Roger, Greg, and Charlie were also at the table.

'The boss caught you by surprise earlier, Richard — I could tell. Is it going to work with him in charge?' John asked.

'Bland has made his decision. That's the end of it — we just get on,' Richard replied.

John recognised that Richard was not happy with what Bland had done, but clearly did not want to get drawn into the pros and cons of Bland leading the squadron.

'Well, I think its bloody stupid,' Greg said. 'He's inexperienced in battle and has no leadership skills.'

'Greg, he is the CO,' Richard responded. 'He has flown on several war ops since getting his medical clearance, and I think he has performed well in those engagements. He is experienced compared to some we have on the squadron at present. Two of them are just off Wings and through consolidation. They'd be lucky to have twenty hours on Spits, and we are taking them into battle with the Luftwaffe.'

'Maybe so, Richard, but they are not being asked to lead the squadron and make tactical decisions in the air when we are confronted by Jerry,' Greg retorted.

'The decision has been made. We will just have to cope with the change. It's no use prattling on about it. Anyway, he may surprise us.'

Charlie tactfully changed the subject. 'I hear we are not up for an early start tomorrow. They're keeping us in reserve for later in the morning. After days of pre-dawn wake-up calls, I'm very happy about that. I felt so tired yesterday I could have had a quick kip as the sun beamed down through my canopy,' he said.

'Hell, Charlie, you wouldn't last long if you did that. I can hear Baron von Richthofen now,' said Roger, grinning. '*I found zee Englander. He vas dozing in his cockpit. I shoot and make his dreams a nightmare. Sehr gut.*'

The others all laughed. The difficult issue of Bland assuming operational leadership was left behind as they talked about other things.

The next morning, the pilots gathered in the briefing room to be given detail of the weather conditions they would probably encounter, the patrol route, and the formation to be adopted for today's operation. Bland confirmed he would be leading the squadron and that he would use standard Vic formations.

'We are to be airborne at ten thirty hours,' he told the assembled pilots. 'Any clarification needed?'

Derek raised his hand. 'Operating in three-ship Vics means we will not get into pairs when we engage?' he asked.

It was a good question. Pairing had been successful in war operations, but it would not be so easy to set up when all the aircraft were in threes to start with. Finger-fours had been simple to split into twos. More organisation would be required to allow Vics of three aircraft to quickly reform as pairs.

'Ah,' Bland began, clearly uncertain as to how the aircraft might best proceed in those circumstances. 'I think we will just stay in threes,' he said finally. He did not give any reasons.

Derek nodded his acknowledgement and said nothing. Nor did any of the other pilots. They were dismayed at the lack of analysis and insight just demonstrated by their new operational leader.

At eleven hundred hours, as they crossed the French coast near Calais, Bland's Spitfire squadron was at twenty-four thousand feet. It was just 415 Squadron this morning. No big wing rendezvous had been ordered. The pilots knew that Bland's plan was to proceed inland towards Lille. He thought that would provide them with an opportunity to intercept any bombers inbound from the east, on their way to bomb the troops and the transport vessels engaged in the evacuation.

As they were passing abeam the town of Saint-Omer, John heard Bland's warning over the radio.

'Bandits, thirty plus, ten o'clock, low,' he called.

John watched as Bland adjusted his heading, clearly intending to intercept the bombers' route.

'Follow me,' Bland ordered.

Two to three miles out from the German aircraft, there was still no order from Bland as to the positioning he wanted the squadron to adopt for the attack. Richard knew it could not wait any longer.

'Red one, this is red two. Shall we open our spacing?'

'No, stay in current Vics,' was the response.

The twelve Spitfires arrowed towards the Luftwaffe bombers in four groups of three aircraft. Bland opened fire first, but at too great a range. His shooting was ineffective, and there was no reaction from the Germans. Soon, however, the bombers were within range. Then all the Spitfires began firing, but not before they had increased their distance from one another in their respective Vics. Maybe the CO had said to stay in current Vics, but that was not going to work once they started firing, so they had opened their spacing anyway. Two enemy aircraft started emitting smoke from their engines. They dropped down out of their formation as they lost power and speed. One of them entered a dive, spinning uncontrollably as it fell from the sky.

'Fighters, multiple, coming down behind us,' someone called.

That sounded like Greg, John thought, as he swivelled in his seat to look to his rear. He saw the yellow noses — Me 109s, lots of them. Like most of the other pilots in the squadron, John began taking evasive action, which meant a reprieve for the bombers. He twisted and weaved, trying to ensure he was an unsteady target for anyone trying to shoot him down. He saw Bland's Spitfire below him, diving and rolling, with a

German on his tail. John set off after them, trying to close in on the Me 109 pursuing Bland. He called him as he did so.

'Red one, this is red three, coming on to your port quarter. Chasing the one-o-nine on your tail.'

Bland did not respond.

As John was trying to position himself for a shot on the Me 109, he saw Bland pull his Spitfire up into a steep climb. After a few seconds, the CO's Spitfire began to slow as it lost energy in its vertical ascent. As his airspeed washed off, John saw that Bland intended to extricate himself from the position into which he had flown his Spitfire by undertaking a stall-turn. His aircraft slowly pivoted around its right wingtip as it moved from a vertical ascent to a near-vertical dive. Watching this, John could not believe what he was seeing. *Stupid bugger*, he thought. *That's not going to help you.*

The Me 109 following Bland's Spitfire was presented with a perfect shooting opportunity. As Bland entered the stall-turn, his aircraft hung virtually motionless for a few seconds at its pivot point. The Luftwaffe pilot did not hesitate. He raked the Spitfire's wings and fuselage with burst of gunfire. Bland's aircraft fell onto its back and entered an inverted dive towards the ground thousands of feet below, smoke pouring from its engine.

Just then, the Me 109's cockpit exploded as it was hit by a hail of machine-gun bullets. The German had not seen John's Spitfire coming.

'I saw the CO go down,' John said at the patrol debrief after returning to Hornchurch. 'I followed him after we all broke up on initial engagement with the Jerry bombers, as the fighters arrived. He was on his own, and I thought there would be value in me operating as his wingman, acting as a pair. I was trying to take out the Jerry on his tail when he was shot down.'

'You saw the whole thing?' Greg asked.

'Yes, he pulled up into a vertical. I thought he would either loop or roll off the top into a steep turn, but he didn't. He stall-turned.'

'What the hell was he playing at?' Greg snapped. 'That's just bloody well asking for it.'

'I know.' John shrugged. 'I was surprised he did that, but at least I got the Jerry who shot him down.'

'That's pleasing to hear, John,' Greg said. 'When we broke up, I lost contact with the CO. There is no doubt in my mind that we would have been better in pairs. Then each leader would have been with a dedicated wingman. As it was, although we stayed in Vics wherever we could, the lads took it upon themselves to open the spacing, and they needed too. Someone might have been hit by friendly fire if we had stayed in close Vics. Couldn't understand the CO saying no to increased lateral distance between us.'

'I think we all agree with that, Greg,' John responded. 'It was a fiasco.'

It had been a bad day for the squadron. There were three pilots missing, including Wing Commander Bland. A recent squadron joiner, not long out of Wings, had failed to survive his first day. The other casualty was Derek Laing. He had been seen going down in flames about two miles off the French coast. No-one had reported any sign of a parachute.

It was a sombre evening in the mess. The three empty chairs at dinner could not be ignored, nor could the absence of Derek's friendly chatter. Greg was the first to voice what was on the minds of many of the pilots.

'Richard, I presume you will reassume ops leadership in place of Bland. And if you do, no more Vics, eh? Let's engage in pairs. It has worked well to date.'

'I suppose I will be, but I need to confirm it with Squadron Leader Sidey.'

The table fell silent again as they tried to eat. Their appetites seemed to have deserted them, as they were consumed by a sense of loss.

CHAPTER TWENTY

That evening, Squadron Leader Sidey addressed the pilots. With Wing Commander Bland gone, he had taken over as acting CO. 'We have been advised that tomorrow is likely to be the final day of RAF involvement in Operation Dynamo. The view at senior level is that most of those who can be evacuated have already been taken out, although there will be some others who, hopefully, can get out over the next twenty-four hours. The costs to the Royal Navy are reaching an unsustainable level. They are losing too many vessels to bombing and mines, and the Germans have set up some long-range and accurate artillery on the coast. They are landing salvos across vessels out in the Channel, probably just as their crews and passengers are starting to feel they have made it.'

Sidey paused, looking around the room. 'It will be a dawn take-off again tomorrow. We won't be part of a big wing. Four-one-five squadron will operate its own patrol. Flying Officer Cowles will be leading you, although you should all be aware that from tomorrow morning, he will be Flight Lieutenant Cowles. Command will formally confirm his promotion later this afternoon.'

There was a smattering of applause.

'Thank you,' Richard said. 'We are down on both aircraft and pilots, so squadron strength tomorrow will be ten, even after using our spare aircraft and reserve pilots. We will operate as five pairs from take-off. The pairs listings are on this sheet, which I will put on the noticeboard. Weather will also go up on the board in the morning, so check it after you have had your breakfast. I want propellors turning at o-four-thirty.'

As the pilots got up and left, John wondered what would come next. The German forces had bombed their way across Europe in short order. Now they were at the western coast of Europe. Holland, Belgium, Luxembourg, and France had quickly been conquered, after initial Nazi forays into Czechoslovakia and the subsequent invasion of Poland. Britain, with troops trapped in the pocket at Dunkirk, was now struggling to get as many of them home as it could. The men were badly needed to defend the United Kingdom as the war progressed. Effectively, Britain was the last man standing against the might of the German military.

At 0430 the next morning, the squadron of Spitfires was again howling across the operational area at Hornchurch, eager to fly. Soon they were climbing steadily towards France.

The Luftwaffe was already over Dunkirk's beaches when the Hornchurch Spitfires arrived in the area. Stukas, more than John had ever seen before, were dive-bombing two large vessels loading troops from an assortment of small boats shuttling from the shoreline. An attack was called and the ten Spitfires, spaced in five pairs, peeled off and dived towards the Stukas. Richard opened fire from an extreme range, while he was still at least seven hundred yards out. *Too far*, John thought as he watched. Richard must have realised the futility of such long-range shooting himself, as he stopped firing almost immediately.

A few moments later, the Spitfires were close enough to shoot and expect some results. John saw Richard fire again, his tracer weaving over and in front of a Stuka, before it finally zeroed in and scored a hit. The Stuka exploded in flames and fell from the air. Richard banked left to line up another Stuka in his sights. As Richard's number two, John rolled his aircraft to follow, and as he resumed straight and level flight he looked back over both of his shoulders in turn. Seeing no German fighters, he returned to looking towards his leader.

As he watched, he saw a group of three Me 109s approaching head-on from above the Stukas' height. He called a warning to Richard, who had not reacted to their approach.

'Red one, three hostiles at twelve o'clock coming down towards us.'

Richard reacted in an instant. He pulled his aircraft up sharply, converting his diving attack on a Stuka into a climb directly towards the approaching fighters. John followed, then they both fired at the Me 109s. The Germans must have been unsettled by two Spitfires coming at them, head-on and shooting. They split up. The leading aircraft pulled up into a climb that would take him safely over the top of the Spitfires. His compatriots banked away, one going left, the other going right.

Richard pulled his aircraft into a tight turn to follow the German who had flown to the right. As the Me 109 appeared before him, Richard fired a long burst after allowing for some deflection. His calculation was perfect. The Me 109 flew into Richard's hail of bullets. John saw it shudder as smoke started to pour from its engine. Then the German aircraft slowly rolled to the right, dipped its nose, and began the long plunge towards a wide sandy beach below.

Looking around to check there were still no other enemy aircraft about to pounce, John saw nothing but empty sky. He continued to follow as Richard turned and climbed.

As they flew clear of a large area of cloud, John could see that the organised formation of Stuka dive-bombers they had attacked was gone. Now it was nothing more than several widely dispersed aircraft, all flying in various directions at different heights. The Spitfires had broken up the Luftwaffe's attacking force. John could see some 415 Squadron aircraft, as well as a mix of Me 109s and 110s. There were several individual dogfights going on.

'John, select your own targets at will,' Richard radioed. 'I think these engagements are just one on one. We can do more individually than as a pair. Good luck. Go.'

John understood Richard's strategic thinking, and he also understood his lack of formality on the radio. This was a friend wishing him well as they went into battle, not his senior officer giving him an order.

An Me 110 flashed across in front of John's aircraft, diving down towards the beaches. John rolled into a steep descending turn, following him. Faster in the dive, John's Spitfire rapidly gained on the fleeing German, but they were getting low. As his altimeter unwound, John saw he had just passed through seven thousand feet. He was almost in shooting range. Passing four thousand feet, John fired a quick burst. The tracer showed him he had missed. He manoeuvred his Spitfire into a better aiming position and fired again. Success this time. Pieces flew off the German's right-hand engine, then it showed some flame. Small at first, the fire rapidly grew and soon engulfed most of the aircraft's wing. They were down to two thousand feet. The landing gear on the Me 110 came down. *Is that some sort of surrender signal?* John wondered.

It was not. John saw that the aircraft was also extending its wing flaps. At the same time, it turned to follow the line of the beach, heading south, away from the town of Dunkirk itself. *He's damaged, and he's landing on the beach*, thought John. *And he's trying to get as far away as he can from our lads before he touches down. What shall I do? Shoot at him again? Break off and climb back up to where the other aircraft are?*

Black puffs began appearing around the Me 110. The British forces on the beach were directing anti-aircraft fire at the German aircraft. After just a few seconds, one of the rounds hit and the Me 110 disappeared in a large explosion. John had to turn steeply to avoid flying through the debris left in the air.

Suddenly, his aircraft was rocked by a shell exploding close by. 'You stupid buggers! Can't you recognise your own?' John screamed out loud in the confines of his cockpit. Evasive action was needed, otherwise he would go the same way as the Me 110. John considered his options as more bursts exploded around his Spitfire. He knew he should not climb. That would leave him in the anti-aircraft battery sights for too long. In any event, there was little point in going back up — the dogfights would be long over. *That just highlights the pointlessness of the required climb to altitude demanded by aerial combat policy, regardless of circumstances,* he thought bitterly. John decided to get down low, below the elevation of the anti-aircraft guns. He dived towards the beach.

Levelling out at less than fifty feet above the sand, he saw figures on the beach zipping past beneath him. He heard some thuds. Two bullet holes appeared on the wing just beside his cockpit. Looking about, John saw some of those on the ground had their rifles up in firing position against their shoulders. *Christ, now the troops are taking pot shots at me,* he thought. He rolled his aircraft into a turn that would take him out to sea, well clear of the soldiers who had decided he was the enemy.

However, approximately five hundred yards off the shoreline, he saw there was an extensive area of low cloud. It was about three hundred feet above the sea's surface. There was some light rain falling, causing reduced visibility in the area below the cloud. What to do?

He knew standing orders required him to get back to altitude, but he had already dismissed that, because climbing would again expose him to friendly fire for no real reason. *On the other hand,* he thought, *if I ignore standing orders and stay down at this level and continue west, out to sea, my in-flight visibility is going to be marginal. I don't want to have to blind-fly at this height.* He considered his options for a few more moments and then decided to stay low and go west, flying at two hundred feet. That was far enough below the cloud base to provide sufficient clearance, but high enough to preserve a reasonable margin from the surface, especially if he lost what little visibility there was. He did not want to inadvertently descend into the sea if he had no horizon to guide him.

John would rather have been flying higher as he crossed the Channel. If he had an engine problem, he knew he would be in the water quickly from just two hundred feet. He was stuck with that situation, though, given conditions, so he had to continue at low level. As a result, he was very conscious of the rhythm of the engine.

After flying westward for a short time, the cloud and visibility had still not improved. The British coast would be looming up in another ten minutes or so. John was picturing accidentally flying into the White Cliffs of Dover when his attention was drawn to the surface of the sea. There was a large line of disturbed water, obviously recently churned up. It was a ship's wake, he realised, looking ahead to where the vessel must have already disappeared into the gloom. John decided to follow, wondering what sort of Royal Navy ship was leaving this trail across the sea.

The wake became more pronounced; the vessel was clearly travelling quickly. *It can't be far ahead now,* John thought. Then, through what had now become misty drizzle, he saw the stern.

A red ensign fluttered on its afterdeck. Though it was not windy, the ensign was standing straight out behind the pole it was secured to, indicating the speed of the vessel. Suddenly, John slammed on full power and threw his Spitfire into a tight one-hundred-and-eighty-degree turn. A risky manoeuvre at that height and in those conditions, but he had recognised the flag.

As he had got closer, he had seen the Swastika at the centre of the ensign. The vessel was an E-boat belonging to the German Navy, the Kriegsmarine.

John doubted he had been seen by any of the crew of the E-boat. His Spitfire, briefly appearing low out of the mist some four to five hundred yards behind, would only have been seen if, by some misfortune, someone on the vessel had been looking back at the very moment he had appeared. John had been quick to turn away and disappear back into the murk.

Checking his fuel, John realised he did not have much more than thirty minutes' endurance left. If he attacked the E-boat, that would use a lot more fuel. His consumption rate in battle mode would be much higher than if he just continued to cruise back to base. *I will make one strafing pass and hopefully knock the vessel out of action, or at least force it to go somewhere for repairs*, he decided. *That won't use too much fuel.*

He turned through another one hundred and eighty degrees to resume his track in the general direction of where he thought the E-boat would be. John was unsure of its actual position, and the reduced visibility was not helping. He set up a weaving track to increase the likelihood that he could again locate the fast German boat. He was looking for its wake, which he would then follow all the way to the vessel.

After a few minutes of searching, John came across the wake. He reduced his power. He wanted to be a bit slower this time as he came up behind the E-boat. When he saw the white foam generated by its busy propellors in the distance, he set up his guns and increased power. John was now flying straight towards the vessel's stern. As he got closer, he saw movement on the aft deck. Sailors were doing something with the torpedo tubes on each side of that deck. *Looks like they are loading them*, John thought. Someone on the E-boat must have seen him.

The sailors ran for one of the bulkheads and a machine gun near the back of the vessel opened up. John saw the river of tracer slicing towards him and passing out to his right as the gunner missed. The E-boat itself started to move left and right in the water, trying to make it difficult for John to shoot. The first burst John fired kicked up a trail in the water along the port side of the vessel. He corrected to the right, and his next burst went along the centre of the main deck and exploded against what John thought was probably the back of the bridge.

Then he was past, clear of the shooting, continuing to Hornchurch. He had no fuel for any more strafing runs. John smiled to himself, pleased he had probably done some damage, maybe even shut down the bridge. Suddenly, out of the drizzle, there was a warship directly in front of him. It was a Royal Navy destroyer, hardly moving. He could see the British ensign, white with a red cross, with the Union Jack in the upper corner.

'Bloody hell!' he shouted as he banked sharply to avoid a collision with the ship's infrastructure, which reached up higher than he was flying.

Christ, that was close, John thought. He also now realised that the E-boat was stalking the destroyer in the reduced visibility. He knew he would have to have another go at the German ship, otherwise the Royal Navy vessel he had just seen would be in real danger. It was obviously damaged and limping through the sea. He circled around, approaching the destroyer from the front quarter. The drizzle was not as heavy here, which pleased him. The Royal Navy would be able to identify him more easily.

He soon realised the crew of this destroyer were not good at aircraft identification. Two guns on the ship started shooting at him. *Damn it*, he thought as he banked away. The firing suddenly stopped — perhaps the crew had belatedly recognised his aircraft as a Spitfire, but John could not take that chance, and stayed well clear. Now past the Royal Navy vessel, his eyes were searching in the direction he thought the E-boat would be as it followed the destroyer.

He saw the E-boat's bow wave first. He was directly in front of the German vessel, so he knew they would have seen him. Sure enough, the gun on the front deck started firing, including some tracer rounds, at his aircraft. John jinked his way closer to the approaching E-boat, trying to make himself a difficult target. At a range of two hundred yards, with the boat plumb in his sights, he pushed the gun button at the top of his control stick, unleashing a hail of bullets. He could see the rounds hitting the front of the E-boat's deck.

Seconds later, John's Spitfire snarled over the German vessel, just a hundred feet above. He banked hard to the left and then rolled right in a steep turn to position himself to make another attack, this time from the boat's starboard rear quarter. John's shots pummelled the side of the vessel as he came in from that direction. Then, once again he was across the boat. He turned to make another run. Halfway through the turn a shell exploded on the fuselage, immediately behind the cockpit. It must have damaged his flight controls, because John found he had no response from his elevator. He could not use that control to make the aircraft raise its nose and climb, nor lower its nose and descend. The damage also affected John's ability to hold the Spitfire in the turn he was partway through when hit. To stop his nose dropping, which would have resulted in him plunging into the sea, John rolled his wings level.

Because he had abandoned his turn, the E-boat remained forty-five degrees off his nose and he had no line of fire at it. He needed to try to get his aircraft turned some more, so his target would be dead ahead of him. But he could not bank the Spitfire in the normal way while he had no effective elevator control. He needed that to hold his nose up as he turned. John dipped his left wing very slightly. That, together with a good amount of left rudder, carefully applied to ensure no upset, eventually got his nose around, pointing at the E-boat. He knew a flat turn at low altitude was high risk, but he had decided it was the only way he would be able to bring his guns to bear, and he was being cautious in his execution of the turn.

He fired a long burst as he closed in on the German vessel, knowing that was probably going to be the end of his ammunition. There was a large explosion. John could not avoid the fireball. He felt a thump as his Spitfire flew through the super-heated and disturbed air. A torpedo in a tube on the E-boat, loaded and primed to go, must have been hit. John had no time to congratulate himself on destroying the German vessel. He knew his controls were gone, literally shot to pieces. Flying through the fireball had also damaged his engine, he realised, as it started to run rough. *Damn, I'm going to end up in the water*, he thought.

The destroyer was now in sight, so John decided he would ditch in front of it, to one side of its path. He hoped that would make it easier for them to stop and pick him up. He had decided that because they had ceased shooting at him earlier, as he had passed, they would probably again recognise that it was a Spitfire. John accepted he had no choice, anyway. His aircraft would not continue flying for much longer.

As he flew past the ship, he reduced his power, allowing the Spitfire to sink towards the surface. Luckily, it was reasonably calm, with no marked swell that he could see. He knew he had to keep his nose up. If it dropped and hit the surface first, it would be like flying into a brick wall. The loss of elevator control meant that was easier said than done. Pulling back on the stick would not lift the nose, because of the damage to his controls. All he had was his elevator trim. It controlled a small tab at the rear of the elevator itself that was used to make limited adjustments to the elevator's position during normal flight, to balance the aircraft longitudinally. Not normally sufficient to raise the nose for landing, it was better that nothing, John decided.

He wanted to reduce the aircraft's speed as much as possible before hitting the sea, but he decided not to use flaps. Lowering flaps would risk the nose of the Spitfire dipping too low for him to lift at touchdown, with the damaged state of his elevator. He kept power on at this stage, although it was a reduced setting, and the engine was still running rough. Some power helped hold the nose up.

John estimated he was only five or six feet above the water when he started winding back the elevator trim as fast as he could. At the same time, he reduced engine power. The Spitfire was dropping towards the surface. The effect of the trim being wound right back meant the elevator moved slightly, stopping the nose from dipping too sharply, although it was a technique that was only partially successful. The trim was less effective at low air-speed. The aircraft touched the surface of the water, and then it was enveloped by a wall of spray as it went deeper into the cold sea. John was conscious of a solid impact as it did that, and he felt himself being thrown forward against his harness straps. He had opened the cockpit canopy as he was about to ditch and his head was thrown violently to one side as the aircraft entered the water. John felt his forehead strike the front windscreen frame. It was a solid bang, and that was as much as he knew.

The bright light was annoying. John screwed up his face and reached up to cover his eyes with his hand.

'Easy, young fellow,' a voice above him said.

'How did I get here?' John asked the voice.

'I'm Commander Bond,' was the reply. 'You are in the sick bay of our ship. The crew picked you out of your aircraft when you ditched alongside.'

'Ah, thank you,' John replied.

'No, thank you. If you hadn't taken out that E-boat targeting us, there would have been a very different story today. We didn't know he was there until we saw it blow up when you attacked it. Our vessel, including our radar antenna, had been damaged while we were off the beaches, so when the E-boat was further away, in the murk, we couldn't detect it. And sorry we shot at you. When you first appeared low out of the gloom, we thought it was more Jerries about to attack us.'

'Yes, I saw that and I was very pleased that you stopped before you hit me,' John replied.

'You had a lucky day on several counts. The fact that our gunners were not on target is one of them. Another is that our captain is an aviation enthusiast. He recognised the special shape of your Spitfire's wings when you banked. He realised you were RAF and ordered a stop to the shooting.'

'I feel all right,' said John. 'Am I injured?'

'A few bumps and bruises, but nothing broken. There is a good gash on your forehead, but we've popped some stiches in and it will heal nicely. We are just entering Dover port, so get yourself ready to disembark, probably in about fifteen minutes. You will be taken to hospital. They want you to go into observation for a short time, just to check you over. Thanks again. Your work was appreciated by everyone on board.'

CHAPTER TWENTY-ONE

'Welcome back, old bean!' Greg shouted, standing up to greet John as he came into the mess at Hornchurch. It was the day after John had crashed into the English Channel next to the Royal Navy vessel that had then rescued him from his downed Spitfire.

'Good to be here,' John smiled back.

'We all thought you were a goner,' Greg went on. They shook hands and Greg patted John's back. 'Tell us what happened and where you've been.'

John took them through everything that had happened to him, from the time he chased the Me 110, to his successful attack on the E-boat and subsequent ditching in the Channel.

'Wonderful, John. Well done,' Richard said as John finished.

'Yes, good work,' Roger added.

'Was the water cold?' Charlie asked. They all laughed at that.

'Flight Lieutenant Cowles, Flying Officer Noble.'

John looked around. It was Squadron Leader Sidey.

'Yes, sir?'

'I need to have a discussion with both of you. Please be in my office in fifteen minutes.'

Quarter of an hour later, John and Richard were sitting expectantly, opposite Sidey, who was behind a large desk, waiting for him to speak.

'We have a short notice assignment,' Sidey said. 'Intelligence has reported that the Germans are keen to show the citizens of the Third Reich how good they are at war. The Dunkirk evacuation is being trumpeted as a huge British defeat, which to be fair, it probably is, despite the fact we successfully got a lot of troops out of France.'

Neither Richard nor John said anything. John was wondering what this was about. Something more than a meeting to summarise Operation Dynamo and to talk about German success, he guessed. He could tell from the look on Richard's face that he was similarly mystified.

'Anyway, Herr Goebbels, the German propaganda minister, is sending several of his senior staff, together with reporters and cameramen, to Dunkirk. That is so they can record the success of the Wehrmacht, showing the equipment abandoned there by the Expeditionary Force as they fled, that sort of thing. We have been asked to put a spanner in the works.'

'Intelligence has advised that the Nazis are sending their publicity team from Berlin, Tempelhof aerodrome, in a Junkers fifty-two. There will be some twelve passengers, and camera gear, aboard, and they will land at Mardyck aerodrome, which the Luftwaffe now occupies. That's about nine miles southwest of Dunkirk. While the Luftwaffe has moved into Mardyck, intelligence doesn't think they have established any fighter squadrons there yet.

'Whitehall does not want this propaganda operation to succeed. I have been asked to arrange an interception of the Junkers, which is to be taken down.'

John was staggered. He guessed that he and Richard were to be part of this operation, and his mind was racing. How would they locate the Junkers, was an immediate question?

'You are to fly on this mission, gentlemen, and I will lead it,' Sidey said, confirming John's expectation.

'The three-engined Junkers fifty-two has the capability to carry the payload required direct from Berlin to Mardyck,' Sidey continued. 'Our intelligence sources in Berlin will notify us when the aircraft takes off. Using that departure time, and the standard cruising speed of a Junkers, we will be able to estimate the time the aircraft will reach Mardyck, and arrange our reception committee.'

John thought about what Sidey had said. Because a direct flight from Berlin to Mardyck was proposed, he realised the aircraft would always be somewhere along a track-line joining those two points. Where it was on that line would depend on its groundspeed.

'We can make a reasonably accurate calculation as to the time it will likely be approaching its destination,' Sidey said, confirming John's initial thoughts. 'Weather conditions will be important, of course. If the flight is affected by strong winds, that will change the position of the Junkers along its route. Similarly, if it has to make a diversion around any adverse weather, that will also alter timing, and thus position. Those are risks we just have to accept. When we have tomorrow's weather, we will have more of an idea about likely effect.'

'We will be notified of the Junkers' departure time from Berlin, and I am hoping there will be no weather that compromises our ability to locate the aircraft. Preliminary forecasts look okay.'

'I propose that we intercept it before it gets to Mardyck, somewhere in the area north of Ypres.'

'Do we have any information on what air defence capability the Germans have established in the area in which we will be flying?' Richard asked.

'There are some fighter squadrons being established at various airfields in northern France, but as I said, nothing at Mardyck itself at this stage. We are not aware of anything yet established in southwest Belgium. We are working on the basis that three Spitfires going in low and fast, and getting out quickly, may not be seen in time for the Luftwaffe to respond.'

You make it sound so easy, John thought to himself, but he understood that it would not be easy at all. It was a high-risk mission. Weather, interception by the enemy, and inability to locate the target somewhere along its route, all loomed large.

'Gentlemen, I want you to complete the planning necessary for this mission. Come back to me when it's done, so I can review it with you,' Sidey continued. 'I understand from intelligence that we will get the departure time very shortly after the Junkers has taken off from Berlin, bound for Mardyck, so that will enable us to calculate its expected arrival time in the area where we will make the intercept. By the way, this mission is classified top secret, so it is not to be mentioned to anyone.'

That night John and Richard reviewed the latest weather forecasts, topographical charts coving northern France, Belgium, and Germany, and plotted the direct track from Tempelhof aerodrome, the proposed departure point for the Junkers, to the airfield at Mardyck. The flight time for the trip was calculated to be three hours, in no wind conditions and based on the cruising speed of a Junkers 52.

No significant wind was forecast, and the weather right across France, Belgium, and Germany looked as if it would be fine the next day, as Sidey had indicated. Similarly, the forecast for southern England and the Channel did not mention any adverse weather issues.

The two Spitfire pilots had soon completed the detail for the planned intercept.

They would leave from Hornchurch, two hours and fifteen minutes after the Junkers had left Berlin, planning to meet it somewhere north of the Belgian town of Ypres. It would take the Spitfires twenty minutes from Hornchurch to the point they planned to cross the French coast, near the small town of Wissant. From that point to the interception area near Ypres would be another ten minutes. Their plan was to position north of Ypres, and to search along the Junkers' expected track, which went right through that area. They had calculated that the German aircraft should be in their planned interception area about two hours fifty minutes after it had taken off from Berlin. 'Let's take this to Dave Sidey now,' John said to Richard.

Sidey was in his office, and it did not take long to go through the detail they had prepared. Off Hornchurch two hours fifteen minutes after advice of the Junkers' departure from Tempelhof. That would have them in the interception area two hours forty-five after that departure. Fly a search pattern along the anticipated flight path of the Junkers, starting from a position just short of its destination. They should see it at some point if they did that, then, after the attack, they would vacate the area as fast as they could.

'I'm happy,' Sidey said, as John and Richard completed their presentation to him. 'Weather looks to be okay. German fighters in the area may be a risk, but Dynamo is not long over and Jerry does not seem be organised with a significant fighter presence in that area yet. If there are Luftwaffe aircraft about, we just have to hope they don't see us for as long as possible, if at all.'

Armed with advice from intelligence the next morning, that the Junkers bound for Mardyck had departed from Tempelhof at o-eight-hundred hours, German time, Sidey, Richard, and John took off from Hornchurch at nine fifteen hours. They flew at low level across the English Channel, and their Spitfires were racing across the white-sand beach near the small French town of Wissant, twenty minutes later.

Turning northeast, and remaining at a height not above fifty feet, as planned, the three Spitfires arrowed towards the planned interception area near Ypres. That was where they expected to locate the Junkers on its flight from Berlin, as it approached its destination, Mardyck aerodrome.

Once established in the area in which they expected to see their target, Sidey ordered that they separate, so there was a mile between each aircraft as they began the long sweeping turns he wanted. The spacing was to widen the area they were able to scan, as they began searching along the corridor in which they anticipated they would see the Junkers. Five minutes passed. Nothing seen. Then, high at his two o'clock, John saw a *schwarm* of Me 109s.

Oh no, not now, he thought. He was unsure if the three Spitfires had been seen. They were low, and probably well-merged with the landscape, he thought.

As he was wondering about that, he saw the Junkers 52 approaching, easily recognisable by its three engines — one in the nose and one on each of the wings. It was about two miles away, at about three thousand feet, tracking in his direction.

John called his sightings to Sidey.

'Don't think the one-o-nines have seen us,' Sidey said, in response to John's warning. 'Let's go for the Junkers.'

'Ah, the one-o-nines have spotted us now,' John replied immediately, as he then saw the four German fighters roll into a diving turn towards the Spitfires.

'I will intercept the Junkers, you two take on the one-o-nines,' Sidey snapped, clearly unhappy that their mission was about to be interrupted by the German fighters.

John saw Sidey turn towards the lumbering Luftwaffe transport aircraft approaching from the northeast, with its load of propagandists and their cameras

Looking away from Sidey's aircraft, and glancing up over his right shoulder, John saw the German fighters were now getting close.

'After me,' Richard called, as he entered a climbing turn to meet the approaching Messerschmitts. John increased his power and followed.

The German fighters were soon shooting and the air was full of tracer, but neither Richard nor John was hit as they flew, head-to-head with the enemy aircraft. Then the one-o-nines were past, and turning hard, trying to get around behind the two Spitfires. Richard pulled his aircraft up into a tight loop, with a roll through one eighty degrees after coming through the top of the loop, to position to again meet the 109s. John, close behind him, did the same. John thought the manoeuvre was a good direction reversal technique, compared to simply steep-turning back to confront the attacking 109s.

The loop and roll worked well. Both Spitfires were now higher than the German aircraft, and in a good shooting position. John and Richard fired extended bursts that hit two of the 109s. But they did not appear seriously damaged and they continued to fly their attacks against the Spitfires. The encounter continued, with the pilots of both sides using all their skills and experience to try to attain a good shooting position behind an enemy's aircraft. Then John saw one of the German fighters break away, and dive towards the north west. *Damn, he has seen Sidey after the Junkers, and he's going to intervene,* John thought. He called a warning.

'One-o-nine coming down on you, red one, on your four o'clock.' There was no reply from Sidey.

A 109 tried to turn in behind John, but John had seen him coming and quickly entered a steep turn to the right. That prevented the German from getting in behind him. After going through a full three-hundred-and-sixty-degree circle, flown clockwise in a prolonged right-hand turn, with the Luftwaffe aircraft still chasing, trying to achieve a good shooting position, John deliberately slipped his aircraft sideways. In his steeply banked turn, that caused him to quickly lose two hundred feet in altitude. The German pilot did not follow immediately, so John knew he would be momentarily out of his view, beneath the Messerschmitt's nose. John rolled his Spitfire into a steep turn to the left, in the opposite direction, taking himself out of the circle in which he and the Luftwaffe aircraft had been established.

Maintaining his turn, the Me 109 that had been trying to position for an attack on him, soon came into his view. John's relative position meant he was able to approach the Messerschmitt from its port rear quarter. No avoidance manoeuvres were being flown by the German, so John decided he was not aware of the Spitfire coming in behind him. John fired an extended burst, and the Me 109 was hit, rolling on to its back and disappearing in an inverted dive towards the ground not far below. *Got you,* John muttered, before looking towards where he thought Dave Sidey would be.

He saw Sidey's Spitfire. It was shooting at the Junkers, which had turned away from its track and was diving, trying to avoid the attacking Spitfire. As he watched, Sidey scored multiple hits on the Junkers' rear fuselage. The German aircraft was turning and twisting frantically, to make it hard for its attacker. The crew and their passengers are probably wondering why RAF Spitfires had unexpectedly turned up over German-occupied territory, so soon after the British defeat and evacuation, John thought, as a torrent of bullets from Sidey's aircraft ripped pieces off the Junkers' right wing. It caught fire and slowly rolled onto its back, before spiralling down out of control, flames getting larger all the time. Within a few more seconds it impacted the ground and there was a large explosion.

No propaganda clips from them, thought John, as he looked around to see where the 109s were now.

'Red section, back to base,' Sidey called. 'Mission accomplished. Break off now.'

John rolled his aircraft into a steep turn and dived towards the coast, trying to get as much speed as he could from his Spitfire. He saw that Sidey and Richard were doing the same.

John kept descending, until he was right down amongst the hedgerows. He had to turn several times to avoid tall trees. A line of bullets and cannon fire kicked up the ground just to John's right. There was a 109 close on his tail and shooting.

John steep turned left, held that for a moment, then steep-turned right. He climbed during that second turn, but only momentarily, he did not go up more than three hundred feet. Then he rolled left again, but went right through an inverted position as he continued in his roll, letting it develop into a steep turn in the opposite direction. A line of tracer streamed close over his cockpit, and then the shooting zeroed in on his aircraft. There was a loud *crack,* and John felt a sting on his left cheek. He saw that the left-hand side of his canopy had taken some fire, and had fractured, with part flying off and hitting him. *Bastard,* he thought, *you cut my face!*

Looking back, John saw two yellow-nosed aircraft behind him. *Like bloody angry bees,* he thought, Then, he entered a maximum rate turn, so tight he almost blacked out, but he held it for one eighty degrees before releasing and flying straight back at the Germans who had been on his tail, chasing and shooting at him. That caught them by surprise. They had not expected the fleeing Spitfire to suddenly turn and fly straight back at them, firing from point-blank range. They pulled up, and turned away sharply to avoid a collision, and John's bullets.

John took the opportunity presented by their momentary confusion and dived to ground level, heading towards the coast. Soon John was over the sea, continuing to twist and weave so as not to present a steady target to his pursuers. He saw some shooting from the chasing Luftwaffe pilots cause the relatively calm sea surface adjacent to his aircraft to erupt in spray.

Then the Me 109s stopped firing. Looking back over his shoulder, John saw that they had abandoned the chase and he was relieved to see that Sidey and Richard had also got away unscathed. They were about a mile out to his left, low over the sea, heading back to Britain.

With Operation Dynamo complete, the squadron was now back at Catterick. The men had been told to rest and repair. No-one was sure what the Germans would do next, but an attempt to invade Britain, effectively continuing the push that had started in Czechoslovakia, then moved into Poland, and eventually, into France, was considered likely. Consequently, every element of the armed forces had been instructed to prepare for the war that was now expected to come to Britain itself.

That evening, as they sat together at dinner, the pilots talked about what might now happen, and when.

'Hitler won't muck about,' Craig said. 'He has knocked us out of Europe. He knows we are damaged, so across he will come if he's got any sense, before we have time to recover and rebuild.'

'Perhaps,' Richard responded, 'but let's not forget the Jerries suffered a fair bit themselves in recent weeks. They may want to pause and rebuild themselves.'

'I hear that over three hundred thousand troops got out in Operation Dynamo,' Charlie added. 'That's an important save. It's a lot of military muscle for us to have right now.'

'I heard the new PM, Churchill, said that the Battle of France is over and now another will begin. He's calling it the Battle of Britain. He talked about fighting on the beaches, in the streets, everywhere, because we are never surrendering,' John said.

'Yes, he's a tough fellow,' Greg said. 'It's all on now. Even if Hitler wanted to stop and seek peace, Churchill would turn him down, I bet.'

They all agreed with that thought.

Squadron Leader David Sidey was sitting at the top table in the mess dining room. With Wing Commander Bland gone, he had taken over as acting CO. An orderly came in and handed the squadron leader a message. After reading it, Sidey stood and tapped his glass with a spoon. The room fell silent.

'Gentlemen, I have just received a message from the Admiralty. I shall read it to you:

'*I have been commanded by the First Sea Lord to convey the appreciation of the Royal Navy to four-one-five squadron.*

'*One of your squadron's Spitfires was responsible recently for saving a fully loaded vessel as it made its way from Dunkirk. The destruction of an attacking E-boat by that aircraft in difficult circumstances saved hundreds of lives.*

'*I formally record my thanks, and my respect, for the skill and perseverance shown by the pilot concerned. I will be recording the detail in a formal report to the Prime Minister.*'

Sidey looked up, smiling. 'That is a wonderful communication to receive, but remember, this squadron is a team. You are all being thanked. Flying Officer Noble's particular attack, mentioned by the First Sea Lord, is highly commendable, but so are many of the other actions by members of four-one-five squadron. Congratulations to you all for a job well done.'

As they resumed their dinner, Richard said, 'I thought the new boss handled that well.'

'Absolutely. Well-balanced and thoughtful towards us all,' Greg added.

'True — we don't want just John singled out, so he gets a swollen head,' Charlie added, laughing.

'Don't worry, lads. I would never do that, and if that changes, then I'm sure you will be the first to tell me,' said John wryly.

After dinner, John telephoned Mary to tell her that his temporary relocation to RAF Hornchurch was over, and he was now back at Catterick.

'Oh, John, I didn't know you were back. Can we meet?' she asked.

'Yes, please. How about lunch tomorrow, at the The King's Head?' John suggested.

'I have a mid-afternoon shift, but I could meet you for an early lunch if I can get away by two.'

That was fine by John, so they arranged to meet at the hotel at midday the following day.

John arrived at the The King's Head first, so he sat down at a small table in the corner. 'You look lovely,' he said as Mary came in and took the seat opposite him.

She smiled and gave him a brief kiss on the cheek. 'I won't ask you about your operations out of Hornchurch, John. I'm guessing it wasn't pleasant, and I can see the stitches on your face that were probably not the result of a fall. We should talk about nicer things, like going away together for a few days. Can you get leave?'

'Yes, I can, and thanks, it's probably a good idea not to talk about the last week. I lost friends over Dunkirk. I don't want to sift through it, so, as you say, let's focus on more pleasant things.'

They chatted happily about everything except the war.

'My mother is getting a few chickens,' said Mary with a laugh, 'to run around in her garden cleaning up weeds and insects, apparently. She wants to be self-sufficient in eggs, and she thinks the chickens will peck her cottage garden clear. And my father is about to plant some hops. I think he's mad, but it seems someone has said it's possible. He fancies himself as a beer producer. More importantly, it gives him an interest he can follow when he takes an occasional break from the pressures of wartime planning. If it works, we'll only have small quantities, I suspect. This isn't industrial scale.'

'Pity, I wouldn't mind a girlfriend whose father was a beer baron,' John said with a grin.

'And you, John, what do you have to report?'

'Nothing much,' he answered. 'I did have a letter from my folks. They tell me the farm is going well, and my younger brother has settled in to working on the property. He's doing the jobs I used to do, before I came here to fly.'

'I'm glad you did, John. Otherwise, we wouldn't have met, would we?'

'Indeed not. Now, speaking of our relationship, seeing as I have forgiven you for not telling me at the beginning who your father was, where shall we go away together?'

'Forgiven me? Ha! I only asked for a wing waggle if you ever went over. You did a lot more than that.'

'Yes, I was trying to impress a young lady who lived there. Didn't know her father was a senior officer.'

Just over an hour later, John was saying goodbye to Mary when a carload of pilots from the squadron arrived.

'John, we are having a few beers. Come and join us later, if you like.'

'Mary is just going. I will be with you shortly,' John replied. He turned to Mary. 'Until next week, then.' He kissed her softly.

As they drew back from each other, Mary looked at him without saying anything for a moment.

'I am really looking forward to our time away together,' she finally said. Then she turned and walked away.

John said nothing, but felt an incredible longing for her as he watched her leave.

When John had joined the group, Craig said, 'Glad you could pull yourself away, lover boy. She has got you, well and truly.'

John ignored him and tuned in to the conversation the rest of the pilots were having. As usual, they were talking about the war.

'This is the way I see it,' said Charlie. 'Hitler won't want to send his armies across the Channel unless he has control of the air. Landing barges, ships and whatever would be too exposed to air attacks by us. I reckon he will try and destroy the RAF, or at least seriously deplete it, before he risks a crossing.'

'How does he do that, Charles?' Richard asked. 'Draw us up to fight, hoping to beat us in the air? Or does he bomb the hell out of us, destroying airfields and aircraft on the ground?'

'He would try everything, surely?' Charlie replied.

'I think you are right, Charlie, and that's why some of the stuff being done by Command is important,' said Roger. 'The new radar stations are going to be critical, but only if the information they provide can be fed to the squadrons in a timely manner.'

'Sidey was talking about Chain Home. It should enable command to put squadrons where they need to be at any time, based on the information the radar is giving them,' John said. 'Apparently, the oversight is out of Bentley Prior, but day-to-day ops control will be from Uxbridge. That's Eleven Group, which is the area that's probably going to see the most Luftwaffe activity — initially, anyway. I saw the Uxbridge control room being established when I did the officers' course there. It looked impressive.'

'Yes, there has been a lot of preparation for what's going to unfold. Hopefully it will all work as planned,' Charlie said.

An hour after he had joined them, John decided he would leave his fellow pilots and head back to the station. He planned to walk. It would only take fifteen minutes. He excused himself and left, promising to catch up again that evening in the mess.

John was soon out of the village and on the road that would take him to the gates of RAF Catterick. A few minutes later, he became conscious of footsteps behind him. He stopped and looked around. Twenty yards behind, he saw three men. They had clearly been following him. Then one of them stepped forward a couple of paces. He was their leader, John decided, noting his shaven head.

'I heard you talking in the pub,' he said. 'You RAF?'

'Yes, four-one-five squadron, Spitfires,' John replied.

'We were in France,' the man told John. 'We got out of Dunkirk on the fifth day.'

'That was a difficult time for you chaps on the ground.'

'Yes, it was. Bloody Jerry bombed and strafed the hell out of us.'

John said nothing, but he had seen what was happening from the air, so he understood.

'My question for you, sir, is where the hell was the RAF?'

The 'sir' was delivered with heavy sarcasm. John realised this was not simply a friendly chat.

'We were there shooting down the Luftwaffe. I flew continuously on offensive ops in the evacuation zone with my squadron.'

'If you had been there, we would have seen you. The truth is that the RAF was absent,' the man responded. 'You Brylcreem boys were too busy sitting in your comfortable digs at base while we copped it.'

'That's just not correct. If you didn't see us, it's because we were intercepting Jerry before he reached you.'

'If you were intercepting them, how did so many get to attack us?'

'We stopped a lot, but we couldn't stop all of them. We just didn't have enough aircraft or pilots.'

'Trouble with you boys is that you don't know real hardship and hard fighting. I'm going to show you what that is now, and you can tell your mates back at the station that it's a thanks-for-nothing from some of us caught on the beach at Dunkirk.'

With that he ran at John, a fist poised to swing at him once he got close enough. His two friends behind him hesitated, before starting to walk forward menacingly.

I need to stop this fellow quickly and cleanly, John thought. He knew he could not handle three at once, but the first man had separated himself by getting ahead. If John could drop him, perhaps the others would reconsider whether they wanted to fight.

When the angry soldier was almost upon him, John leaned back and kicked out his right leg, aiming at his attacker's left kneecap. He hit it hard and heard a snap as the knee tried to fold back. It broke as it was forced the wrong way by John's well aimed and solid kick.

His would-be assailant collapsed to the ground, holding his knee and screaming. 'You bastard! Oh, Christ, you've broken my bloody knee!' he wailed.

His two supporters stopped, wary of John. They were in no hurry to risk a similar fate. John did not hesitate. He turned and ran towards the station, some distance down the road. As he entered the gates, one of the soldiers on duty there saluted and then addressed him.

'Sir, welcome back. Good news about the CO.'

John was nonplussed. 'Thank you, Corporal. What are you talking about?'

'Wing Commander Bland, sir. He has turned up after surviving being shot down. He got back on one of the last boats out of Dunkirk.'

John could not believe it. He had seen the damage to Bland's aircraft. He did not think he could have survived. He made his way to the officers' mess and went into the bar. There he was: Wing Commander Christopher Bland was indeed alive and having a cup of tea.

'Flying Officer Noble,' Bland said, 'I want to talk to you.'

'Sir, I'm very pleased to see you back. To be honest, I didn't think you would make it when I saw you go down.'

'Well, I am back, and I'm in good shape, as you can see. But my question for you is this: how did Jerry get me when you were meant to be watching my back?'

John was surprised but instantly alert. He recognised the signs. Bland was gunning for him, again. The fact of the matter was that John had tagged on as Bland's wingman when he had seen him below by himself, being chased by a Messerschmitt. He had gone to help and now Bland was blaming him for the outcome.

'I would be happy to have that discussion with you, sir. Perhaps I could come to your office sometime?' John was not going to let this develop in front of others in the mess bar.

'Yes, let's do that. Ten hundred tomorrow.'

CHAPTER TWENTY-TWO

Early next morning, heavy showers were falling from the dark grey clouds that were hanging low over Catterick. It had been raining since before dawn. The pilots of 415 Squadron were in the ante room of the officers' mess, awaiting the arrival of their CO, Wing Commander Bland. He was to brief them on Fighter Command's analysis of the current situation.

Normally, with all the squadron pilots present, the constant chatter of multiple conversations would fill the room. But not today, John could see. Instead, they all just sat quietly, looking troubled. Apart from the occasional comment to someone sitting adjacent, little was being said. There were thirteen pilots there. That was less than the normal number. Usually there would be sixteen. The problem was, John recognised, times were far from normal. It was nearly a week since the squadron had finished its operations over Dunkirk, and there had been losses of both aircraft and pilots.

The atmosphere in the ante room was not a surprise to John, as he continued to look around the room, taking in the sombre attitude of those there. He guessed why no-one was saying much; they were all caught up in their own thoughts about what might now happen. He could feel his own anxiety. German forces had routed the armies and air forces of the countries invaded to date, and the Expeditionary Force sent by Britain to stop Germany's expansion had been lucky to escape from the beaches of the small French coastal town of Dunkirk. While he knew there was a general recognition of Britain's success in rescuing so many troops in that evacuation, the very fact it had been necessary was a prime concern. The German war machine appeared to be superior, and now it was positioned just a few miles away, across the English Channel. John understood the concern he could see and feel in the room.

The previous evening, John and some of the other squadron pilots had been talking in the mess about what it meant for Britain now it faced the might of Germany on its own.

'No-one really knows what's next,' Roger had said. 'Deciding what Jerry will do, or, at least, when, can be little more than an educated guess.'

'To me, the worst thing would be the Germans continuing their push, and coming across the Channel very soon,' Richard responded. 'We need more time to recover and prepare. Mind you, having said that, I don't think they will attempt an invasion without first gaining air superiority. Jerry won't want to risk being caught by us in the open, on the water.'

'Maybe that's the answer. Jerry will try to cross, but only when safer from air attack. That might mean the RAF will be specifically targeted. Taking us out would make an invasion more likely to succeed,' John suggested.

The others all nodded their agreement to that proposition. John's view seemed logical, and if he was correct, they all knew what that would mean. Providing cover for the troops during the Dunkirk evacuation had tested them, but the next battle would be harder. The Royal Air Force itself would be the main target.

'You're right, John, and bloody important we can successfully resist the Luftwaffe in that case. The outcome would be critical,' Richard said. 'Failure by us would encourage Germany to get on and cross the Channel, knowing they would be largely unaffected by any attacking RAF aircraft.'

'Sure, but on the other hand, if they can't knock us out, that might also firmly shut the door in Jerry's face, so far as German forces crossing the Channel are concerned. At the very least, successfully resisting the Luftwaffe will give Britain more time to bolster its position,' John replied.

'Absolutely. Our ability to hold off the Luftwaffe is going to be decisive, no question. The PM said it when the Battle of France was lost; now we face the Battle of Britain. I think he was being quite literal with that comment. It's a battle that could well decide Britain's future.'

As Richard said that, John thought he looked grim. *Not surprising,* he decided, *because, right now, the German forces are looking unstoppable.*

John's thoughts were interrupted as Bland strode into the room, went to the front, and began addressing the waiting pilots.

'Gentlemen, sorry about the delay. I was getting some last-minute updates. Fighter Command has completed its analysis of what we may now be facing, and what it is we must do to prepare. I will outline the key things anticipated, and how we plan to respond.'

The tension in the room was palpable. John could see everyone there was anxious.

'With Operation Dynamo complete, and the evacuation largely successful, Britain must now prepare to defend itself. The view at the top is that Hitler will come across the Channel as soon as he can get himself ready. In any invasion, landing craft, gliders, and paratroopers, operating in concert, and supported by dedicated air cover, are thought the most likely scenario.

'Command expects the Germans will spend some time re-organising and strengthening their supply lines before attempting an invasion. Those lines may have been over-extended with their recent advances.

'There is also a view the Luftwaffe will want to have air superiority before German ground forces try to cross the Channel. An invasion force would be too exposed on the water if we could mount substantial air attacks. It will also want to be confident about its aircraft having a relatively unimpeded run against our naval assets.

'This all makes the RAF the key tool in Britain's defence at present. Consequently, Fighter Command has been ordered to ensure all squadrons are at optimum capability as soon as possible.'

Bland paused, and looked around at his pilots.

'In a nutshell, Command's view is that the Luftwaffe will likely be ordered to make annihilation of British air capability its priority. Germany will want control of the air as a precursor to launching an invasion.'

John agreed that it was likely the Royal Air Force would be the Germans' prime target. He saw the glances exchanged between the other pilots, and knew what they were thinking. When over the French beaches in their Spitfires during Operation Dynamo, they had all seen the power and strength of the Luftwaffe.

'We don't know the enemy's actual intent, but that's the best guess. We anticipate the Luftwaffe will seek to destroy the Royal Air Force,' Bland went on. 'We also don't know when they may begin any campaign against us, but our job is to prepare. Squadrons are to get damaged and unserviceable aircraft airworthy, and any advanced pilot training completed as soon as reasonably practical.

'There were significant demands on four-one-five squadron throughout the Dunkirk operation, and we came out of that reasonably well, and learnt a lot. That will stand us in good stead for what comes next.'

As John listened, he found himself worrying not only about what the Luftwaffe may do, but also about the capabilities of the squadron's leadership. In his opinion, and in the opinion of the other senior pilots in the squadron, Bland should not be in charge in the air. Particularly now, when the RAF was going to be required to fight for its own survival, and, consequently, the survival of Britain itself.

Bland's performance had been sub-standard during Dunkirk, where he had failed to provide adequate strategic and tactical leadership.

'The only thing missing in action is the CO's leadership,' Richard Cowles had said to John at the time, summing up the view of many in the squadron. There was no question that the CO had been fine as an administrator, running the station with the assistance of his adjutant, but in war-operations all the pilots thought he was well out of his depth.

As he was mulling all this, John could feel himself becoming angry. *The man is an idiot*, he confirmed to himself, as he returned his focus to the briefing.

'I am confident we will be able to deal with the Luftwaffe,' Bland was saying. 'The Spitfire is a superb aircraft, and you are capable pilots, with most of you having some experience in war-ops, following Dunkirk. I'm going to hand the briefing over to Squadron Leader Sidey now. He will take you through the actual programme developed for four-one-five squadron. Thank you, Squadron Leader,' he said, nodding towards David Sidey.

Following completion of the briefing, John went to the administration block which housed Wing Commander Bland's office. As he went in, he was met by Flight Lieutenant Gardiner.

'Morning, Flying Officer, what can I do for you?'

'I have a meeting with the CO at ten hundred hours, sir.'

'Really? It's not noted in the diary.'

'He asked me to come and see him in his office this morning, sir. Wanted to discuss a dogfight we were involved in over Dunkirk.'

'Just a moment. I will check.'

Gardiner disappeared into Bland's office, emerging just a few moments later to tell John there was no meeting.

'The CO says he has no arrangement to meet you, Flying Officer Noble.'

John was flabbergasted. He was clear in his mind; Bland had nominated a meeting time of ten hundred hours today, in his office, to discuss the circumstances of him being shot down at Dunkirk, when John had been acting as his wingman.

'Very well, sir. My mistake.'

He left and made his way back to the mess, thinking about what had just happened. John knew he was not wrong. A meeting had been scheduled, but for some reason Bland did not want to follow up with him to discuss whether John had been at fault in the Me 109 shooting him down.

John knew why Bland had fallen victim to the German. He had flown badly, making a stupid mistake, trying to escape by stall-turning his aircraft. That manoeuvre might have caused the CO to feel he was undertaking effective avoidance, as it involved unusual aircraft attitudes, but all it really did was present his attacker with an easy shot. In a stall-turn, an aircraft momentarily hangs in the air as it slowly pivots around its wing-tip. Bland had made it relatively simple for the Luftwaffe pilot chasing him.

'Dave Sidey seems very confident that we will have no trouble intercepting Jerry using the Chain Home equipment,' said Charlie. He and John, together with Roger and Richard, were enjoying a pre-dinner beer in the mess. A standard practice for the pilots most evenings.

'Absolutely Charlie, Chain Home is going to be very important. We will know where Jerry is, how high, and how many,' Roger responded. 'We will be able to get out there and meet the buggers, before they get to their target.'

'Raises the issue, doesn't it, that an efficient command and control system is in place?' Richard noted. 'No point in knowing where Jerry is if you don't have your various squadrons positioned up there to greet him, is there?'

'Well, it all worked fairly well when used to vector squadrons into positions to enable big wings to be formed during Dynamo, so it should work just as well to locate enemy aircraft and direct us for an intercept,' John said.

'It will need to,' Richard responded, 'the chat is that the Luftwaffe can muster over two and a half thousand bombers and fighters. We have about six hundred battle-worthy fighters to meet that at present, although I am sure someone in London will have ordered a ramping-up of aircraft production.'

'Christ, we are going to be busy, aren't we?' Charlie said, 'and you are right, Richard. We will need to be bloody well organised to be in the right position, at the right time.'

Murmurs of agreement from the others, and silence for a few long seconds as each of them privately contemplated what it all meant for them. Roger broke the silence.

'Look, what I heard at the briefing today says to me we can be confident Chain Home will tell us where the enemy are, and that control will be able to vector us to them. John is right — it did work quite well during Dynamo, well, most of the time anyway, when we were asking for vectors to meet up with other squadrons, so we could form a big wing. There was one day the weather was too bad to enable us to link up, but that was the exception. It's a relatively simple step to take it from that to a system that enables our engagement with the enemy. I think Chain Home will give us critical information about Jerry, where he is, how high, and how many, and we will be able to use that to our advantage, even though we have less aircraft than the Luftwaffe. While they have more aircraft, they can't continually put them up as flights of hundreds at any one time. We will most likely face them in the same numbers as we did over Dunkirk. There, we typically saw groups of thirty to forty bombers with the same number of fighters as escorts. We dealt with them then. We can do it again.'

'That's all very well, Roger, but our encounters with Jerry are going to be in a different environment now,' Richard responded.

Roger looked at him, enquiringly.

'First, at Dunkirk, the troops on the ground were the principal target. The Luftwaffe's attacks were consequently focused on them, in a relatively small area. Compare that to air warfare over southeast England. The conflict area is much larger, and there is a variety of dispersed targets available. That means more enemy aircraft in the air at any one time, spread over a wide area, and that will stretch us.

'Second, let's not overlook the RAF itself may be the Luftwaffe's principal target this time, and that would mean comprehensive tactics designed to take us out,' Richard said.

'What do you mean by comprehensive tactics, Richard?' Roger asked.

'As well as meeting us in the air, I think Jerry will attack our airfields, aiming to disrupt our operating bases and infrastructure. He might even try to catch us on the ground, because while we can launch to counter any attack we see coming, we must land and refuel at some point.

'Because of their superior aircraft numbers,' Richard continued, 'Jerry can send aircraft in continuous waves. Their additional aircraft will count when they start coming over here.'

'That's a very jolly picture you paint, Richard,' Roger said.

'Sorry, I don't mean to be the doom merchant,' Richard replied, 'but realistically, all we can do is try to have our aircraft in the right place at the right time, and for us to fly better than them when we actually meet in the air.

'Britain has very capable fighter aircraft in the Spitfire and Hurricane, and our pilots are well-trained. Nevertheless, only some of us have useful war-ops experience following Dunkirk, so getting the new chums up to speed as soon as possible is a big issue. A Wings course doesn't teach a new pilot how to deal with a Jerry ace on his tail.'

No-one said anything as they pondered the difficulties Britain faced, and the importance of everyone involved in its air defence operating well, both pilots and controllers.

Then Charlie broke into everyone's thoughts.

'Did you know that *Luftwaffe* means *air weapon*?' he asked.

'Air weapon. Very Germanic,' John responded, 'but they will have to face our air weapons of course, Spitfires and Hurricanes. So, we will show them bloody air weapons.'

'Yep, Jerry won't find us as easy as some have been so far,' said Charlie with a wide smile.

There was a general muttering of agreement with that sentiment. They were feeling their patriotism and determination.

After dinner, as he was making his way up to his room, John found Richard on the stairs. It almost appeared as if he had been waiting for him.

'Everything all right, John?' Richard asked.

'Yes, all good thanks.'

'I thought you looked a little pensive tonight. You sure everything is all right?'

'Well, apart from a bloody big enemy air force about to have a crack at us, sure,' John grinned.

'We just prepare as best we can, John, and take some comfort from the good things being put in place, as we covered when we were talking about preparedness and defence planning earlier.'

'Yes, got that. I agree. But I will share this with you. I worry about Bland leading us on war-ops. I don't respect his judgment, nor his abilities in the air.'

Richard didn't reply immediately. He just looked at John, but not with any indication of disagreement, or suggestion that what John had said was inappropriate.

'Actually, I agree with you, John, and we are going to have to manage Bland.'

'Not an easy man to manage,' John replied.

'Actually, I have already started,' Richard said, with a grin. 'I heard him talking about your failure to stop Jerry shooting him down at Dunkirk. I had an off-the-record chat with him, and suggested he was being unfair.'

John realised then why there had been no meeting that morning between him and the CO. Richard had put a stop to it. Richard may be junior in rank to the Wing Commander, but the CO would listen to him, because he was from the aristocracy. Bland's elitism had worked in John's favour.

'Thanks,' John said, smiling at Richard, 'I appreciate that. I'm off to bed. Need my beauty sleep. Goodnight,' he said, and headed off to his room.

As he lay in bed, John's mind was active. *God knows how this will develop, and where it will end,* he thought. *All we can do is prepare and then do our best with what we have. Won't be easy. Christ, I hope Bland doesn't ruin things. We need to be on our best form.*

Then, as the pressures and commitment of recent days caught up with him, John fell into a deep sleep.

CHAPTER TWENTY-THREE

The four Spitfires of 415 Squadron were patrolling from RAF Catterick at twenty thousand feet. They were over the North Sea, approximately eighty miles off the coast from Hartlepool, tasked with looking for any enemy activity. The briefer had made it clear that if the patrol did have any sightings, it was unlikely to be anything other than a sole Luftwaffe aircraft intending to undertake some reconnaissance.

'You aren't going to see any bombers in the patrol area. They don't seem to be initiating any raids on targets in Britain at this stage,' he had said, confidently. It was over three weeks since the Dunkirk evacuation had been completed and, to date, the Luftwaffe had not been seen over England, and certainly not in Catterick's sector.

'In any event,' the briefer had continued, 'they are not going to send bombers this far north, even if they do become active. There was a small group of German fighters seen over the North Sea by a patrol yesterday, but they were well to the southeast, some distance off the Dutch coast. They weren't seeking engagement. Nothing has come anywhere near us to date, so I don't expect you will meet Jerry today.'

The Spitfires were patrolling in their finger-four formation.

Bland, was leading red section. He was red one. Roger was red two, John was red three, and Charlie was red four.

'Eyes peeled everyone,' Bland called on his radio.

The Spitfires cruised along, heading southeast. The day was relatively clear, with only a few cloud build-ups and there was little wind forecast. A lovely day for flying, John was thinking, when a warning call was made by the CO.

'Bandit! Eleven o'clock, low.'

John searched the sky below, in his forward port quarter. At first, he could not see another aircraft, but then he recognised the long thin shape of a Dornier Do 17, with its twin tail. He guessed it was about five miles away, flying past them in the opposite direction. It was on a northerly heading, and looked to be some five thousand feet lower.

What's it doing? he asked himself. *He's not going to see anything this far off the coast, so what's he reconnoitring?*

John, number three in the formation, called on his radio.

'Red one, it's a Dornier.'

'In for the kill chaps, follow me, in line astern,' Bland responded.

John felt uneasy. The flight profile of the Dornier made no sense. It was much too far off the coast to be undertaking land reconnaissance, and shipping would not normally be the subject of such a flight in this area. Why was it just cruising easily along, at the mid-teen altitude chosen, well out over the North Sea?

Not only could he not understand why the German aircraft may be there, he did not see the point in all four Spitfires swooping down on it in a line astern attack. One pair would have been more than enough, with the second pair staying back and keeping watch for any other aircraft. Then it dawned on him.

John had heard stories of bored Luftwaffe fighter pilots, not yet fully released to participate in attacks on Britain, setting aerial traps for RAF aircraft out on patrol. He lifted his head, searching the sky above, as the four Spitfires rapidly closed their distance with the Dornier. Then John saw them.

High to his right, there were eight Me 109s, travelling together as two *schwarms*. The Dornier, he realised, *was* on a mission, but it was not reconnaissance. It was there to act as a target, drawing in any RAF fighters that spotted it, so that the flight of Messerschmitts, thousands of feet above and behind it, could then attack the attackers. He called a warning.

'Red one, one-o-nines coming down on us from our three o'clock, eight of them.'

There was no reply. John wondered if he had not transmitted clearly. He repeated the call.

'Heard you the first time, red three,' Bland responded, but said nothing further.

After a few more moments of silence, John decided some decisions had to be made. In the absence of anything from Bland, he would do it himself. He knew that would not help his already strained relationship with the CO, but this was a dynamic situation and action was needed. John thumbed his radio button and called.

'Red four, we will break away. Follow me in pair towards the one-o-nines. Red one, you have red two with you for your attack on the Dornier.'

With that, John pushed his throttle forward to full power and pulled his Spitfire up into a climbing right-hand turn. Behind him, Charlie did the same. They were soon head-to-head with the approaching Germans.

With the speed the Luftwaffe aircraft had built up as they dived, their rate of closure with the two Spitfires climbing towards them was very high. When they were within shooting range, John saw lazy arcs of tracer searching him out. He fired a long burst in return and broke hard right, with Charlie on his tail. The 109s were travelling so fast they could not easily follow the turning Spitfires. Four of the German aircraft continued straight ahead in their dive, chasing the two Spitfires now closing on the Dornier. The other four pulled out of their dive, and began a climbing turn back towards John and Charlie.

Here we go, thought John, looking down at the four enemy aircraft coming up towards him. *Need to warn the CO and Roger about the four going for them.* He called a warning.

'Red one, four one-o-nines chasing you. Coming down at you on your six o'clock.'

Charlie, who had repositioned his aircraft about fifty yards to John's left, unleashed a prolonged burst of fire at the Me 109s climbing towards them. John did likewise. One of the Messerschmitts was hit immediately. Pieces flew off its fuselage and its left wing. The aircraft literally fell from the sky, clearly out of control. *Either damaged controls or a damaged pilot*, John decided. Another of the German aircraft began emitting smoke from its engine cowls, and dipped away.

The two remaining 109s then rolled away towards the distant Dutch coast, diving to build speed and get away. John did not bother chasing. He knew they would be hard to catch. He looked around to see where the CO and Roger were. He soon spotted them. They were shooting at the Dornier, which was also trying to escape. It was making for a nearby cloud formation. Bland had not responded to John's warning about the enemy aircraft, and now they were almost on him. John called again.

'Red one, four bandits, very close, targeting you at your six o'clock.'

Bland reacted to that call. As he watched, John saw red one, followed by red two, break off from following the Dornier and execute a hard steep turn to the left, to meet the approaching Luftwaffe fighters. When the Spitfires came out of that turn, they were head-to-head with the 109s. The Germans then had to make a tight turn themselves, to avoid the risk of colliding with the Spitfires.

John and Charlie were diving down to help. Confronted with attacks by four Spitfires, two climbing towards them and two coming down on them from above, the Germans decided they would break off. They turned towards the Dutch coast. Their trap had not worked today.

'Red one, red three and four are back with you, approaching from your four o'clock,' John called.

'Roger. Back to the airfield,' Bland replied.

The Spitfires reassumed their earlier finger-four formation, and followed their leader on a heading to take them back to RAF Catterick.

'I was surprised you took off on your own mission when we encountered that Dornier,' Bland said to John. They were being debriefed on the patrol they had just undertaken, by the station's intelligence officer.

'I thought it best to leave the Dornier to you and red two, sir, given the approach of the Jerry fighters. We would have been sitting ducks if we had all remained in line astern attacking the Dornier as they came from above.'

'All right, it worked out today, but wait for my order next time, Flying Officer. Don't start making decisions like that on your own account.'

John was seething, but he said nothing, simply acknowledging Bland's admonishment with a curt nod as he left. He needed to leave, otherwise he knew he might say something to his Commanding Officer that would only make matters worse.

CHAPTER TWENTY-FOUR

That evening, six of the squadron's pilots met in the reading room on the ground floor of the officers' mess at Catterick. It was a small space, dimly lit, with only a limited amount of natural light.

The room's windows were narrow. Ivy encroaching over their panes outside made it even duller inside. Dark timber bookshelves covered most of the internal walls, exaggerating the lack of light.

There were two brown leather couches at one end of the room. They showed their age. Scratched and scuffed leather surfaces, with cushions flattened by years of use. Opposite the couches were three small armchairs, covered in a lurid red material.

'Put the light on, would you, John?' Roger asked. 'I know we've got long summer evenings, but there is damn all sunshine getting in here.'

John thought the lack of natural light suited the room's purpose. It was a reading room. Intimate and quiet. But that was not why they were there tonight. For want of a better term, this was a plotting meeting. Dimly lit was appropriate, given the circumstances.

He turned on the light.

'There you are lads. You can all see clearly now,' John said with a smile.

As well as John and Roger, the other squadron pilots with extended war operations experience were there for the meeting; Richard, Charlie, Greg, and Craig.

'I have given Richard a heads-up on what I want to talk about. He agrees this meeting is as good a starting point as any to consider the squadron's war-leadership capability,' John began.

'You all know that when the CO got his medical back and was able to participate in the Dunkirk operation, we were concerned he did not have the experience nor the aerial warfare skills required to lead four-one-five squadron on air operations. So, when he said he would take over war-ops leadership for Operation Dynamo, we pushed back, subtly. Consequently, we were able to put in place arrangements that kept him out of that role, at least initially.'

There were affirmative nods and murmurs from the group, as they recalled what had happened. John continued.

'But then the CO decided he would take over leading us at Dunkirk, and managed to get himself into that role. In the last days of Operation Dynamo, when he was in charge in the air, his performance during engagements left us in a difficult position during several encounters with Jerry. I think we all agreed at the time that he was limiting our effectiveness, and exposing us unnecessarily. Today, I saw yet another episode of his lack of capability, and I've concluded that something needs to be done. We can't go on like this, particularly with the Luftwaffe expected to increase its operational intensity against us in coming days.'

Richard spoke up. 'Before the discussion develops, I want to tell you that we are not being disloyal, nor are we challenging authority. This is about an important operational issue to ensure our capabilities are maximised and our losses are minimised. Not only is this important for us, it's also important for Britain. With what is coming, every fighter squadron must be able to operate effectively and efficiently. Consequently, no-one should feel this meeting is out of order. Is anyone concerned that what we are discussing here is inappropriate?'

Nobody said anything. They all understood the problem they would have with Bland if he continued to lead them in battle.

Richard dipped his head towards John to continue.

'Today I was on a four-ship patrol led by the CO. Roger and Charlie were also there. We were some distance out from Hartlepool, at twenty thousand, when Bland called a sighting. He had sighted a bandit five or six miles east of us, and about five thousand below. It was a Dornier 17, and it was just cruising, south to north parallel to the coast, but about eighty miles out. The CO ordered a line astern attack. That was not the optimum attack plan to utilise for a single aircraft, but that wasn't my main concern. I was looking for any other aircraft.

'I was doing that because the Dornier didn't appear to be undertaking any particular mission, and I recalled the recent stories about some of the things the Luftwaffe has been doing. I scanned about, because I was suspicious. What the hell was this Jerry doing, all by himself, at that height, on that track, in the middle of the North Sea?

'Turned out it was one of the traps we have heard about. Offer a slow, easy target, meandering through the sky. Totally unthreatening and tempting, but above and some miles behind, position your fighters. They were there this morning, waiting to dive in if the bait was taken. As we went after the Dornier, eight Me one-o-nines pounced on us. When I saw them coming, I called the CO, to warn him. He didn't reply, nor did he order any action. We all just continued in line astern towards the Dornier.'

'What did you do?' Greg asked.

'I repeated my call, but when I got no response, I called for pairs. Charlie and I turned to meet the one-o-nines, and the CO and Roger continued after the Dornier.'

'What you did sounds a sensible plan of action in the circumstances, John,' Greg said.

'The one-o-nines split in response. Four went after the CO and Roger, and four came at Charlie and me. We damaged two, and that caused the other two to vacate the area. The four following the CO and Roger took off when they were confronted with Charlie and I diving down on them, and the CO and Roger turning to face them. They left the area as quickly as they could. The Dornier escaped into some cloud.'

'I might have got him,' Roger said, 'but Bland wanted to do all the shooting and required me to tuck in behind him, to watch his tail. He didn't score a hit, despite expending most of his ammunition. We should have opened our positions laterally, to allow us both to attack. I could have still had some value as wingman, even in that situation, but he didn't want me involved in the attack on the Dornier for some reason. Wanted to do it all himself.'

'Let's keep this focused, chaps,' John said, keen they all remain objective in assessing their Commanding Officer's performance. 'We have an operational issue that requires a solution, and we should approach it in a careful and considered way, so that we can find a suitable resolution.'

There was a general acknowledgement from those in room.

'We can't just tell the CO we don't want him leading on war operations,' Craig opined. 'I don't think he would ever accept we had a valid concern. It's not in his nature.'

'That's right,' Greg agreed. 'Ideally, we need to give him something that doesn't embarrass him, but leads to him happily accepting a change. It probably needs to be his idea.

Better if he sees himself as the driver of change, rather than having it forced on him.'

They all agreed with that comment, but at the same time recognised achieving it was the hard issue.

'As far as I'm concerned,' Richard said, 'our leadership in war-ops must be by someone who is experienced as a pilot in those operations, someone with a good grip on the agreed airborne strategy and able to implement the required tactics. A leader must be able to make tactical decisions quickly in the air, and effectively communicate those decisions to accompanying aircraft. It's a fact that the CO isn't experienced in war-ops, and his strategic thinking and tactical implementation are below par. We have seen it in previous engagements, and John saw it again today.'

'I did,' John confirmed, responding to what Richard had just said. 'I outlined earlier what happened, but, basically, the CO ordered an inappropriate attack method. Then, when the dynamics of the situation changed, he didn't react in *any* way. The appearance of some fighters protecting the lone hostile we were preparing to attack did not elicit anything from him at all. In the end, I had to act on my own initiative and call the required response. That's not good enough.'

The group was silent. Then Greg spoke, summing up what was in their minds.

'We know the Luftwaffe is probably going to specifically target the Royal Air Force. It must neutralise us if Hitler is to have any chance of successfully crossing the Channel and invading Britain. I expect our current occasional enemy encounters will soon change into something much more. We can't afford not be at our best when we meet them. That says to me we must come up with a way to take the CO out of leading us in the air, and we need to get on with it sooner rather than later.'

Squadron Leader Sidey was in his office when there was a tap on the door.

'Come in,' he called. John and Greg entered.

'Good morning, sir,' John said with a wide smile. He had decided to make every effort to engage well, and get Dave Sidey on side with the issue the pilots had agreed must be addressed.

'Good morning, gentlemen,' Sidey responded, nodding to both. 'What can I do for you?'

For the next fifteen minutes, John and Greg took him through their concerns about current squadron operational leadership. Sidey said nothing as he listened.

'All right,' Sidey said when they had finished what they had come to say, 'I understand the issue. I have seen some of the matters you raise myself, and I have been wondering about what we might do to improve matters for the squadron, especially now that we expect the Luftwaffe to make us the focus of its attention. Trouble is, the CO's abilities when leading us in the air is not an easy issue to address. Persuading him to give up in-air leadership will not be easy, and I'm not sure anyone in Fighter Command will want to get involved with the issue. They will see it as something that is too hard to deal with, I suspect. You can bet that the CO will fight tooth and nail against any suggestion he be replaced. '

John knew Sidey was correct in that assessment. Bland would be very unpleasant if he felt pushed. *How the hell can we change things without disrupting squadron cohesion?* he wondered. *Bland will never accept he is not doing things well. Something is needed, though. Now is not the time for us to have to worry about the quality and competence of whoever is leading us into battle with the Luftwaffe. Too bad the CO got his medical back… Ah, that's it,* he suddenly realised. *If Bland does not have a medical clearance to fly, the issue would resolve itself.*

'Sir, I wonder if there would be some value in talking to Doctor Berryman about Wing Commander Bland?' John asked, with a knowing look.

John knew that the station's chief medical officer, Brian Berryman, was a good friend of Sidey's. The two men had known one another at university, and had rekindled their friendship upon finding themselves both in 415 Squadron. *Old friends, thrown together by the war,* John thought.

Sidey looked long and hard at John, and then started to smile. 'Yes, Flying Officer, I will have a chat with him. I understand the point you are making. Leave it with me, gentlemen, and I will come back to you in due course.'

'Thank you, sir,' John said. 'We appreciate your assistance.'

'I think that went well,' said John as he and Greg walked back to the officers' mess.

'It did,' Greg responded, with a grin. 'You weren't that subtle in your hint that without a medical clearance to fly, the Bland problem would go away.'

'Fingers crossed then that Sidey can persuade Berryman to ground the boss on medical grounds. Big ask, but something has to be done. Jerry will be ramping up operations any day now, and, as we all expect, specifically targeting the Royal Air Force. We need to be at our best, and that requires Bland to be on the ground, not trying to lead us in the air.'

'Right, we are in the hands of Sidey, so we just have to wait to see what he can do,' Greg said.

'Indeed. Now, I'm off for a long, hot bath. I feel the need to soak and relax,' John said. 'It's been a hectic day.'

Back at the mess, John filled the bathtub near to the brim with piping-hot water, slipped in, and lay there, luxuriating. He did not want to let thoughts concerning Bland spoil his relaxation, but found himself thinking about the CO. He could see Bland was going to be a problem if nothing could be done. *A problem we don't need as we move onto the next phase of this war*, he concluded.

John put that out of his mind as he contemplated the squadron's operations over Dunkirk. It was a melancholy moment.

Alastair Bayliss had been a wonderful mentor. Now he had been so badly hurt he would not fly again. He might not even walk again. And Derek Laing had been a close friend. John had got to know him well as he had completed his Spitfire consolidation course. Now he was dead. And the squadron had also lost two young pilots who John had not even had the chance to properly speak to, as they had been brand-new to the squadron.

Let's not get maudlin, John told himself. *You need to be able to cope with all this, because there is going to be a lot more. Hitler will send his Luftwaffe soon, instructed to take out as much of the RAF as it can. If he is successful, his army will be crossing the Channel shortly.*

What had Churchill said in his recent broadcast? *The Battle of France is over: the Battle of Britain is about to begin.* John knew the Luftwaffe was a powerful force; its aircraft far outnumbered the RAF's. John and his comrades would need to fly well and defend ferociously. He understood that what they had been through in recent months was just the beginning.

Am I ready for what is to come? John asked himself. *Yes, I am, and so is my squadron.* The RAF would be stretched, but John was determined the Luftwaffe was not going to find the Battle of Britain easy, despite the odds.

A NOTE TO THE READER

Dear Reader,

I hope you enjoyed *Spitfires Rising*, the first novel in the *John Noble Fighter Ace Thriller* series. In writing the series, the abundance of publicly available historical material has been very useful. It has enabled me to weave my fictional stories through actual events and activities of the past. I researched RAF Fighter Command's WWII practices and procedures, and reviewed notes and records from the time. I also had access to a Spitfire pilot's logbook. What I saw in that logbook helped me develop the stories in a way that I hope will give readers some understanding of the trials and tribulations a fighter pilot would have faced in the air, at the time.

While the books are works of fiction, the stories they tell are inspired by real people and actual events. In some cases, the missions reflect war-time operations flown, and aerodromes used, but I invented the squadron numbers. They were not allocated to a fighter squadron at the relevant time.

While the *John Noble Fighter Ace Thiller* series is a fictional series, the stories told can serve as a reminder of the debt owed by many of us, to the fighter pilots of the RAF during WWII.

Thank you for taking the time to read *Spitfires Rising*. If you would like to leave a review of the book on **Amazon** or **Goodreads**, that would be appreciated. Readers are welcome to get in touch with me via my **Facebook Author Profile**.

Kind regards

David Mackenzie

Sapere Books is an exciting new publisher of brilliant fiction and popular history.

To find out more about our latest releases and our monthly bargain books visit our website:
saperebooks.com